D1402204

ELLA'S WISH

ELLA'S WISH

JERRY S. EICHER

THORNDIKE PRESS

A part of Gale, Cengage Learning

Detroit • New York • San Francisco • New Haven, Conn • Waterville, Maine • London

GALE
CENGAGE Learning™

Copyright © 2011 by Jerry S. Eicher.

Little Valley Series #2.

Unless otherwise indicated, all Scripture quotations are from the King James Version of the Bible.

Thorndike Press, a part of Gale, Cengage Learning.

Thorndike Press® Large Print Christian Romance.

The text of this Large Print edition is unabridged.

Other aspects of the book may vary from the original edition.

Set in 16 pt. Plantin.

LIBRARY OF CONGRESS CATALOGING-IN-PUBLICATION DATA

Eicher, Jerry S.
  Ella's wish / by Jerry S. Eicher.
    p. cm. — (Thorndike Press large print Christian romance) (Little valley series ; 2)
  ISBN-13: 978-1-4104-3987-1 (hardcover)
  ISBN-10: 1-4104-3987-9 (hardcover)
    1. Amish—Fiction. 2. Loss (Psychology)—Fiction. 3. Motherless families—Fiction. 4. Large type books. I. Title.
  PS3605.I34E45 2011b
  813'.6—dc22   2011020840

Published in 2011 by arrangement with Harvest House Publishers.

Printed in the United States of America
1 2 3 4 5 6 7 15 14 13 12 11

ELLA'S WISH

ONE

Ella Yoder looked to the south through the living room window of her new home. Chapman Road made its way through the gently rolling hills and was lined with the Amish farms and businesses of Cattaraugus County. Thick clouds, faintly tinged with the red of the setting sun, hung on the horizon. After a moment she moved to the couch and sat beside her sister Clara.

"It's been such a long day," she said, leaning back and trying to relax.

Clara nodded. "And now you're in your very own house. It doesn't seem possible."

"And unpacked," Ella added with a sigh, realizing she felt not just tired but older and alone.

That morning her daett had said, "I hope you make it well on this wild idea of yours." Then with his eyes twinkling, he had added, "You'll always be welcome back home."

And so she would be, and that was *gut,*

7

was it not? It was just that tonight was one of those unexpected times when her heartache returned with a vengeance. Aden, her betrothed, was gone from her life — suddenly dead. And then, the money he had saved for their house had been used to build this, *her* house. Aden's brother, Daniel, had insisted that's what Aden would have wanted.

Tonight she was finally in her house. It should have been *their* house. Ella could still see Aden's face, with his eyes aglow with joy, in stark relief on the walls of her mind. *Oh, if the memory were not the only thing left of him. What would it be like to really see his face again, to know what I had loved, and to forget that I had ever lost him?*

"You're sad tonight," Clara whispered, "but you're in your new house, and it's a really nice one."

"Yah," Ella whispered back, "it is a nice big house. It's just that I'm thinking of Aden and how much I wish he could be here to share it with me. I never want to leave."

Clara moved closer to Ella. "It will be lonely here for you. You know I'd like to come and live with you all the time. Would that help?"

"I would love that," Ella said, squeezing Clara in a hug, "but you know that can't be. You're just out of school, and Daett needs you at the farm, especially since I'm not there. He couldn't manage with two of us gone."

Clara smiled faintly. "Well, at least my drawing was used to build the house — my drawing and Daniel's help."

"Yah," Ella said, trying to smile, "your drawing inspired this house." She looked over to the wedding quilt with Clara's drawing as the centerpiece. "It was a very *gut* drawing."

"I've decided I'm going to draw some more," Clara said. "Of course, I won't draw in school since Katie still wouldn't like it, but I can do it somewhere else. I just love to make up stories and draw."

"Maybe you can write true stories someday about the life of our people," Ella said, adding "Just don't write about me."

"No, I won't. Besides, now I wouldn't know what to write about you."

"I suppose not. My life shall be a quiet one, I imagine," Ella said.

"You'll find a nice man again someday," Clara offered. "This house needs a man."

Ella shook her head. "That's what I don't want. And, besides, there's no one out there like Aden and never will be." Determined to change the subject, Ella said, "Now shall we eat some of Mamm's casserole? It's late already, and I'm sure you're hungry."

"Yah," Clara said, pushing herself up from the couch.

The two sisters moved to the kitchen. Ella brought out the casserole as Clara stretched to reach the plates in the upper cupboard.

"I'll have those moved lower for you later. I want you to visit often."

"You know I'll come anyway," Clara said, bringing the two plates to the table.

"It would be good to have everything down lower, anyway. With so few dishes, they look lonely up there all by themselves. Kind of like me, I suppose."

"That's why I said you need a man," Clara said, teasing, "but I know what you're going to say."

"I'm too old," Ella said. "Is that what you were expecting?"

"Too old? You're only twenty-two. And, no, I wasn't expecting that excuse. You have to stop making excuses, Ella."

"That's awful big advice coming from a fourteen-year-old, don't you think?"

"Not if it's true."

Ella carried the casserole to the table, placed a large spoon beside it, and then waited for Clara to join her.

Somehow I will make it through life. First

comes tonight, then tomorrow, and then day by day, I'll move through the years ahead. Whatever pain happens, it will just have to be. I'll be lonely, yes, but this house will become my refuge, mine and perhaps my brother Eli's if he follows through with his plans with that Englisha *nurse.*

Eli had an awful stubborn streak in him when it involved things of the heart. *Maybe Eli has forgotten about Pam by now.* Ella hoped so. *We simply cannot lose him to the world.*

"Ach," Ella said, lost in her thoughts. "I'm so absentminded tonight. I've got so many things on my mind."

"It was a hard day," Clara said. "We could both use some sleep."

"We should pray, then," Ella said as she sat down and bowed her head. Out of the corner of her eye, she saw Clara follow. Her father wasn't there to lead out, and she waited in the silence. *Does a woman dare pray out loud without a male present? Isn't that an awful violation of tradition?* A few moments of silence later, she glanced up to see that Clara had already raised her head.

The fact would just have to be accepted that prayers could not be said in the house — at least, not out-loud ones. The desire to hear them would have to remain unfulfilled.

11

So many of the other experiences would be lost too, like seeing Aden's eyes when he first saw her on Sundays or feeling his arms around her in one of his precious hugs. Nothing could be done about it.

Life swirls heavily around me. I can feel it tonight. It is in the sound of the wind under the house's soffits and in the noise the little legs of the couch made when Eli and Monroe pushed it into place on the hardwood floor. It is in the vast emptiness of the upstairs bedrooms and the huge basement beneath. The rooms are unfilled, unlived in, and waiting. Life wants something from me, but what? It's even in Clara's eyes, lifted to me with expectation. Clara thinks I am capable, energetic, and a safe guide for her journey to adulthood. She looks to me to be an interpreter of Amish peculiarities, offering her sense when life seems senseless. Yet I am only Ella — simple Ella with a heart that beats in broken rhythms.

I loved a man with all of my heart, and Da Hah *— for reasons only He understands — has taken him from me. I still believe in* Da Hah *for many reasons, some of which are the same incomprehensible reasons I've grown up with, but mainly because He is God. One doesn't go around throwing taunts at the Almighty. Does my faith not demand it? Even more and on a deeper level, does my heart* *not demand it?*

"You don't like Mamm's casserole?" Clara asked, puzzled. "You haven't eaten anything."

"Ach, of course," Ella said, grabbing her spoon. "Silly me. Mamm's food is always good. My mind was somewhere else, that's all."

The casserole tasted like home. It melted in her mouth and brought back the memories of what she had just left — her mom, her room upstairs, the morning rush, the evening chores, the smell of the barn, and the joys of life on Seager Hill.

Ella saw that Clara was watching her and felt the need to say, "I'm going to cry yet, just like the *bobli* I am. Mamm's casserole has me thinking about home."

Clara laughed. "If that's all that's bothering you, you'll be okay. I've felt like that sometimes, like the time I stayed overnight at cousin Emma's house for the first time."

"But I'm older than you are," Ella said.

"Maybe," Clara allowed, "but that just means you'll get over it sooner."

"Perhaps." Ella forced a smile. "I'm glad you're here for the first night."

"And I'll come back some more," Clara said with a chirp, "as often as Mamm lets me."

"I'll have you. That's for sure." Ella didn't have to force a smile. She thickly buttered a piece of fresh bread that had been made that morning before they left with the spring wagon for the move. Ella mounded on the raspberry jam and then wondered whether she could actually eat the whole piece. It looked huge in her hand.

Carefully she lifted the bread to her mouth. The rich aroma of bread flooded her senses, and the jam exploded with flavor in her mouth. The creamy butter mellowed the tang of the berries, and the whole mouthful became a sensuous delight as she slowly chewed. Suddenly, the piece of bread no longer looked too large. It looked much too small. She could go on eating buttered homemade bread and raspberry jam all night.

"Ach, that helps a lot," Ella whispered between the next bites.

Clara smiled and said, "I think I'll have a piece myself."

She prepared the bread quickly. A pleased expression spread over her face even before she bit into it. They chewed together in rapturous silence and then burst into laughter.

"Well," Ella said, "that makes one feel much better, and now we don't even have a lot of dishes. So why don't I do them while you're off to bed."

"It's still early," Clara protested, "and I want to read. I'm too excited to sleep."

"Another thirty minutes," Ella said, giving way. "I guess there are no chores tomorrow morning, but we're still getting up early. I'm not forming any bad habits just because we're not at home."

"No, you wouldn't. I know you too well for that." Clara laughed and carried her dish to the sink. Ella dipped cold water from the bucket into the sink while Clara nestled down on the couch. Tomorrow she would light a fire in the stove. Tonight soapy cold water was good enough. Ella finished the few dishes and then walked over to check on what Clara was reading. Unable to see, Ella lifted the jacket up to glance underneath.

"Nee!" she exclaimed. "What is this? *The Adventures of Tom Sawyer*? Where did you get the book?"

"It's not bad," Clara protested. "Eli said it wasn't, and he got it for me. I just brought it along to read."

"I know what it is, but where did Eli get it?"

"The library."

"Does Daett know he goes to the library?"

Clara shrugged. "Mamm's seen me reading it, and she didn't say anything."

Ella's mind whirled. *What business does Eli have at the library in Randolph? None, that I know of. He is almost eighteen and never has been much of a reader, and it is highly unlikely he has suddenly become one. My brother is up to no good, and it takes little imagination to figure out what that is.*

TWO

Ella lit the gas lantern and hung it on the nail in the kitchen ceiling. In the silence of the house, its soft gush of sound filled the room. Clara, on the verge of sleepiness, sat on the couch. Every now and then, her copy of *Tom Sawyer* would tilt downward and then jerk back up again. Ella returned to the kitchen table as thoughts of Eli's possible actions rushed through her head.

It has to be Eli who has filled Clara's young mind with such things. Not that Tom Sawyer *causes any serious trouble with Amish traditions — Mamm would have taken the book away if it had. The problem is with what else Eli is doing in the library.*

There can only be one possible answer and it is the Englisha *girl, Pam. Eli has obviously made further contact with her and determined the safest place to meet is the Randolph library.* Ella hadn't been in the library that often, but she knew the layout of the place.

From the main entrance, the bookshelves extended in both directions. *There are plenty of places to act like you had found a book and page through it while in conversation with someone else. On the slim chance an Amish person saw you, it would look quite innocent.*

How like Eli, with his stubborn mind, to go and push things to the edge. If caught in this deception, it would be more serious because Eli was a conscientious boy who planned to start instruction class this fall.

Not all the youth joined church this early, but Eli wanted to. Apparently his heart wasn't totally in the effort, or else he had been seriously sidetracked. Which was correct, she wasn't certain, but this situation wasn't needed. *I have enough problems to deal with already. Problems like how I am supposed to support myself.* Distracted, she scribbled figures on the paper in front of her. None of the totals that came up looked acceptable.

There was still some money left from when the house burned in the midst of the construction project. The Amish community, their compassion stirred by her already great loss, rebuilt the house on two Saturday frolics.

Also, the possibility of marriage to young Bishop Wayne Miller would mean an adequate income. His unexpected proposal hung heavy on the horizon. He would return soon for her answer, and she needed to be ready to give it.

After Aden's death, she would have been fine climbing into a hole and pulling dirt right down on top of herself. Instead, life had gone on as usual. Days turned into nights, the chores still needed to be done, and family life continued. Then it all changed.

She often wondered what Bishop Miller was thinking by approaching her so soon. *Am I a rubber band he can just stretch out however he pleases?* She was surprised at the nerve of the bishop, coming over and stating his intentions while her heart still throbbed with pain.

He had said he would give her time to heal and would return for an answer in six months. That would soon be up. The thought caused Ella to shiver in the early evening chill. *Bishop is a good-looking man — there is no doubt about that. He's almost as handsome as Aden.* She could admit that much without any disloyalty to Aden's memory, but beyond that she was not prepared to go.

"Bishop Miller's attentions are a great honor," Dora had reminded her last week.

"Just think how quickly he came over. I think it's a sure sign of *Da Hah*'s hand in the thing."

"I don't think so," Ella had retorted. "I wished he'd have left me alone. I was just fine the way I was."

"You were not," Dora said. "You haven't been right since Aden passed. Now with this fresh start offered to you, the good days could start again. You'd be happy and cheerful, like you used to be. He's a *gut* one to love, Ella. He really is."

"So why are you suddenly so cheerful about something?" Ella asked. "Normally we'd be hearing the dark side of things from you."

"It's because this is such a good chance for you — a chance to start over with a *gut* man. That's why. I can feel it all the way down to my bones. In time, the bishop's love might be almost as *gut* as Aden's had been. The second time around usually happens that way."

"My heart hasn't healed up, and that's that." She had glared at Dora, who only shook her head in response.

"Mamm and Daett approve wholeheartedly." Dora got in her last and best shot.

But as someone else's wife. Ella shivered again. Her coming wedding to Aden had been close enough that she had almost imagined the promises being said in front of the bishop. *No, I won't marry another man. I will choose my own way. Having my own house helps.*

Still, guilt gnawed at her. *Am I being stubborn and displaying the family trait like Eli? Do I have the right to live my own life while others might need me — such as young Bishop Wayne Miller?* He had not yet found a girl whom he considered worthy of marriage. *Can I survive as a single woman if I reject him? Will it be allowed? Can I allow it myself?*

Ella glanced toward Clara, who had fallen asleep. Her book was crooked on her lap, her head was tossed back, and her white covering was crushed against the couch fabric. She was the picture of innocence; of what life was like before adult burdens descended.

Oh, for youth! For the carefree hours when life seems like an open road on a summer morning, and the horse stands rested and ready for travel! But I am so tired now. True, it is late, but that does not cause my weariness. It's life that has left me weary despite my being so young.

With reluctance, she got up and walked over to where Clara slept, her body slumped

21

in a half upright position. Clara was too big to carry to bed, and so Ella gently shook her shoulder. Clara sleepily opened her eyes, and her hands grasped the cover of the book before it slid to the floor.

"Did I fall asleep?" she murmured.

"Kumma," Ella whispered. "I'll help you to bed."

Clara got up with Ella's hand on her shoulder, and the two walked toward the bedroom. Ella found Clara's night clothes in her suitcase and helped her change and crawl under the covers. She tucked the quilt around her and whispered, "Good night."

Clara simply rolled over and gave no response.

Ella returned to the kitchen table and thought of sleep, her eyelids heavy. The gas lantern hissed above her. Its sound was like that of her people's lives — steady, quiet, private, and at peace with the world around them.

Ella struggled to think. *There is the matter of money and Eli.* Those looked like the first two things needing attention. The amorous bishop would have to be dealt with when he showed up, and each moment would have to be taken from there. Da Hah *helped me before — even if I couldn't understand His ways — and there is no reason to believe He*

22

won't continue to do so.

He will surely help me with Eli's stubbornness. I will have to tell my parents, but how will Eli react from the pressure that's to descend upon him? Will he give the girl up? Eli has several good prospects among the Amish girls, and all might be lost if even the slightest report of his actions becomes known.

Can it be kept in the family? Ella almost thought it could, and a moment later, she was certain it could. Relief flooded through her. *I will tell Mamm what I know, and Eli can be dealt with at home. Further secrecy on my part is no longer in order. Tomorrow I will take Clara back and tell them everything.*

What then to do about the money? Ella frowned. It felt distasteful to look at things in such stark terms, but there was no doubt she needed a source of income. With quick scribbles her pen added up numbers on the paper but again found no concrete answer.

To her surprise and amidst deep thought, there came a sharp knock on the front door. The sound vibrated through the still house, and Ella jumped. *Who could be at the door at this hour of the night?* She pushed against the table to scoot her chair back and stood up. The motion caused her papers to slide across the table. Her pen rolled across the tabletop and dropped noisily to the floor.

THREE

Ella listened quietly but heard nothing. *How could someone come to my door without me hearing them?* The blood suddenly pounded in her ears. Never had she felt such fear at home. Daett was always there to answer the door. *Is this fear and distress when visitors call to be a part of my new life? Is this even a visitor?*

With a deep breath, Ella got up slowly while pressing her hand against her chest. *It's nothing,* she told herself and walked toward the front door with as steady a step as she could manage. She opened the door slowly. Her breath caught in her throat when she was unable to make out the form in front of her. At least he wore the familiar broad hat. At the moment, anything familiar was a comfort.

"Sorry to be botherin' you at this time of the night," Daniel timidly spoke through the darkness.

24

"Ach, that was a bit of a start!" She sighed in relief, her hand on her chest again. "Maybe I'm just uneasy, this being my first night in the house and all. But do come in."

"It's kind of late," he said, nodding and stepping inside. The soft light of the gas lantern fell on his unsmiling face.

"You look troubled," Ella said. "What brings you out on this late night visit?"

"I need to speak with you," he said.

"Are you wantin' to sit down?" she offered as he nervously turned his hat in his hands. "I don't have much seating space, yet. Just the couch and kitchen chairs."

"It's nice." He seemed to relax a little, and the hat fell to his side. "I just needed to speak with you. The matter's been heavy on my heart for some time."

"Yah?" She offered him a seat by motioning with her hand and stepping toward the couch. Daniel followed her and sat down after she did. Ella studied his face, but he didn't meet her eyes.

"I've been meanin' to say this for some time," he said with an unsteady voice. "Ever since the house was done, and I'm sorry I haven't got around to it before now. I guess I'm not like Aden, who was so certain of himself. I'm clumsy, and I hope you don't hold that against me."

She laughed suddenly. The sound bubbled up from inside of her. "I like you for that. It's one of the *gut* things about you."

"It is?" His face lit up, and relief showed plainly on his face. "It's nice to hear you say that since I'm clumsy with words and with other things like that. Sure, I can build a house okay, I guess, but . . . Well, it's just the way it is."

"Yah, this is a *gut* house but a little lonely tonight." She smiled, hoping to place him at ease. "I will always be grateful to you for it. You put in many long hours for not much money."

"I was paid enough, considerin' it was for my brother."

"I had hoped so. I expect you could have made more working for regular carpenter's wages from some of the *Englisha* people."

"I was glad to do it for you and for Aden." He managed a weak smile. "The deed is transferred, and I think the lawyer's office just drew up the last of the papers this week. I talked to him when I was last in Randolph. It's now your house, clear and free. I also put your signature on Aden's bank account and took mine and Daett's off. There should be enough money to do you for a while. Everything else — the horse and the buggy — is paid for."

"I am thankful for all you and your daett have done," Ella said. "For what you did and for what everyone else did, I am so grateful. I can never repay everyone."

"It's as Aden would have wanted it." Daniel nodded, keeping his eyes focused on the floor. "We were pleased to do what we could."

"I was just trying to figure out how to make some money," she said, laughing and pointing toward the papers on the kitchen table. "I've got to do something soon. I can't just keep living on what Aden left me."

He cleared his throat. With a pained expression on his face, he said, "That's what I wish to speak of. Well, in a manner of speakin', it's about you and me."

"Yah?" She gave him a strange look. The sudden thought of what he might be prepared to say startled her. *Surely he wouldn't.*

"I have been meanin' to say this. Many times I have, but now is the time. I'm thinkin' — what with you in your new house and startin' over and all — perhaps you would think of . . . somethin' else that's new even though it's not new for me."

She lowered her head, not daring to look. *He does mean to ask the question!*

"I know I'm not Aden, and I can never be, but my heart has been drawn to you

27

during all this time we've worked together. I suppose you might not have thought of it, and I'm thinkin' that's also a *gut* thing for both of us. It made our time together more comfortable. I know it did for me, at least. Now, even though I can never take Aden's place, perhaps we could make a new place for each other in our hearts. Start over, sort of. Perhaps we could start over with a new life — which neither of us planned for — but *Da Hah* has opened up the way for."

"You and me?" she mouthed the words barely above a whisper and pointed a finger toward herself. "You are thinking we could —"

"Yah," he said. A light now lit up his face. "I know I am not as good as Aden, but I am still Daniel, and you said you liked that."

Ella paused but only for a moment. "But not in that way. More like family — like my brothers. You know I've always thought of you like Eli and Monroe." She almost choked on the words.

"That was the best way." He nodded as if the thought wasn't new to him. "That is the way of our people. But what could be better than someone you already know like your own family? We could love each other, Ella. With time we could. We have already built a house together."

"But what about Arlene?" she sputtered. "You have a wedding planned surely by now. You can't be calling it off. She has been your girl for years already."

He shook his head. "We have never planned anything, let alone gettin' around to speaking of a wedding date. And now I know why, Ella. I know why it was not to be with Arlene. I was meant to be with you, Ella. This love I feel for you, I never felt it while Aden was here, and I am glad for that. It would have been dishonorable. But now, *Da Hah* has given His permission."

Ella couldn't find words. "You had best just go home," she finally managed. "If Arlene ever finds out anything about this, tell her you made an awful mistake. Perhaps your mind was confused . . . or something like that. But you must not do this, Daniel. You and I are family, but we cannot love each other — not in that way. It cannot ever be."

He looked at her with genuine pain on his face. "Then I am not *gut* enough for you. You think me unworthy?"

"Daniel," she said, meeting his eyes, "I feel like a sister to you, and I will say what I would say to my brothers. You must come to your senses. You must go back to Arlene right away. At least in your heart, you must make this right with her. I will never love you, Daniel — not as my husband and not like Arlene does. Can you understand that?"

He hung his head. "Then we can never have what you and Aden had. That's what I was wantin', and I was wantin' it bad. Arlene and I don't have what you and Aden had."

"Daniel," she declared, "everyone is different. You can't go looking at other people and wanting what they have. You and Arlene are made for each other. She loves you. I know she does because I've seen her when she looks at you."

"But I'm wantin' something better," he said. "Aden was always better than I was."

She stood up. With exasperation filling her, she took a deep breath and tried again. "You're needing some sense pounded into your head, Daniel, but I'm not knowing how to do it. Nor will I be trying. You can't go through life muddling around like this. You need to be a man and appreciate what you have. You need to enjoy what you have — someone like Arlene — and accept who you are. Arlene's a *gut,* nice girl and the best one for you. She's the best you'll be seeing in a long, long time. There are a lot of other boys out there, Daniel, who would love a chance with her."

"I'm sorry," he said while holding his hat. "I was just speakin' my heart."

"Then it's best you don't speak your heart," she snapped and then softened her tone at the look of dismay on his face. "You are like a brother to me, Daniel, but you best be growin' up. And that right fast."

"I'll try," he muttered. "I'm awful clumsy about such things."

"You'd best not be saying stuff like that either," she said. "Arlene doesn't want to hear it. No one wants to hear it. You are what you are, and you can't be changing that. Arlene likes you because you are Daniel, and don't be forgetting that or trying to be like someone else. Now you'd best be going, and I hope Clara hasn't been awakened to hear this."

"Then we cannot be . . . . together? Ever?" he asked as he got to his feet.

Her exasperation returned. "I see nothing I said got through that head of yours. I wouldn't have thought it so thick. But, no, it cannot be. If you don't quit soon, we can't even be what we are now, which is friends."

"It's best not to be that either, then," he said, placing his hat on his head and turning to go. "Good night. I'm sorry to have bothered you."

She followed him to the door and would

have given him a smile had he looked back, but he went out into the darkness without a backward glance. Moments later, his buggy wheels rattled on the gravel. Ella remained at the open door until the last sound of his horse's hooves on the blacktop had died in the distance.

The stars were out, and their bright twinkle called to her. A few steps took her out from under the porch roof and into their full glory. From wherever he was, she wondered if Aden had watched this exchange. Had he seen his foolish brother tonight? Then she felt a twinge of guilt. *Did I encourage Daniel in some way? Did I give him reason for this, even perhaps unintentionally?*

Carefully she searched her memory and her heart. To her relief, no accusation arose to blame her. Ella sighed, thankful that no further burdens descended to her shoulders. The least she could do was stop in and speak with Arlene. Perhaps that would smooth things over if she ever found out. Beyond that, the boy would not be her responsibility.

With a weary heart, she stepped inside, forgetting the stars. In the kitchen, she turned out the gas lantern and found her way to the bedroom in the dark. She climbed into bed beside Clara as sheer exhaustion swept over her. Sleep came quickly.

FOUR

Bishop Wayne Miller wrinkled his brow and
continued to study for his Sunday morning
sermon. He reached over to turn the kerosene lamp beside his couch still brighter.
The flickering flame lit up the off-white
pages of the *Martyrs Mirror,* but still he
squinted his eyes. *Is it worth lighting the gas
lantern?* he wondered for a moment and
then settled back on the couch.

The testimony and life story of the mar-
tyred girl fascinated him. *It would make an
excellent addition to the planned sermon.* It
was his turn to preach, but as bishop he
wouldn't have to abide by it if a visiting
minister was present.

On the pages before him, the young
widow from a long ago day had withstood
both the thumb nail torturer and the insis-
tent interrogation of her capturers. But in
the end, she bravely faced the flames and
through death was, no doubt, rejoined to

her husband.

He saw the story in his mind so clearly and with great intensity. He would tell the story with great sober tones, and surely there would be no one who would sleep through it. At age twenty-three, the young man's first ordination had come, and two years later, the lot had fallen again on his shoulders — this time for bishop. And he was still not married. He felt the pressure of time pressing in and desired a *gut* woman to live with him in his house. It was time the matter was settled.

How that fit in with martyrdom, he wasn't certain, but another girl stirred his thoughts. She was definitely not a martyr. Ella was young and beautiful and he was definitely a man and a bishop. He had desires like other men, and they were not to be ashamed of. He owned his farm and had his cabinet-making business out in the shed.

No woman had ever stirred his emotions as Ella Yoder had. Perhaps he shouldn't have been so quick to make a move after she lost her boyfriend. He could have waited longer before going to speak with her, but there was plenty danger to waiting. She would not stay unspoken for long. He was certain of that.

He pondered the situation as he watched

the kerosene lamp flicker and lightly stroked the *Martyrs Mirror* he held in his lap. How holy these people of long ago had been. They were great in their faith; solid under physical torture and faithful in death. How he wanted to measure up to them and reach the heights they had obtained.

Were any of these martyrs ever racked with longing like I am? Had they ever wanted to love a woman like I do? I want to hear the sound of her feet on my kitchen floor, see her hands pick up my dishes, watch her prepare my food, feel her fingers on my hand at our wedding day, and see a smile in her eyes when they meet mine.

What did the fire of the stake, the loneliness of the dungeon cell, or the joy of a martyr's death have to do with what I feel? Little, he was sure, and yet he had these feelings, and he was certain he would claim Ella Yoder for his wife.

Ella took his breath away with the poise of her bearing, with the sound of her voice, with her presence of mind, and with her loyalty to Aden's memory. She was all he wished for and so much more. *Da Hah,* who supplied all things in their own good time, had given him a chance at a great gift.

Soon he would go to speak with her again. He lay his *Martyrs Mirror* aside, unable to

36

concentrate any longer. The time was late anyway, and he really needed to be in bed. He shifted on the couch, attempting to find a more comfortable spot. *That will all change when Ella marries me. We will purchase new furniture.* They wouldn't buy anything fancy because he was a bishop and needed to set the example, but the new one would be better than the old couch he had found at an *Englisha* garage sale. He had driven by in his spring wagon, not meaning to stop. Usually it wasn't worth the time to check for furniture at such places because the *Englisha* often had flowers or patterns on the upholstery, making them unusable for an Amish home.

This couch, though, was simply a soft gray color. He gladly made the purchase for twenty dollars, loaded the couch on his spring wagon, and drove home. Afterward he had discovered how lumpy it was but had endured the situation. *Ella deserves better. She will also know how to manage a home far beyond my feeble abilities.*

Will Ella say yes to me? The question disturbed him as it hung in the air. *Surely she won't deny me. Does she have reason to say no? Is someone else after her affections?* He knew of no one and had kept his ear open to be sure. Ella had promised she would give no one else an answer before she spoke with him again.

Could any other man make an offer better than mine? He searched his mind and tried to be honest. There were not that many marriageable men available. Boys or girls of twenty-one years or older either had firm dating relationships or were already married; some only months after their birthdays.

He was the exception but had never worried much about his limited choices. Ella must have been the reason. *Da Hah* must have known she would come along and had given him the patience to wait.

He got up and used the dipper to pour a drink of water from the water bucket, splashing water on his shirt. His clumsiness disturbed him, and then he smiled in the dim light of the kerosene lamp. *I might not know how to pour water from a dipper without spills, but I certainly know how to touch a woman's heart.*

All his life he had known how. He couldn't remember a time a girl made him blush or tremble like the other boys in his class. His cousin Amos had turned as red as beet when Esther May so much as walked close to him. When Amos was well over nineteen, he still reddened when Esther smiled at him in the public youth gatherings. He couldn't imagine those kinds of nerves when it came to girls.

Thomas became all tongue-tied around girls in grade school. He chuckled. *I am a bishop now and shouldn't really be thinking such judgmental thoughts about the other men.* Yet they just came. Ella did that to him. She made him feel his youth again. *Isn't love like that? Ella doesn't turn me into a stammering mess and neither will her smile once she finally gives it to me out of the deep love of her heart. I can already see the glow on her face.*

Bishop Miller turned down the light of the kerosene lamp and picked it up to take with him. He would find Ella's love, when it came, a great honor; a thing he would always be grateful for, even unworthy of. *Have I not waited all my life for this, and has* Da Hah *not seen fit to send Ella my way?*

He bowed his head in thanks, guilty and yet glad that martyrdom wasn't ahead of him. *Soon I will hold Ella's hand in marriage. Soon this house will know the step and steady hand of the woman I love.*

He felt the urge to sleep and prepared for bed. Tomorrow would be busy with orders to fill at the cabinet shop. Kneeling by the bedside, he opened the prayer book and

read the evening prayer. His voice was full,
confident, and open before God.

FIVE

Preacher Ivan Stutzman sat in his rocker. His oldest daughter, Mary, sat on his lap. He was fully aware that the time was well past their regular bedtime. The squeak of the old hickory rocker filled the living room with its rhythmic sound. All day Mary had complained of an earache, and aspirin seemed to give little relief.

Tomorrow she would need a visit to the clinic. For now little could be done. Mary had dozed off, a fitful sleep from which she would awaken if he dared move. He knew this because he had tried.

Slowly he continued rocking. The kerosene lamp was turned down low, and his other two children were fast asleep. The baby slept downstairs in her crib in his bedroom, and two-year-old Sarah slept upstairs, where her sister should have been by now. Never in his wildest dreams had Preacher Ivan Stutzman imagined having to raise three daughters on his own.

His older sister, Susanna, lived across the road, taking care of their elderly parents. During the day, he took his three girls over to her. Evenings, mornings, nights, and weekends, they were in his care.

He continued to rock as tears formed at the edges of his eyes. It didn't seem fit for a preacher to be crying, but still the tears began to roll down his cheeks and mix with his lengthy beard. A few fell on Mary's long black hair. He thought to brush them away but was afraid Mary would awaken.

Since his wife, Lois, had passed, he hadn't cried often, though the pain was intense at times. Preacher Stutzman considered himself a strong man, able to work outdoors for most of the daylight hours and handle his farm in summer's heat or the harsh unrelenting winters. Yet his loss and the sorrow that followed had broken his heart and nearly crushed his spirit. He knew now how greatly he had loved her.

Among his people, he was feared for his fiery sermons. He was known to take on all men, holy or unholy, who threatened what he loved — God and the Amish tradition. And yet it was he who had loved a woman so greatly that he gave her the place in his heart that belonged only to the holy One.

Guilt gripped him and compounded his agony. *Is this not why I've been left alone to bear the weight of the children without the care of a mother? Will* Da Hah *have mercy on me?*

Da Hah *must have His reasons for what He has taken and what He has left behind. That usually involves rebuke and chastening. Is that not my faith, the one I've always preached with such vigor? Is that not the value system that applies equally to my own life as well as those I preach to? I've failed not only God but also my beloved Lois, for she would have surely lived out her full years if I'd kept my heart in the right place. Beyond a shadow of doubt, I've sinned beyond measure by loving my wife so greatly.*

Da Hah *in His wisdom has found a way to reach me and cause the necessary pain to punish me.* Preacher Stutzman could have borne untold distress, discomfort, and even death, but when these things were laid upon his children and his beloved, he was crushed to the ground.

"*Da Hah* has a case against me," he whispered. "I must have been grievin' him somethin' awful."

His lament turned to gentle sobs, which stirred Mary in his lap. She rubbed her ear vigorously and whimpered.

"You want to try to sleep in your bed now?" he asked.

"It's hurtin'," she moaned.

"Daett knows," he said with a voice filled with regret. "We'll take you to the clinic tomorrow to get some help. You just have to endure this for the night."

"I'll sleep upstairs, then," she said, "with Sarah."

He got up, cradled her in his arms, and found his way carefully upstairs in the darkness. At the top, he found the bedroom knob and pushed open the door. The half moon gave enough light to find the bed. He pulled the covers back and gently lowered Mary into bed. He stood, waited for her to resume her sleep, and then he retreated.

Outside the door he waited a few moments longer and then moved downstairs in the silence. Perhaps there would be peace for the rest of the night. The girl was exhausted, worse than he was, and sleep sometimes came even when there was pain. Some nights his body took over and demanded the rest he had no desire to experience.

It would have seemed more appropriate if he never slept again and suffered in that small way in payment for what he had done.

On the last stair step, even with the light of the kerosene lamp on the desk, he stumbled and caught himself awkwardly. The clatter across the floor echoed in the house. He reached for the couch edge to help regain his balance and listened in the silence. *Did I wake the baby?*

Hearing no sound, he walked over and blew out the lamp. Gently he opened the bedroom door. He contemplated the thin rails of the crib outlined against the wall but heard no sound. *Baby Barbara must be fast asleep. This can simply not go on. Something has to be done, but what?*

"You have to get married," his sister Susanna had lectured him a month ago already.

He had shaken his head, resisting her. Not only was it too soon, but he knew he could not love another woman again.

"A man in your situation needs a woman," Susanna had scolded. "Look at yourself. You have three small children to care for. It's not my place to be mentioning names, but you know I could do so. There are several widows around who would jump at the chance to fill the place Lois left. You have to think about it, Ivan. Think hard and long about it."

He hadn't answered, but on nights like

this, it was hard not to consider her words.

A widow lived in the district south of them. Nancy Weaver was a year older than he was, and her husband had been dead for four years already. She had three children of her own; all boys. *My memory of Lois is too fresh. It's too soon to take another woman as my wife and allow her to hold the place that Lois had held. Plus, have I not sinned once in this area already? The sin, though driven out, can easily return.*

Then why not take Nancy Weaver as my wife since I do not love her? Nancy would understand my reasons and might even feel the same way. Surely Da Hah *would accept my marrying a woman I do not cherish as I had Lois.*

Perhaps Susanna is right. Perhaps it is time to consider a wife. In the darkness he found the bed and lowered his weary body. The night air was too warm for the quilt, and so he pulled only the sheet over himself. *A marriage to the widow Weaver might be the right thing. But I need to think of my girls. How would they survive, thrown suddenly into the company of three strange boys?*

Necessity is the issue now. I need someone to keep house and run to the clinic tomorrow with Mary. I need time in the hay field, which is ready to cut. Susanna can't go tomorrow, but someone must. He tossed onto his side, unable to sleep. *Without a doubt, I need a wife — and quickly.*

Still, a wedding takes time. Is it possible to hire a girl temporarily? That would take the pressure off until I can approach the widow Weaver, have a proper engagement, and set the wedding date. But where would such a girl come from? She would have to be someone who wants the work and is available. Those girls are few and far between. Many of the families help each other out but usually only for short periods of time. Most older girls are either married or needed on the family farms.

A thought came to him, unheeded at first, fuzzy because of the lateness of the hour. *Didn't Ella Yoder move into her new house just this week? Wouldn't she have plenty of time on her hands? Sure, she's a little strange. What young Amish woman has her own house and remains unmarried? She's also, no doubt, still grief stricken from losing Aden Wengerd.*

Would she possibly consent to work for me — in the daylight hours, of course. Ella Yoder has a house of her own. Why couldn't I board the girls there until I've made other arrangements? I could then bring the girls back home on Friday nights to spend the weekend with me.

Would Ella Yoder consent to such an arrangement? He searched his mind and couldn't find any reason why she wouldn't. He could afford to pay the usual fee. The farm didn't bring in much more than enough to live on, but there was money in the bank he saved mostly because of Lois's wishes. Surely she wouldn't have objected if the monies were spent on her girls.

Will Ella think me untoward? Surely not if I explain myself. I'll tell her the situation is only temporary and until something else can be done. Even Susanna will approve of this plan. What the widow Weaver thinks about it, I need to find out.

Will Ella think I'm after her as a wife and presenting some hidden marriage proposal of sorts? He tossed in bed and decided she could figure that out herself. *Ella is a smart girl, from the little I know of her, and will see by my attitude what my intentions are.*

Why not ask Ella to marry me? The thought pressed in on him as he looked out the window at the starry sky. He wished the idea hadn't come. It was wild and stirred him deeply. It was a troubling notion.

Yet for what he had in mind — a marriage in which he would never give his heart — this seemed grossly unfair to anyone but a widow. Ella might feel like a widow, as close

48

as her wedding date had been. Yet he knew that nearly married wasn't the same as married. Any girl, he figured, deserved to marry for love and experience the affection of a husband who could give her his whole heart.

He, of course, could never give his all again — couldn't even if he had wanted to — out of fear the Almighty would smite the object of his desire. Preacher Stutzman stirred again and reached for sleep. *Perhaps a confession at church might be in order; a confession for the sin I've committed. Yet how would I do such a thing?* A knee confession in front of the whole church — a punishment saved for only the serious offenses — would be appropriate, but Bishop Mast would have none of such a confession. To love one's wife too much was not a matter to be confessed in church.

At the very least, I could preach about the matter and warn others of the danger I've stumbled into. I would have to speak in vague terms, of course, to protect the honor of Lois's memory. Thoughts of Ella kept running through his mind. He pushed them away, realizing his body was so tired it ached. For a long moment, he listened to the silence of the house and then involuntarily dropped off to sleep.

Six

Ella awoke with the alarm, feeling the strange stillness of the house around her. She swung her legs out of bed, groped for a match on the dresser, and lit it by striking it against the underside of the drawer. The little flame flickered in the darkness. She transferred it to the wick and then got dressed. Clara, still asleep, groaned in protest as Ella gently shook her awake. Clara pulled the covers tighter up under her chin and then rolled over.

"You're at my house," Ella whispered, and Clara's eyes opened to her sister's voice. "You're not at home, silly, and there are no chores this morning."

Clara sat up so fast the covers slid off the bed. Ella laughed quietly, the sound echoing in the large bedroom.

"Then I'm gettin' out of bed quickly!" Clara declared.

"That would be a change."

Clara ignored her and slid her feet to the floor. "Dora and the boys are choring by themselves."

"They have less to do with a quarter of the cows dry," Ella said. "Otherwise I don't suppose Mamm would have let you come."

"What's for breakfast?" Clara reached for her dress, which was draped over the dresser.

Ella smiled and placed her hand on the doorknob. "We can fix anything you want because this is our special day. It's just you and me. The morning is ours. Then I really need to get you back home since Mamm probably has housework aplenty for you."

"Scrambled eggs," Clara declared, her spirits undaunted.

"So let's do it," Ella declared, caught up in the moment. "Scrambled eggs and what else?"

"Oatmeal."

"Just plain oatmeal? Is that all? And on your special morning."

"They go together," Clara said. "Scrambled eggs are *gut* too, even if Daett says *Da Hah* made the yoke and white separate and that they weren't intended to be mixed up before the stomach saw them."

Ella laughed. "That's just Daett's reasoning because he doesn't like them scrambled.

You know that. He eats cake and bread just fine, and they have the eggs all mixed up."

"I guess so," Clara said. "I guess he can't see the eggs in the cake batter."

Daett's opinion on all matters carried weight for all of them, and Ella supposed this would always be so. *Will my news about Eli's caper have a similar end? Will Eli finally listen? Perhaps I should have spoken up sooner. The weight of Daett's opinion might have persuaded Eli from his unwise actions with the* Englisha *girl.* Still, she dreaded the upcoming conversation at home later in the day.

"I'll get the fire going," she said, leaving the bedroom door open behind her.

The rays of the morning sun would soon warm the kitchen through the large living room windows, a feature Ella had requested when she instructed Daniel about the kitchen layout all those many months ago. When the house was rebuilt after the fire, she forgot to mention the kitchen layout again, but Daniel had not forgotten, perhaps for reasons other than family ones.

What a shame Daniel had to go and muddle things up. Arlene might very well not take him back if she ever finds out. The boy has problems, greater than I'd imagined, but I've got my own, she reminded herself, *and so*

52

too does my family.

Ella stood in front of the cold stove, ready to make the fire but discovered the firebox was empty. That was one of the many things that had been forgotten yesterday.

"I'm going outside to get wood," she hollered toward the bedroom. Clara opened the door fully dressed and nodded.

Ella opened the front door and stepped outside. All around her the first streaks of dawn lit the sky. There was no red in the color of the sunrise, just the pure light of a beautiful day without a cloud in sight. She took a deep breath and looked up at the sky. With summer well on its way, the farmers could use the rain soon. The gardens needed the rain too. She would not have a garden this year, but for certain, she would have one next summer.

The light was just bright enough to see by, and Ella found her way around the corner of the still unfamiliar house. She looked everywhere near the wood pile but could find no ax. It must still be in the barn. With quick steps she walked toward the building. She pushed open the barn door, and the horse whinnied heartily.

"Good to see you," she said, laughing. *Why am I talking to my horse?* Likely because they already had a friendship of sorts, for which she was deeply thankful. A disagreeable driving horse or one who balked would have been a heavy burden to bear — and another horse would then need to be purchased at a cost she couldn't afford.

New driving horses were always a gamble of sorts.

"We can drive anything," Eli and Monroe often boasted, but she doubted their tale.

All the horses they ever drove had been hand selected by Daett, and so they didn't qualify as evidence for Eli and Monroe's theories.

"Will you come along to the sale barn and select mine?" Ella had asked her dad.

"You know I would," he said, shaking his head, "but I just can't get away today. Eli can go along, though."

"Yah, I can take care of it," Eli said, delighting his father.

"Like I trust you," Ella had told him with a touch of sarcasm, but he came anyway, sure of his prowess.

"That one," Eli said, pointing toward a high-spirited gelding prancing into the ring, led tightly by its handler. "It will outrace the best of them on Sunday evenings. It will last you for years with plenty of speed and stamina."

"I told you I don't trust you," Ella had

said much to his chagrin. Thankfully there were other opinions available. She left Eli and walked across the bleachers to where Daniel stood with his dad.

"What do you think?" she had asked the man who would have been her father-in-law. "I need a good driving horse, and Eli's got some high-spirited thing in mind for me. I don't want one that runs away from me or won't go when I want it to either."

"We just saw a nice gelding back in the barn. Number 305," Daniel said, and his dad nodded in agreement. "The price may go a little high, but the horse is worth every penny."

"Like a good man," Daniel's dad said. "I think you're right son."

Ella had followed Daniel's advice, to the consternation of her brother.

"Every other horse will pass that one on the road," Eli said, his nose turned up while she bid.

Ella smiled at the memory. He, of course had been wrong. The little gelding had plenty of speed.

Ella finally found the ax and walked back behind the house. *Daniel had been so right about the horse. How could he, then, be so wrong about my feelings? Have I ever thoughtlessly encouraged him?* Last night the question had seemed answered, but now the strangeness of it all came to her again. She stopped and looked long at the dawning sky. *My relationship with Daniel has always been that of a brother — Aden's brother. Never have I given him reason to think otherwise.*

Ella sighed, placed the first piece of wood on the chopping block, and brought the ax down. *The world is a strange place, and people don't always do what I expect them to do. God doesn't always do what I expect, and so how can earthen vessels, as the preachers says, be held to a higher standard?* She opened up the little doorway on the side of the house and tossed the pieces of wood inside. They landed with a thump.

Clara's faint voice called from inside, "Shall I start the fire?"

"You'll be needing kindling," Ella hollered back. "I'll split some in a minute."

"Yah," Clara answered.

With her ax in hand, Ella carefully took little slivers off the sides of a block of wood. Her left hand held the block firmly in place as her thumb and fingers wrapped around the side. The ax rose and fell, and she trembled slightly. She had always disliked chopping kindling. One slip and the ax struck one's hand, laying the flesh wide open.

Dora and Ella could have left the cutting of kindling to their dad or to Eli and Monroe, but they chose to do it themselves. It was a part of their world and, thus, worthy of mastery. Still, Ella's hand twitched with fear, even after all these years. The ax was so large, the wood piece became ever smaller, and her hand was always just inches away.

After a few more chops, she finished and tossed the little pieces through the doorway. She then walked around the corner of the house and set the ax inside the porch. She stopped for a moment again and studied the just-risen sun over the valley. It glowed red now, flaming large with still no clouds in sight. Peace filled her, even with the knowledge of what the day might hold. God was still in charge of His world. Her faith declared it, and her heart refused to abandon the belief.

Clara had the fire going when Ella entered the kitchen. The flames already reached out greedily for more fuel. Ella checked over Clara's shoulder and was satisfied things had been done correctly. *Now, everything will be fine just so long as the chimney doesn't burn down. Wouldn't that be something! I certainly wouldn't want to burn down the house on the very first full day here.* Ella pushed the thought aside and went to retrieve the eggs from the basement. The stair boards were brand new and wider than their basement stairs at home.

"The new codes require it," Daniel had said when she noticed the difference.

The eggs wouldn't keep long in her basement, even back in the darkest corner of the root cellar where a patch of concrete had been left out. Eventually she would need ice stored here, covered with sawdust, but for now, eggs and other perishables could be kept in small quantities.

Ella selected what she wanted and went quickly up the steps, walked to the kitchen, and set the eggs on the counter. Clara immediately began cracking the eggs into a bowl. After she cracked the half dozen eggs, she whipped them vigorously with the hand beater and added salt and pepper. With a twirl of her hand, she poured them into the pan and over the dab of melting butter. The pan sizzled and popped. Clara split the eggs into smaller chunks with the hand spatula. Then, only minutes later, she flipped the results out of the pan.

"Now isn't that the way to make eggs?" Clara's eyes glowed. "This is truly fit for kings and queens."

Ella laughed. "I think I do agree with you,

58

but you'll never convince Daett, let me promise you that."

"It's enough that I convince you," Clara said, smacking her lips.

From how the result looked on the plate, Clara knew how to make scrambled eggs. The water boiled moments later, and Ella poured in the oatmeal, stirring slowly so the mixture wouldn't stick on the bottom. When the oatmeal was ready, Ella waved her hand toward the table and asked, "Shall we eat? The sisters two!"

Clara giggled her answer and sat down. After a silent prayer, Ella waited for Clara to start.

"You taste them first," Clara said.

Ella raised her eyebrows. Clara nodded sharply. Ella shrugged, placed a sample of eggs onto her plate, and then took a taste.

"Not as good as fried eggs but good for scrambled eggs," she teased.

Clara relaxed and took a large helping of eggs, pulling them onto the plate with her fork, then filled her oatmeal bowl, and placed a big dab of brown sugar on top. Carefully she stirred in milk and then buttered a piece of bread.

"It's good," Ella said. "It really is."

"I'm going to just take my time," Clara said. She took her first bite of eggs and chewed slowly while holding a thick slice of well-buttered, homemade bread in the other hand. "Mmmm, this couldn't be better."

"I think I do agree," Ella said, her eyes turning to the living room window as a buggy came up the road from the south. The horse trotted slowly against the grade, passing the house and moving on down the road. It was a delightful sight — and sound. This was going to be home for her. She could begin to feel it.

The sisters finished at the same time, and as Ella washed the dishes, Clara swept the kitchen floor and made sure the stove was properly banked. They walked out together to harness the horse, which had stuck his head over the stall door and was glad to see them. Clara rubbed his nose while Ella threw the harness on and tightened the straps. His bridle went on easily — another of his good points. Horses could be downright stubborn when it came to such things. Nasty ones clenched their teeth or shook their heads from side to side.

Ella led him outside while Clara shut the barn door behind them.

"He's a nice horse," Clara said, holding up the shafts of the buggy.

"Daniel picked a good one," Ella agreed.

"He's *gut* with such things."

"Yah, he is," Ella said. *Would Clara still think Daniel was* gut *if she knew about his visit last night? Clara is a little young for such information. Likely she would blame me for a lost opportunity rather than Daniel for his muddled state of mind. I guess Daniel's visit best remain my secret.*

Clara climbed in and held the reins as the horse stood patiently until Ella had climbed in.

"Getup," she said softly, slapping the reins. The gelding threw his head in the air and took off with a jaunty air.

"He is a nice horse," Clara said, smiling.

"A real nice horse," Ella said as they pulled out of the driveway, wondering whether everyone had as many secrets as she did.

Seven

They drove south and turned east at the river. A fog hung heavy along the banks, making a mist that increased the early summer morning chill. Ella searched for and found the light buggy blanket under the seat. Clara pulled it up well over her knees.

"I don't like this spooky weather," she whispered.

"It's just the clouds come down low." Ella smiled. "Aden always liked a fog along the river, and I think I learned to enjoy it from him."

"Not everyone's like Aden."

"I know," Ella said, feeling her mood dip. She slapped the reins, and the horse responded quickly enough by settling into a steady climb up from the river. They broke out of the mist to see the crest of Seager Hill in front of them.

Her parents' place sat on the ridge, surrounded by Amish farms on either side. A sweep of the valley opened toward the east and west to the low mountains. Ella had always loved the place.

"Mamm will be lookin' for us with all the work that's to be done," Clara said.

"I know." Ella slapped the reins again. "I think I'll stay awhile and help out. Perhaps I can make up for the use of you last night."

"I wanted to stay," Clara said, "and I hope Mamm lets me come some more — even often."

Ella agreed with a nod of her head, pulled to a stop at the bottom of the valley, and then turned left. The horse slowed on the climb up the hill, but Ella was glad to see he wasn't winded as they pulled into the driveway.

While Clara held the shafts, Ella unhitched the horse because she planned to stay at least till noon. Clara waited until Ella returned from the barn, and together they walked toward the house. Ella expected their mom to meet them at the door, or perhaps Dora would. She hadn't been gone so long but that their arrival still warranted some level of interest.

With no one to greet them, Clara walked on in without a knock. Ella supposed she would have done the same, and yet the feeling was a strange one now that she didn't

63

live at home. *Do I just walk in without notice? I suppose so. Some things are just like that — home, family, and where one belongs. They grip the heart with roots that can hardly be dislodged. It's the way things are supposed to be.*

Ella followed Clara into the silent house. Surely her mom was close by, occupied with some task, which kept her from a friendly greeting at the front door.

Through the familiar living room opening, the muffled cries they heard stopped them short. Clara glanced at Ella but said nothing. When Ella stepped forward, Clara followed. Cautiously, Ella entered the living room to find her mom and Dora seated on the couch. Mamm held her handkerchief tightly. Her tears were thick on her cheeks, and a muffled sob still hung in the air.

"What's wrong?" Ella gasped while a hundred fears raced through her mind. *Has there been another accident? Has Daett been injured? Maybe Eli or Monroe?* Since there was no sign of her two brothers or dad, she expected the worse.

"Sit down," Mamm said, motioning with her hand. "We have just been brought news — something I never imagined possible. A terrible thing has happened. Eli's seein' an *Englisha* girl."

Ella's mind raced. *Obviously Dora did not bring the news, I haven't yet confessed to prior knowledge, and so who brought the news?* Ella imagined her face was a picture of guilt and was thankful her mom's eyes were occupied.

"Aunt Sarah stopped by," Dora volunteered as she set her hand protectively on her mother's shoulder. Ella wanted to ask Dora the obvious question but didn't dare. Dora, as if she understood, glanced up and shook her head.

"I just can't believe this! My Eli. And the oldest boy. Why would he have done such a thing? Settin' such an example for the rest of the family. And with no warnin' at all. It's like the sky dropped on our heads."

"Has Daett been told?" Ella asked, her guilt becoming stronger. *Perhaps I should make my confession before Daett arrives.*

"We haven't sent anyone to call them in," Mamm said. "Daett's out in the fields with Eli and Monroe now. The day is completely full of work already with the hay just ready to bale this morning. We are supposed to help load soon — probably starting before lunch. If we say something now, it will end the day's work."

"Mamm, I have something I'd best be tellin' you first," Ella said quietly, so softly her mom apparently didn't hear. Dora looked wildly at her and vigorously shook her head.

Ella felt she must do what was right. Confession was good for the soul, especially in this situation. She gathered herself to speak louder this time, but Mamm spoke first.

"This will break Daett's heart," her mom said with a trembling voice. "His first born son is visiting an *Englisha* girl."

"He was seen leaving town with her Friday night," Dora said, clearly hoping Ella had said all she planned to. "He tied his horse at the Quality Market, and they went out somewhere together in her car."

"It will be all over the world before long," Mamm said in despair.

"Aunt Sarah won't spread this around," Dora assured her. "She wouldn't."

"Maybe not," Mamm agreed, "but someone else will see him. They may have already done so."

Ella decided it was confession time, regardless of the consequences. Dora might not feel guilty, but she did. Her dad would have to be told eventually, and things would only go harder for her and Dora if this came out later.

She cleared her throat, but Dora read her

face and spoke first. "No one's to blame for this. Really, they aren't. We couldn't have done anything about it."

"It falls on our shoulders. Me and Daett," Mamm whispered. "If only we'd known earlier. He must have been seeing her for some time, it would seem."

"I knew," Ella said, kneeling down in front of her mom, placing her hands on her knees. "I knew some time ago that Eli was up to something but thought it best to not say anything. I thought Eli might come to his senses."

"You knew?" Her mom's handkerchief fell from her hand, and her eyes searched Ella's face.

"I'm so sorry," Ella whispered. "Eli's so stubborn about these things."

"Did you help him?"

Ella shook her head.

"I knew too," Dora spoke up. "We both thought Eli wouldn't go this far and that the matter would stay with just talk."

"Perhaps you'd best be telling me everything," their mom said, sitting upright. "Should Clara leave the room?"

Ella shook her head again. "There's not much to say. And Clara can stay."

"Then tell me quickly and don't be leavin' anything out."

Ella got up from the floor and stood weakly in front of her mom. Her heart felt heavy with guilt. Her judgment of Eli hadn't been correct.

"Perhaps I should speak," Dora offered.

Mamm said, "No, I want to hear Ella. The oldest had best tell the story."

As always, Ella thought, *the duty of age comes down with a crash. I am the oldest girl and so held to a higher degree of responsibility.* She cleared her throat, but the words still came out of her mouth with great difficulty.

"I first learned of Eli's attraction to the *Englisha* nurse after he came home from the hospital."

"That long ago." Mamm's voice was a whisper.

Ella continued. "He told me her name was Pam. He said he had invited her to stop by on her way home from work to check up on him while he was still sick in bed . . . since she lives north of here somewhere."

"She came to my house? When I was not at home?"

Ella felt guilt grip her hard and take her breath away. Back then the decision had seemed the right thing. Now, with Mamm's pale face in front of her, she trembled. This had not been her house to allow such privileges, yet she had done so.

"She came when you were at the funeral of David's girlfriend," she managed. "I didn't know she would come, and Eli had seemed uncertain himself."

"But she did come." Her mom shifted on the couch, and her fingers reached for the handkerchief on the floor.

"That day she did stop by," Ella said, "in her nurse's uniform, and so I figured she just wanted to check up on Eli. I couldn't just turn her away. I figured Eli would get over her if he saw her again."

"You made this decision by yourself?"

"I'm sorry," Ella whispered. "It looks different now, and I know now I should have told you. I did try to persuade Eli. I really did. I spoke long and hard with him."

"You tried to instruct your brother?" her mom asked, standing to her feet. "I'm ashamed of you, Ella. I thought we taught you better than that. Have the lessons of our leaders no meanin' to you? In these spiritual things — in matters of Scripture and the tradition of the fathers — it is not up to us women to teach the men. We will always fail. As you have failed. Do you not know this? The matter belonged to your daett . . . by the design of *Da Hah* Himself. Do you not know that after all these years?"

Ella's face burned like fire, and she could say nothing in her defense.

"I knew too," Dora offered in what Ella knew was an attempt to share blame. She felt a rush of emotion at her sister's thoughtfulness.

"Ella is the oldest girl," her mom said, "and she shares the greatest blame. But, yes, you should have known better too, Dora. I am ashamed of both of you. Let this be a lesson for you, Clara, and let it be a good one. This is what happens when women step outside of *Da Hah*'s place for us. You must never be teachin' and sayin' these matters to the men."

Mamm sat down suddenly on the couch. Her face was drawn up in pain.

"But you tell Daett things," Clara said. "I hear you all the time."

Whether this was true or not, Ella wanted to clamp her hand across Clara's mouth, but the words had been spoken. She held her breath and watched her mom's face.

Mamm seemed lost in her own world of grief, but slowly she turned toward Clara. "I know, child. I do," she said, her voice soft. "We all do whether we should or not. I'm just overcome at the moment. I know Ella and Dora meant no harm. I might have done so myself if my brother had been seein' an *Englisha* girl. But what are we to do now? Eli is seein' a girl of the world, and your daett must be told."

"I can tell him," Clara whispered as Ella and Dora sat on each side of Mamm with their arms around her shoulders. In the silence of the living room — the familiar scene of a thousand family gatherings — they all wept together.

EIGHT

"Ach," Mamm finally said, "here we sit like *boblis,* and the day's work has not been done yet."

"I can go tell Daett," Clara repeated her offer and looked relieved the tears had stopped.

"No, I'd best go tell him," Ella said, getting up from the couch. The action seemed right to her, that she — the one who had known before — should be the one to break the news to her father.

"Not now." Her mom stood. "There is hay to put up, and we have the wash to do."

"But I have to get home," Ella said, the words sounding strange in her mouth. This had been her home, and now it wasn't.

"We must speak of this . . . as a family," her mom said, "but it cannot be done now. Not with the hay in the field. Could you stay for the day and help out? Perhaps stay for supper? Then we could talk afterward.

72

You can even stay for the night if you want to."

Ella considered the question with surprise. *I really am grown up. Only last week Mamm would not have asked.*

"It would help out . . . a lot," her mom added with a worried look on her face.

"Then I will," Ella agreed with a weak smile. "The house can just wait."

"Is the place locked up? Did you bank the stove before you left?" Mamm asked.

Ella nodded. "Things will be okay."

"Then it's decided, and you're staying. There is something I needed to tell you, but I had forgotten, what with the news of Eli's doin's. Sarah also said Joe and Ronda are lookin' for a place to rent."

"They're getting married soon," Dora said loudly from the kitchen.

"But what's that got to do with me?" Ella asked.

"Well, I was thinking. With you in that big house — why, it's big enough for three families — they could live upstairs, and you could make some extra money. I know you'll be needing money since you're living on your own now."

"For how long?" Ella asked, trying to imagine another family in her house. She did need the money, so she was slow to

73

express her concern.

"Think about it," Mamm said, "but you do need to let Ronda know soon. I expect they could live in her mamm and daett's *dawdy haus* for a while if they have to, but this would be much better."

"They're startin' to bale," Dora hollered from the kitchen. "It's time to go. Are you comin'?"

"I sure do appreciate this," Mamm said as Ella and Dora left the house together.

"This was nice of you," Dora added once they were outside, walking quickly up the long lane where their dad had the baler parked.

"I couldn't say no," Ella replied. "It's not like I have much to do at home other than sit around and think about how to live my life."

"Looks like Eli's got our evening taken care of," Dora said, glancing across the knee-high grass in the center of the lane.

"I sure was wrong on that one," Ella confessed. The words felt good to say. Not that they changed the situation, but confession did benefit the soul.

"I suppose I was too," Dora agreed.

"I shouldn't have tried to straighten him out by myself like Mamm said. It wasn't my place."

"You know she does the same." Dora bent over and caught a long stem of grass in her fingers. The piece refused to tear, and she refused to let go or break her stride. With a jerk the grass came up by the roots. The heavy end snapped forward, and Dora stepped sideways without even a backward glance so that it missed her legs. She let go on the upward arch, and the whole thing flew over the fence.

Ella watched the grassy missile land with a thud and wished she could get rid of her troubles that easily, to just sidestep them and let them go.

"She does," Dora repeated.

"I know. I suppose we all do, but it still doesn't make it right."

"I'm thinkin' of quitting Norman," Dora said, her voice quiet. "There are too many things I want to change about him."

"Just because of what Mamm said this morning?"

"Maybe in part." Dora shrugged. "I've been thinkin' about all his faults lately anyway."

"That's just the dark side of you speaking," Ella said, trying to sound hopeful. With Dora it was hard. "You'll get over those feelings. Norman's a nice match for you."

"He asked to marry me. He asked on Sunday night."

"Then why are you moaning?" Ella smiled. "That sounds like good news to me."

"I haven't even told Mamm, and I don't want to until I know for certain."

"But you told him the answer, surely?"

Dora shook her head. "I told him I'd have to think about it. Ella, did you ever get scared with Aden once you knew for sure?"

Ella wished she could say she had been, if for no other reason but to comfort Dora. Dora took her silence as the answer, and her face darkened. "See, that's what I mean. I want to have what you and Aden had."

"It's not the same for everyone," Ella said. "Love comes in all kinds of ways."

"That's what you say, and yet you'll always be lookin' for the same thing again all the days of your life. You'll even turn down the offer from the bishop just because he's not like Aden. And still you want me to accept that love's different. Don't you think you should be doin' the same?"

"What makes you say that?" Ella said a little too sharply even in her own judgment.

"Because it's the truth, and you need to hear it." Dora plucked another stem of grass. This time the stalk detached itself easily. She bit off a piece and tossed the rest by the lane.

"I'm not marrying anyone," Ella said firmly. "I've told you that before — you and Mamm and Daett."

"You should listen to your own words — the ones you just spoke to me."

"That's different. You never lost the one you loved with all your heart. There is just one Aden. That's all. Only one, Dora. There will never be another one."

"I might not have lost my beloved, yet losing and never havin' come much closer than you think."

"I'm not taking Bishop just because someone thinks I ought to."

"Many of the girls would fall over backwards in their rush to take his hand. You know that, Ella. Are you too high and mighty for his offer?"

"Would you take his offer?" Ella asked.

"I don't know," Dora shrugged. "I don't think I'm the bishop's high and mighty wife material. The match really would make us both unhappy."

"The sun has addled your brain, Dora. As sure as it's shining, it has."

Dora laughed. "It's the truth that hurts, they say. This sure sounds like its hurting, sure as Norman's buggy's wheels will be heard here on Sunday."

"I think we have enough trouble with Eli without adding in the dear bishop."

Dora laughed again. "I suppose so, and I guess Eli's out of our hands now. Daett would be whoppin' his tail if he wasn't so big already."

Ella shook her head. "I wish it were that simple, but people do grow up. And Eli's grown up, I'm afraid." Her face darkened. Serious trouble lay ahead this evening, and there seemed little she could do about it. Ahead of them the baler sat, already fired up. Its diesel engine belched black smoke. The wagon, full of loose hay, sat beside it. Eli stood on top, ready to pitch the hay to the ground for Monroe to heave into the baler.

Both of the brothers noticed them at the same time and waved their hats high in the air.

"Someone's glad to see you," Dora muttered.

"Look who crawled out of her fancy house," Eli shouted. "The queen of the south has come down to walk on the ground."

"With her robes lifted high," Monroe added, laughing. His voice could barely be heard above the noise of the engine.

A lump caught in Ella's throat. How could Eli be so normal, so cheerful, so like her brother, when he did such awful things on weekend nights? She wanted to run to him, shake him up, order him to behave, stop what he did, and make him return to the straight and narrow way, but it would do no good. Eli was way too stubborn to listen to her. Soon her father would be involved, and Eli might still not change his ways.

"She is silent. Her pride has gripped her," Eli shouted with a laugh. "My, it's good to be seein' you. It seems like years since we moved you away."

"You are a naughty boy," Ella shouted back.

Eli, oblivious to her true meaning, replied, "Ach, she speaks!" while waving his fork around in mock joy. "I guess the big house hasn't spoiled her yet."

"Take care with that fork of yours," Monroe hollered up at him. "I'm not likin' the possibility of being punched through by your carelessness."

"I'm going to help Daett," Ella said. "Dora can stay with your wagon."

Dora nodded. Either way, they would switch wagons as the need arose. Across the field, her father was driving the team of horses with his voice. He could start and stop them easily. Directing them left and right was the problem. Few work horses were so highly trained.

Ella walked toward him, his broad back bent away from her. How old he looked with the sun shining so brightly on him. It seemed to bring out his age like light on cloth reveals uneven stitches.

"Life has been kind to me," he often said. "I thank *Da Hah* for the *gut* family I have, my health, and so many great blessings in life."

Yet Ella could see his condition with her own eyes. *Daett won't be with us forever.*

He turned to greet her with a smile as she approached the side of the wagon, but his shoulders were still stooped. She wondered if they would go even lower tonight when he learned the news of what his eldest son was up to. Consorting with *Englisha* girls was a nightmare no Amish parent ever hoped would be their lot and a matter to be spoken of with fear.

"You've come to help," her dad said with joy in his voice. "This is a great delight for my old eyes."

"Mamm thought I should," she said, "and I was glad to. The big house can live by itself for a day."

"Ach, your house. Yah, it is a house that

needs a husband. Now is this not true? But my daughter should have no trouble findin' one. Has the good bishop come callin' yet?"

"No." Ella almost choked on the answer.

"Then he will soon," her dad said with a look of satisfaction on his face. "I am so pleased *Da Hah* has seen fit to give you such a chance at a *gut* husband. You lost so much when Aden was taken from you."

Ella hadn't the heart to tell him she planned to turn down the good bishop. She stuck her pitchfork into a thin line of loose hay and heaved it upward, toward the top of the hay wagon. Today the sun was on her face, she was in the hay field with her father, and life couldn't be better. Why spoil the joy with hard words? Tonight they would be spoken soon enough.

NINE

They loaded the wagon with the loose hay until the stack swayed from side to side and Ella could no longer reach the top with her fork.

"I'm going up," she hollered lest her dad order the horses forward while she stood on the tongue of the wagon. Quickly she stepped up, climbing high on the top of the swaying hay wagon with the help of the slated wooden supports.

The lines for the two horses were wrapped around the top rail. Ella unwrapped them with one hand before she pulled herself on up. Her legs sunk three quarters of the way in, and she leaned backward quickly to avoid a fall forward.

A thrill went all the way through her, despite all her years of riding on stacked hay wagons. Ella laughed for sheer joy. Here she was, a grown woman, once nearly married, and now sought out by the bishop himself, and, still, she felt like a schoolgirl on the first day of class. She gripped the reins and yelled for the horse to move. Her dad looked up at her and grinned. The wagon lurched forward, and Ella swayed wildly. The steel wheels bounced through a ground hog hole.

This is my life. This is where I belong — safe and secure from the world and its evils. How could Eli breach this safe way of life? The question ran through her with a sharp pang. She looked across the field to where the other wagon rolled along. They had just started to load. Dora and Monroe pitched from one side while Eli, his back turned to her, threw great fork loads of hay high into the air.

How strong Eli is, and Monroe too, like men are supposed to be. Why, then, does Eli's judgment fail him in one of the most important decisions of his life? Ella pulled the lines hard to the left and brought the wagon to a stop in front of the baler. The engine's roar was loud in her ears again.

"A little forward," her father shouted above the noise.

She yelled to the horses, and they tightened the traces with a jerk. She pulled back on the lines, wrapped them around the upper rail, and then walked clumsily to the center of the stack and began to pitch hay down.

Below, her dad forked in the loose pieces she threw down and what he could detach himself. The baler groaned and moaned and then spit out the square bale of hay on the other side. When several piled up, Daett walked around and threw the bales onto another wagon. An hour later, it was half full, and Daett and Ella were back with their second load.

Ella's back began to ache, and she straightened up for a moment. When the wagon was filled with bales, they would drive up together and unload at the elevator. Likely she and Dora would stay at the bottom and toss in the bales. The three men would be up in the vast loft. There, the fresh bales tumbled out, bouncing wildly in the air. The men grabbed them and stacked them high against the walls.

The ancient ways of my people, she thought. There were not that many *Englisha* farmers around for her to watch at work, but those she had seen farther down in the valley drove their tractors in the hay fields and towed the balers behind them. Likely their work was easier than this. Easier, perhaps, as their Amish preachers would often point out, but this hard work was the lifeblood of their Amish lifestyle. To preserve this life, each modern change must be questioned and usually said no to. She decided it was well worth it even if one could not always understand the reasons why.

"Almost lunch time," her father hollered from the ground.

Ella jerked herself out of her thoughts to stick the fork deep in the hay. She brought the fork up with both hands and saw the great lump of hay on the end. For a moment, she thought it wouldn't come loose and her arms would give out. Then gravity came to her rescue, and the whole thing slid downward.

Her dad's face — sporting a broad grin — came into focus through the strings of hay.

"Just thought you might have gone to sleep up there," he said, laughing. "I'm about starved myself. We'll go eat after this — when Eli's wagon is down."

Ella wanted to tell him that things other than food were on her mind, even though her stomach growled in hunger. She wanted to explain that strange thoughts stirred her — thoughts about Eli, about her new house and the bishop, and now questions about why they did things the way they always did.

Yet, how do I ask such questions in the hay field, where the very air settles them before they can come out of my mouth. To settle all questions, the preachers say to do what is right. The answer is evident here in the open field, under the blaze of Da Hah's bright sun, and with Daett's strong back bent to his pitchfork and practicing what he believes. Is this not answer enough for anyone?

Ella climbed down when the last of the hay was unloaded and then drove forward so Eli could pull up. She stayed on the ground and helped fork hay into the baler. Dora and Monroe tossed down the loose hay from their load. With two people working, the load decreased quickly, and Eli jumped back on the wagon when they were done. He hollered to the horses, drove forward, and turned toward the house. Ella followed with the other empty wagon while her dad brought up the rear with the wagon full of baled hay.

Slowly they drove up the lane, making the steel wheels rattle loudly. Pulling the empty wagons, the tired horses soon trotted in anticipation of water and their noon meal of oats. Daett, with his full wagon, was left far behind. Ella pulled into the barnyard and parked behind Eli. Her hair was pushed back under her head covering, and her emotions were flushed with pleasure after the run.

How can Eli think about leaving this life? Is that not what he is planning, or are his thoughts, instead, just all muddled up thinking about the girl? Muddled up thoughts can be straightened out. On purpose would be another matter.

They unhitched the horses quickly and were back outside to help Daett when he pulled up.

"Runnin' away from the old man?" her father said, throwing his lines on the ground as they all pitched in to help unhitch.

"Can we unload the bales after dinner?" Eli asked. "I'm starved."

"I suppose so," Daett allowed. "They aren't goin' anywhere."

Their mom, Lizzie, had sandwiches and glasses of lemonade set out on the table. They gathered quickly without many words and followed Daett as he bowed his head.

"Thank You, dear Lord," he prayed, "for this day You have given us. Thank You for Your loving kindness, for breath in our bodies, and for grace for our souls. Thank You that Ella could be with us again. You know we need the help, but more than that, we are glad she could be with us.

"Let Your Almighty power be with us and

bless this food. Be with those who have not, the orphans and the homeless who suffer. We ask that Your hand reach them and that You comfort their hearts. In our plenty, we lift our hearts in great thanks. We are not worthy. Only You and Your great name are worthy. In the name of the Father, the Son, and the Holy Spirit."

Ella let the air out of her chest with a long sigh. The sandwiches in front of her eyes drifted in and out of focus. She pressed back her tears as she realized that such moments with her family would now be rare not just because she'd moved away, but because of the moves the others would make. Life moves on. Things could not be stopped, even if one wanted them to.

"How are things comin' along?" Mamm asked to no one in particular.

"Three wagons full already," Daett declared. "Pretty good, I would say. It sure was nice of Ella to help."

"I'm glad to," she said, reaching for a second sandwich.

"This is a good year for hay," Eli said. "The second and third cuttings might be just as good."

"Yah," Daett agreed, "if the rains come like we hope."

"They have come so far," Monroe said.

"That can always change," Daett said in a solemn voice. "Everything can change — and so fast."

Ella wished with all her heart that the evening was here already, that things would never change, and that she could be certain they never would, but, of course, that could never be. *Great change could well be ahead for us — changes none of us could imagine or anticipate. When boys go out with* Englisha *girls, anything can happen. Things can also happen if I say no to a marriage proposal from a certain bishop.*

"You're enjoying your house?" Monroe asked, interrupting her thoughts.

"It's really nice," Clara said, and Ella nodded. "I want to move over to Ella's house," Clara continued. "I want to live with Ella and stay there all the time."

"You're a little young for that," Mamm said. "You'd best be thinkin' about stayin' home. And, besides, we need you here."

"Ella's putting ideas into the child's head," Monroe said, "because she's lonely there in that big house, that's why."

"That's why she needs a husband," Eli offered, "right quick, I'm thinkin'."

"You can keep your thoughts to yourself," Ella informed them.

"I'll be speakin' them if I want to," Eli

said with a laugh. "I think Dora agrees with me, don't you, Dora dear."

"Tell me why I should stick up for you?" Dora retorted.

"Cause I'm such a nice fellow." Eli smiled an evil smile.

He sure is mighty full of himself. Tonight is just ahead, and with this attitude, things do not look well at all. "I think your hat's a little big for your head," Ella told Eli just so he would know how she felt about it.

Dora chuckled, and Eli laughed heartedly. "You are a good one, if I must say so myself."

Ella felt a rush of emotion swell up in her heart. *How I love him and so much the more now that he's in trouble.* Tears stung her eyes, and Eli gave her a strange look. She managed a smile, and it seemed to satisfy him at least enough to make the conversation move on to other topics — safer conversations than what surely lay ahead.

TEN

The sun hung red in the evening sky by the time they pulled the last wagon of bales up to the elevator.

"I haven't felt so exhausted in a long time," Ella said, "but it feels *gut* anyway."

"It's *gut* to get you out of that big house," Eli said.

"Would you two quit chattering? There are still chores to do," Dora snapped. "Let's get the bales of hay up to the mow."

Eli and Monroe looked at each other, shrugged, and shook the straw off their hats.

"I think I'll save my breath with her," Eli muttered as he and Monroe headed into the barn to climb back into the haymow.

"They are *gut* brothers," Ella said, making a point to look at Dora. "You don't have to snap at them."

"I guess I'm tired, and discussing Eli's troubles is still ahead," Dora admitted.

Ella stretched her arms, brushed the

strings of straw off her head covering, and got ready to throw down the first bale of hay.

"I'm too tired to worry how I look," Dora muttered as she pulled the starter rope of the elevator motor.

The engine took off with a sputter. The steel chain engaged and caused its usual racket as Ella threw on a bale of hay. For a moment, she thought she had lost her aim. The bale teetered on the edge and then jerked upward as the teeth on the elevator chain caught it. Dora shook her head and climbed up and over the wooden slats. Together they swung in turns. The long line of bales angled off toward the haymow above them until the last bale left the floor of the wagon visible.

Dora jumped off the wagon, fetched the water jug, and drank deeply before passing it to Ella. Ella let the stream of water run into her mouth and overflow before she swallowed. The taste was heavenly. She took the jug with her into the barn in case the thirst returned before they were done milking.

Ella pulled the three-legged stool off the wall and sat down beside the first cow. Relief spread all the way through her as her back and leg muscles relaxed. Driven by their hunger for the evening meal, they all milked as fast as they could. Eli had half the cows loose by the time Ella finished her second cow. She jumped back against the wall, her full milk bucket held high, as the cows moved out. Eli could be excused for his haste, so she didn't say anything. They were all in a hurry.

Eli let in the second round of cows as Ella emptied her bucket of milk into the strainer. She picked up her stool again and sat down, careful the one leg didn't settle into the gutter in her tired state of mind. Dora, looking as tired as she felt, finished her third cow first.

"I'll finish the last two," Eli offered as he let the cows out again. "We have a lot of dry ones, so there are only two more." He slapped a few backsides to speed things up.

Ella followed Dora to the house. Neither of them said much. Dora's usually dark face was even darker than normal. Ella noticed the look of concern on her mom's face when they arrived in the kitchen.

"Need any help?" Ella asked.

"You girls can set the table. I'm almost done here."

Ella opened the silverware drawer and took out an assorted handful while Dora got the plates from the cupboard. Out in the washroom, the door slammed, and water splashed roughly in the bowl.

"They still make a lot of racket, even when they're washing," Dora muttered.

"*Da Hah* be praised," Daett said loudly as he stepped into the kitchen. "We got all the hay up — with Ella's *gut* help. She will be an honor to any man who can claim her as his wife."

"Daett," Ella said, but even Dora had to smile a little.

"Well, it is true," he said.

"The food is ready," Mamm said, bringing two bowls to the table.

"Then let's eat," Daett said as they all took their seats at the table.

"Our gracious and mighty heavenly Father," he prayed almost before Ella could get her head bowed. As he finished, Mamm began passing the food around.

"We've got plenty now, so don't be afraid," she said.

"As if I would," Eli laughed.

"Yah, you all have *gut* manners," Mamm said warmly but with a noticeable catch in her voice.

Ella glanced at her dad, but he seemed lost in his food. *What will he be saying after supper?*

Only minutes later Mamm said, "And now

for the cherry pie." She rose and brought out three pies from where they sat on the counter. "We've got plenty. I've made sure of it."

"You'll spoil us all," Daett said. "Ach, can I really find room yet? Perhaps a small piece."

"A *big* one," Mamm said, sliding the piece onto his plate.

"Right *gut* service tonight," Daett said with satisfaction and a twinkle to Mamm.

Daett ate slowly and then bowed his head in silent prayer when the last plate had been scraped clean. Eli and Monroe got up immediately and left for upstairs. With a long look at Lizzie, who stood at the counter turned away from him, Daett went into the living room. He returned a moment later to retrieve the gas lanterns from the utility room. He set them on the bench, pumped air into them, and then lit both, leaving one on the nail in the kitchen ceiling and carrying the other stream of light with him. Ella, with her hands deep in soap suds, turned for a quick glance at his retreating back. *When will Mamm bring up the subject of Eli? Apparently she wants all the work done first.*

Dora and Mamm cleared the rest of the table while Clara stood at Ella's right side, drying the dishes. She practically grabbed each item the moment Ella set it on the rack so she could dry each piece quickly.

"They're supposed to drip-dry a little," Ella whispered.

"I know, but I'm in a hurry."

"You'd best be going upstairs," Mamm whispered from behind them. "I'll finish wiping the dishes."

"I already know about . . . tonight," Clara said. "I want to hear what Daett says about it."

Mamm shook her head. "This is for grown-up ears. And don't go getting your feelings hurt over it. I don't want Monroe here either."

Clara's expression fell, but she offered no comment. They all followed Mamm into the living room, and Ella and Dora found seats on the couch. Clara opened the stair door, gave one last beseeching look to her mom, and then disappeared.

Mamm waited at the doorway until the sound of Clara's steps on the hardwood stairs had stopped. "Eli," she called, "will you come down, please."

"What?" the answer came, muffled by the closed bedroom door.

"Come down here now," she repeated with a firm tone to her voice.

Ella saw her dad drop the edge of *The*

Budget. He had a solemn look on his face, and she thought he would say something, but then the paper went back up again.

"We need to speak of a serious matter," Mamm said to Daett as they heard Eli's steps on the stairs.

"So what's this?" Eli asked from the bottom step. Wearing a weary grin on his face, he continued, "A family gatherin'? And that after this long day."

"You'd best keep your jokes to yourself," Mamm said. "Sit yourself on the couch. We need to speak with you."

"Oh." Eli's mood sobered as he sat down beside Ella.

She avoided his eyes. *If he's honest, he already knows what this is about. Sins are that way. They always get found out, and Eli knows that as well as any of us.*

"So," Daett said, folding *The Budget* completely and setting it on his lap, "you have somethin', Mamm? I thought you looked bothered at the supper table."

"I am more than bothered," she said.

"But you haven't told me?"

"I only learned of the matter this morning. This is too serious to discuss before the work had been done. We need time to think and to talk without the day's burdens on our shoulders."

"You have always been a wise woman," Daett said. "*Da Hah* also waited for the cool of the day to discuss the matter when the first man and woman sinned. I'm supposin' this is serious, then."

"Eli is seein' an *Englisha* girl," Mamm said straightaway, allowing the words to tumble out.

Ella felt some relief now that it was out in the open.

"An *Englisha* girl?" Daett said. His voice rose in surprise, and his paper slid off his lap and sprawled in separate pieces across the hardwood floor. "Eli? Are you sure of this, Mamm? Is this true, Eli?"

"It is true," Mamm said.

Eli's face was pale. "Did you girls go tellin' on me?" he asked, turning to Ella and Dora. Both girls shook their heads.

"That's another thing," Mamm said. "The girls are here because they knew about this, but they decided to keep their silence."

"So, who did this come from?" Eli asked, his voice rising.

"Son, look . . ." Daett said. "You really shouldn't be accusin' someone else. This sin lies at your door."

"Pam," Eli said, rising from the couch, "is not a sin. She is the best thing *Da Hah* has ever given me. Her love warms my heart when I am with her. How can that be a sin?"

"But she is *Englisha!*" Mamm exclaimed. "And what of the girls, Daett? They both knew of this and tried to teach Eli themselves. They thought they could turn him back from his error."

"Is this true?"

Ella felt her dad's eyes on her and struggled for breath. All day she had prepared for this, yet the moment still caught her by the throat.

How could I have prepared for Daett's disapproval, his judgment on my actions, and his disappointment in me? The hiss of the gas lantern filled the room, and somehow she found her voice. "It is true that I knew and told Dora. And I did try to correct Eli, but Dora did not. In this the error is all mine."

"You always took too much upon yourself," Daett said, his voice low, "but our son is our business, and he will answer to us."

"I will answer to God," Eli retorted. "I am not a member of the church, and in this matter of love, I will follow my heart. Did not Ella and Aden have the best? Should I not also have the best?"

"Aden and Ella?" Daett asked with a voice filled with surprise. "What has this to do with them? Did Aden know also?"

Eli shook his head. "I mean their love. How true it was. It was one of a kind, like a cow that gives twice the milk. I saw it with my own eyes — how they loved each other. And I want that kind of love."

Ella felt the tears begin to trickle down her face. She restrained her instinct to wipe them away.

"You believe *Da Hah* cannot give you such love with one of our girls?" Daett asked, leaning forward in his rocker.

"He hasn't," Eli said.

"That is not a good answer," Daett said. "We are all tested in our faith, and you did not seem to pass this one, it looks like."

"I am not a wild boy. You know that. I have given you no sorrow and no reason to doubt me, as some sons have. Can you not believe me on this? I must see whether this love is true to the end."

"You are seein' an *Englisha* girl," Mamm said. "Is that not sorrow enough? How can that ever be made right?"

"How can you say that?" Eli asked, distress in his voice.

"Eli, look," Daett said. "I have no complaints about you. You have been all a son could be. You do not hold back from your work on the farm. You are up with the dawn as any good man should be. Your mamm and I have no regrets. Yet in this you have chosen the wrong way. You might think it a matter of decidin' later, but that is not how it is with these matters of the heart. They become their own road. Once started, they cannot be left easily. It would be best if you let this girl know that you will not be seein' her again. You can ask your sisters if you don't know of any suitable girls among our own people. They can tell you of them. Then *Da Hah* will be mendin' your heart before you know it. And your mamm and I will be at peace in our old age."

After a brief silence in which Ella held her breath, Eli said, "I cannot do this, Daett. I love her too much."

Mamm's silent tears became gentle sobs.

Eli's face was fixed and unmoving like a rock in the field. "I will leave — tonight even — if that is for the best. I will find a place in town, perhaps, if this will keep you from shame and sorrow."

Ella heard Dora gasp, and then silence settled again. The lantern hissed loudly above them. *What will Daett say? Is this the end for Eli? Is this how I am to remember him — white faced, on his feet beside the couch, and determined to love the one he's chosen? Can I dare offer my home to him now and give him a place of shelter?* Suddenly the question was a mountain over which she could see no pass to cross.

Daett leaned back in his chair and focused on the ceiling. Ella thought Eli would say something more, but he was silent.

"You cannot send him away," Mamm said in a weak voice.

"We must do what is right," Daett said to Mamm. He drew out each word slowly. "Yet this is not the time. I will speak more with my son . . . perhaps later. We can surely reason with him." Turning to Eli, he continued, "No, Eli, you can stay. You have not yet sinned so greatly that it calls for leavin'."

Eli's head came up, and relief flooded his face. Brave as he had been, his heart had not wished to leave. Ella reached out to him, squeezed his hand, and saw a tear spring to his eye. He loved them all, she knew. Surely, by the grace of God something could be worked out.

"It is well, then . . . for now. We will speak more of this later," Daett said as he began rocking slowly. "But I would speak with Ella and you too, Mamm, after the others have gone."

Dora went to stand with Eli. Glancing at each other, they walked to the stairs and climbed them one by one without comment.

Ella gripped the side of the couch till her fingers hurt. *Is Daett now going to deal with me for my silence on the matter?*

ELEVEN

The sound of Eli and Dora's footsteps on the hardwood stairs faded into silence. Ella could feel the tightness in her chest while an intense fear gripped her entire body.

"I know I have sinned with my silence," she whispered, "yet I meant this for good."

Daett cleared his throat. The sound blended in one seamless note with the gas lantern on the ceiling. She turned to face him and take his judgment with courage and his rebuke with an open heart.

Instead a smile played on his face and a gentle look softened his eyes. She drew her breath in astonishment. The sudden burst of air burned her throat.

"I wished to speak in private," he said gently, "because this also is a matter of the heart — not of judgment. I wish to speak to you about the bishop. Has he come to visit yet?"

Ella's mind whirled in an effort to bring

her thoughts around. The memory of the bishop's visit here many months ago flashed before her eyes. She remembered his knees on the chair close to hers as he focused his full attention on her face.

"He hasn't come," she said in a voice barely above a whisper.

"Then *Da Hah* has been kind to us. But is it not about time that he comes?" Daett said. "I cannot keep track, but it seems like it's time. My mind is not like it once was."

"He should come soon," Ella said. *What is the connection between this and Eli?*

"Has he perhaps changed his mind?" Daett asked, leaning forward in his rocker.

"Of course he hasn't," Mamm interjected, "but I'm not seein' what you mean. Is this your daughter's mind you're askin' about?"

"Well?" Noah smiled.

"Then you'd best leave it alone," Mamm said. "We both hope she makes it up in the bishop's favor, but you'd best not be pushin'."

"I'm not," Daett said, "but my heart was just hopin' she could help out with Eli's problem. Perhaps she could ask the bishop to speak with him. I think Eli would listen then."

"I had not thought of that," Mamm said.

Noah nodded. "Perhaps if Ella speaks to

him — the bishop is a wise man beyond his years — and if he would speak to Eli, maybe his words may well turn Eli to his senses."

"Have you made your mind up yet?" Mamm asked.

Ella opened her mouth, but no sound came out. She saw clearly what her father saw. Her relationship to the bishop could well be the answer to Eli's problem. Eli might listen and mend his ways if he were instructed by a person of such spiritual authority.

"Then *Da Hah* be praised," Daett said. "Who can account for the wisdom of the Most High? I will have a daughter married to a great man and save my son from the folly of his ways. Can a man be more blessed than that?"

"There's always trouble down the road," Mamm said, but a smile played on her face.

Ella tried to collect herself and tell them she could not give the bishop a good answer, but the face of Eli rose before her, and her voice remained silent.

Daett searched the floor for his paper, reached out, and gathered it up. "Then *Da Hah* has sent comfort along with our trouble."

The full impact of her father's words gripped Ella. *How can I disappoint them?*

What had seemed almost finished now looked like it would never end.

"You can have your old room tonight," Mamm said, smiling and wiping her eyes of tears. "Dora hasn't moved in yet. I asked her to wait awhile."

"I think I'll go to bed, then," Ella said, getting up. She felt dizzy, her body was weary to the bone, and her heart beat wildly in panic. *How am I to get out of this dilemma? Surely a continued relationship with the bishop — and perhaps marriage — is too great a sacrifice to ask for, even to get help for Eli.*

She found the door to the stairs. Although the floor appeared fuzzy in front of her, she successfully climbed the steps and made it to her room. Her hand turned the bedroom doorknob and pushed open the door. By the dim light from the window, she paused and then walked slowly forward. She found the matches in the same old place and lit the kerosene lamp.

Everything was as she had left it. Even the quilt on the bed hadn't been changed. Ella walked to the window and pulled the blinds back. There was no moon in the sky, which made the stars bright overhead. She let the tears come as the blinds slipped from her fingers and back into place. Her heart was so weary.

Beside the dresser, she blew out the light but lay under the covers wide awake. She wished she had her journal with her. At least then she could write for a while and get her muddled thoughts onto paper.

The evening's decision couldn't or, rather, wouldn't be turned back. The strength wasn't in her to do so. Nor could she pretend affection when the bishop returned for his answer. *How am I to fool him even for a time?*

She tossed and turned and tried to imagine what would happen. The bishop's handsome face rose before her, and she heard his earnest words at his first visit. His interest in her was all too obvious. In a way Dora had been right. He was not unattractive, but her heart twisted at the thought.

Aden was my love — the sole focus of my attention — for so many years. His place can never be filled, not even if I want it to be, which I don't, regardless of how well-thought-of and self-confident the bishop is.

There must be a way out somehow. Da Hah *hasn't forsaken me yet, and surely He isn't going to now.* Wearily, she climbed out of bed, walked to the window again, and pushed back the blinds. A few clouds scurried across the starry sky, hurrying along as if they had places to be.

"Dear God," she prayed. "I need strength, direction in this matter, courage to speak the truth, and help for Eli."

She waited and let her breath out slowly. *Somehow I have to face the bishop and tell him the truth — that I cannot give him my heart and that Eli needs help. If he is a gut man, as they say, perhaps he won't deny us the help we need. I owe him honesty, and surely Mamm and Daett will understand.*

A measure of peace came, and she let the curtain down again. She climbed into bed but set no alarm, knowing that the familiar household sounds would awaken her as they always had.

When the gentle morning noises began, she awoke gently. They wouldn't expect her to help chore, but she got up anyway, lit the kerosene lamp, and dressed quickly. Downstairs, the sounds of her mom's usual morning bustle came from the kitchen.

"You could have slept in," Lizzie said. "You're on your own now."

"I know. I guess I'm finding that out."

"I hope you won't think I'm pushing," Mamm began, "but when the bishop comes, you will be sayin' yes? Is that what I understood from your silence last night?"

Ella felt some relief that the question was directly put to her. She mustered up her courage and said, "Mamm, I don't know if I can marry the bishop. I don't think so. I don't feel for him the way I did toward Aden, and I'll have to tell him so when he comes."

Ella could see the look of disappointment on her mom's face. "I might never love a man again," she continued. "I have to be honest about this."

"Well, don't make your mind up too quickly," Mamm said sadly, shoving another piece of wood into the oven. "Perhaps *Da Hah* will make a way. The bishop's a good man, Ella. He would make a *gut* husband for you. Please just let him have his say and listen to him. He might say the right words to turn your heart toward love."

"I can't promise," Ella said as she began to set the table.

"Just keep your mind open. That's all we ask."

"I will speak to him about Eli. That much I can do."

"That would be good. Your daett has his heart set on it." Then Mamm turned the conversation back to the bishop's intentions. "He's good lookin', nice too, and a great man of our people. Your children would be

110

brought up well . . . solid in the faith."

"Mamm —"

"Just keep your mind open to him, Ella. That's all I ask. That's all your daett asked. I know Aden left a great hole in that heart of yours, as he left a hole in all our hearts, but we must go on. Life continues in the way *Da Hah* wishes it, and we had best listen to Him and to what He wants."

"I'll try." Ella set the last plate on the table.

"I know you will," Mamm said. "That's all anyone can do."

They finished breakfast preparations with a peaceful silence between them. Ella was thankful. She couldn't imagine how awful it would be to have discord between her mamm and daett. *How does Eli stand it?*

The screen door snapped out in the washroom, and the water could soon be heard splashing in the washbasin. Ella moved the last of the food to the table while her mom sliced bread. She retrieved butter and jam from the lower shelf in the pantry and then went upstairs to call her younger sisters and help them dress before coming downstairs.

When everyone was seated at the table, Daett said, "*Gut* mornin'." Ella took his good spirits to mean that he was confident that the bishop would speak to Eli and

111

convince him to give up Pam. She looked over to Eli and noticed he looked a little guilty.

After prayer her dad cleared his throat, and Ella knew more was to come.

"Ella, your mamm says you might have a chance to let the house out to cousin Ronda."

Ella nodded and took a bite of her eggs.

"That's a good idea," he said. "Why don't you just let the whole house out and come back here? We could stand having you — if you could stand us."

Ella weighed her words. "I like the house," she began. "I'll be stayin'. It gives me a good feelin', making my own way."

"Well, you're always welcome," he said and then with a twinkle added, "until someone picks you for his fine wife."

Monroe laughed, and Ella glared at him. Eli was silent.

"You shouldn't tease the girl so," Mamm said, coming to Ella's defense.

"She can take it," Daett said with a smile. "All my children can. Look at what she has already gone through. And now she has her own house. I did try to raise them well, but this is *Da Hah*'s blessin'. His grace, that's what it is."

Ella kept her eyes down, feeling the

warmth of her dad's praise. He wasn't aware the bishop might get turned down. But hopefully, if Eli was still helped, her dad wouldn't react too harshly.

"*Da Hah* will continue to help us," Daett said, turning his gaze to Eli.

They finished breakfast, and Dora helped Ella harness her horse while her brothers made a dash to get the Belgians ready. The upper hay field was ready today, and she felt guilt about her departure.

"You shouldn't be feelin' so," Dora said as if reading her thoughts. "We all have to leave sometime. And you're just doin' it a little different. If you were married, it would still be the same."

"I guess so," Ella said, getting in the buggy.

"Keep that chin up," Dora said. "There's always more trouble down the road."

"How does that help?"

"Keeps you in condition to face it properly," Dora said quite soberly.

"Be seeing you, then." Ella laughed, slapped the reins, and urged the horse to pull forward. She turned the buggy sharply to the right and drove down the blacktop.

TWELVE

Her house needed attention, but more importantly Ella needed to speak to Ronda. Ella wasn't sure she could live with another couple. In the short time she had been there, Ella had grown to love her house and was reluctant to give up any part of it to another person, much less a married couple. Yet the practicality of it was obvious. It would bring in some income and help out Ronda and Joe too.

Ella slapped the reins and turned down the road toward the house where Ronda still lived with her parents. Moments later she pulled in the driveway and came to a stop at the hitching post. No one seemed to be around, but she tied up anyway, then walked up to the house, and knocked on the door. The sound was loud in the morning stillness.

All around her were the signs of wedding preparations. The grass looked like it had been cut yesterday. A lighter spot in the yard showed where some farm implement had sat. The wood siding on the house looked scrubbed. Across the yard, the pole barn had been completely cleared of farm tools and swept clean. It sat empty now but would soon be filled with benches and tables, set up in long rows for the noon and evening wedding meals. For a brief moment, the unfulfilled plans for her own wedding to Aden stung at her heart, but she quickly dismissed the memory.

The screen door rattled in front of her, and her aunt Sharon opened the door.

"Ach, it's you!" she exclaimed. "We were all busy upstairs, but Ronda did say she thought someone drove in."

"I won't be keepin' you long, then," Ella said. "Mamm mentioned that Ronda and Joe might need a place to live."

"Come inside." Sharon held the door open. "Yes, it did cross my mind, and I said something to your mamm. Ronda really thought the plan a workable idea when I asked her. It's certainly much better than the one we have now. But we don't want to be imposin' on you. I know you just moved into the house and all."

"I think it might work, and I need the income," Ella said.

Sharon smiled. "Don't we all." She walked over to the stairs and called, "Ronda, Ella's here."

A quick patter of feet came down the steps, and Ronda appeared.

"Good morning!" she exclaimed. "I'm glad it's you. I did so want to talk to you."

"Sit down, then," Sharon said, waving her hand and taking a seat herself. Wiping her brow, she continued, "Am I glad this is my last wedding. I'm gettin' much too old for this."

"I'm sorry," Ronda said, moaning and laughing. "I do have to get married, though, and this seems the only way to do it. Do you know a better way, Mamm?"

"Of course not," Sharon said. "I wouldn't want it any other way. And you have been as good a girl . . . as the rest of them have."

"Seven, right?" Ella asked and ran the count in her mind.

Sharon leaned back on her chair. "Seven girls and six boys, and I'm ready to let someone else do the work, I'd say. But we don't want to keep you. So you think you could rent one floor of the house to Ronda and Joe till they can find a farm?"

"Joe thought he had found one," Ronda added, "but the sale fell through. The man decided not to sell."

"Ben will take over the farm here," Sharon said, "since he's the youngest boy."

"I guess we could live upstairs or even in the basement," Ronda said, wrinkling her brow.

"I guess you could call off the weddin'," Sharon said with a straight face.

"No, we can't!" Ronda exclaimed.

"I wasn't serious," Sharon said, laughing. "Don't be gettin' your dander up. I wouldn't keep you from a good husband like Joe. He'll be a *gut* one for you."

Ronda blushed, and again Ella felt a pang in her heart. *Why is love allowed for one and taken away from the other?*

"You must be missin' Aden a lot," Sharon said softly, "especially on weddin' days."

"I do," Ella said, a catch in her voice.

"I'm sorry," Ronda whispered. "I was so caught up in my own joy."

"It's okay." Ella reached out to touch her cousin's hand. "Life goes on, and yours must too."

"Yes, it does," Sharon said, leaning forward and bringing the conversation back to the matter at hand. "And we need to get this house cleaned. So what about the movin' in? Are you two at an agreement?"

"Ronda, you and Joe can have the first floor, and I'll move upstairs. With the way the house is built, the stairs are right by the front door. I can come and go and won't be disturbing you."

"But you'll have no kitchen," Sharon said. "It would, after all, be awkward to share the downstairs, and Ronda will feel equally uneasy, knowing your discomfort upstairs."

"I can put in some cabinets in one of the bedrooms," Ella said.

Ronda was silent for a moment. "Joe can install them, but perhaps your basement would be better. Did you think of that?"

"That could work," Ella said, considering the possibility.

"Ach," Ronda said, "I'm still a little uncomfortable with this plan. I don't like putting you out of your kitchen. Cabinets take time to build."

Sharon spoke up and said, "Hostetlers — they're just down the road — he can make them in no time. I'll talk to James about it."

"They're always months behind," Ronda said. "How could they get them done so fast?"

"He'll make an exception when I explain things to him," Sharon said, getting up. "Now I suppose you two have an agreement, and we have to get back to work. Right, Ronda?"

"I'll be glad to have you," Ella said, standing to go.

"We didn't talk of payin' yet," Ronda said. "Joe told me a number he could afford, but that was when he expected to pay for Mamm and Daett's *dawdy haus.*"

"I don't want a lot of money," Ella said quickly. "Whatever number Joe said is fine with me."

"Three hundred a month." Ronda blurted out the figure. "Is that enough?"

Ella nodded. The answer would have been "yes" no matter what Ronda had said. A little money was better than no money.

"Are you sure?" Ronda asked, breaking into a smile.

Ella nodded again.

"Then it's decided," Sharon said, "and your weddin' is closer than it was this mornin'. We need to get back to work."

"I can't wait," Ronda said, a look of delight on her face.

Ella somehow got out the door and into the buggy before the tears came. She drove out to the end of the driveway and pulled the reins at the corner to turn south toward John Darling Road.

I'll go and visit Arlene at her parents' house. This might not be a pleasant stop, and it might end with the rupture of our friendship — if Daniel's actions hadn't already done so. Do I really want to do this? Why can't I just drive on by and let the situation take care of itself? That was the problem. In a close knit community, no problem really stayed away for very long.

Ella drove on, and the horse seemed to take the extra miles well. *Daniel does know how to pick a horse, even if he's muddled up when it comes to choices on love. I've no doubt Arlene is exactly the kind of girl he needs — calm, sunny, and steady while Daniel is given to dark moods.* Gut *people, both of them. Daniel took a chance with me — reaching out to grasp what his brother had held. And so he missed what his own hands contained in Arlene. Yet, surely all is not lost. Arlene seems like a sensible girl, and so surely she will understand.*

Ella turned left into the driveway and pulled up to the hitching post. Arlene's two brothers, Norman and Mervin, raced out to the buggy, hollering, "It's Ella's buggy!"

120

THIRTEEN

"Is Arlene home?" Ella asked the brothers, still holding the tie strap.

"It's wash day," the oldest, Norman, said, pointing toward the wash line hanging between the house and the high side of the barn. "Arlene's got the first load done. She chased us out, so we wouldn't bother her."

"Norman got his hand caught in the wringer once," Mervin said.

"Not today, though," Norman said, shrugging. "It was when I was smaller."

"I never had my hand caught," Mervin said.

"Arlene doesn't want either of us caught," Norman said, glancing at the ground.

"That makes perfect sense," Ella said, tousling each boy's hair. "Let me tie up my horse, and then I'll go look for Arlene."

The two boys followed her to the house and ran past her when she got to the porch. Since she figured they would announce her presence, she didn't knock but waited.

They came racing back a moment later.

"You're supposed to come on in," Norman said, holding the door open for her.

Ella stepped inside. When they followed, Ella wondered if she should tell them to go play. The conversation ahead certainly wasn't fit for little ears.

Before she could say anything, Arlene awkwardly opened the washroom door — or rather shoved it open — because of the large hamper of wash in her arms.

"You boys go out and play by the barn," she said as if she suspected something about the conversation to come. Ella wasn't sure if this was a good sign or not.

"We don't want to," Norman said. "Ella just got here."

"She's come to talk to me. Now, get," she said in no uncertain terms. Then her face softened. "Good morning to you, Ella. I'm glad you came."

"Come on," Norman muttered. "We can play horse in the barn since they don't want us here."

"Don't fall through the haymow," Arlene said, lecturing their backs.

"We won't," Norman said, but he didn't turn around. The screen door snapped shut behind them.

"Well," Arlene said, shifting the hamper in her hands.

Relief flooded Ella. *At least Arlene isn't angry.*

"Here, let me carry that," Ella said, reaching for the hamper.

"How about one side of it?" Arlene said, letting go of one side. The two walked through the front door together and toward the wash line as Ella searched desperately for the right way to begin this conversation.

"Daniel came over the other night," Ella began when they reached the wash line and had set the hamper gently on the ground.

"That's not that unusual," Arlene said with her eyes on the hamper. Gingerly she reached for a dress, clipped it onto the line, and pulled the pulley to move the wire along. "So what did he have to say?"

"Well, I'd rather not tell you. It's a little embarrassing, really."

"For him or for you?"

"I was thinking of you," Ella said, wishing this conversation wasn't necessary. "Perhaps I should let him tell you his side of the story."

"I'm really interested in your side." Arlene met her eyes. Her smile was now gone. "I already know Daniel's side of it."

"He has spoken to you, then?"

"Not since he spoke to you, but I know his side of things. I've dated him for more than four years."

"That's what I told him. That and some other things. Perhaps I was too hard on him."

"I doubt it," Arlene's said, but her face softened again. "I'm sure he needed it. Sort of a big sister talking-to, yah?"

"I suppose so. He would have been like my brother when Aden and I married."

"So he asked you to be his sweetheart?" Arlene asked.

Ella detected a tremble in Arlene's voice. "Yah." Ella kept her eyes focused on the clothes hamper. "I feel bad about this. I have searched my heart . . . to see if I encouraged him. I really didn't, Arlene. I don't think I ever did. He was like a brother to me — always helpin' out after Aden died."

"Sometimes things turn into what they weren't intended to be. I suppose I could have spoken up, but I wanted to see how far Daniel would take it. He's always dreamin' about things that are never to be his. He thinks he's so much less than Aden. I guess he thought with Aden's girl, he might be more like his brother."

"But I'm not better than you," Ella said,

feeling the words burst out of her.

"It depends. In *Da Hah*'s eyes, no, but men and women aren't made the same."

"You are the one for him, and I told him that."

"I know," Arlene said, wiping the tear that had dripped onto her cheek. "*Da Hah* and I know it, but Daniel apparently doesn't."

"But he'll be back. That's the reason I came to talk to you — or part of the reason. The other reason I'm here is to tell you where I stand, so you would have no doubt. I thought it would be better to hear it all from me — for yourself."

"He's got dreams in his head, Daniel does."

"Mostly muddled thinkin', I would say."

"He can't see the road ahead for the stars in the sky. I don't know, Ella. Sometimes such a mind has to be cleared first before it can walk very far again."

"I'm sorry for my part in this," Ella said, hesitating. "I had no idea. I guess I was so caught up in my own world of grief that I never thought about where I was going."

"I'm not blamin' you," Arlene said. "I could have spoken up if I'd wanted to."

"Maybe it's just Daniel who's to blame," Ella said haltingly. Daniel still seemed like her brother, and one was careful about speaking of family.

"He is," Arlene said, laughing for the first time.

"And who best to straighten him out than the one who loves him the most, yah?"

Arlene laughed again, clipping the last of the clothes onto the line. The rolled-out wire went off high into the air. The pieces were wet and hanging heavily on the line.

"I'll be seein' to him, then," Arlene said. "That is . . . when he comes back around."

"Oh, he will," Ella said, although her heart wasn't so sure. Daniel had looked about as stubborn as Eli when he left her the other night.

After a silence, which signaled to Ella that there was nothing more to be said, she spoke, "Well, I need to get back to my house. I've been gone all day yesterday, helpin' out at home."

"Glad it's not me with that big house," Arlene said. "I have enough to do, the way it is."

"Ronda and Joe will be rentin' the first floor," Ella said, relieved the friendship had been preserved. "I need the money, and I don't need all that house."

"No husband comin' up?" Arlene asked with a twinkle in her eyes.

Ella shook her head. "My heart was already taken."

"You got your eyes in the stars too?" Arlene said. "Don't let it keep you from findin' your way around down here."

"I loved him," Ella said. "I can never love another like that."

"I know," Arlene said, "but *Da Hah* might still have other things in mind for you. And don't be sayin' no just because you remember the past that can't be no more."

Ella felt a shock of horror. *Does Arlene know about the bishop? If she does, then the whole world knows. It will only make things more difficult if people begin assuming things.* "Do you know anything?" she asked through tight lips.

Arlene laughed. "No, I only knew about Daniel, but it looks like there's more to be known. That's not hard to imagine, Ella. Really, now just be thinkin' straight, will you? Aden snatched you right up the moment he saw you. You know that's true."

"There are others who have had the same experience," Ella said, but her voice trembled.

"Yah, but we're not all the same. Look at me. Daniel has never even asked me to marry him. Sure, I know we're for each other, but the waitin' is hard sometimes. He should have been askin' a long time ago. I

127

expect Aden never had that problem."

"He wanted to marry two years ago," Ella said, feeling the tears sting her eyes. "It's one of the sorrows of my heart — that I was never his wife and could have been if we hadn't waited. It would have made it easier, I think, to have had his child with me now."

"You mustn't trouble yourself with such thoughts," Arlene said, taking her arm with a firm grip. "You really mustn't, Ella. Those eyes of yours are always on the stars. You and Aden would have had your share of troubles just like everyone else. Some of us have ours first, and some of us later. But they do come. They really do, Ella. So be thinkin' about your life *now.* I know you won't be left without an offer from some man who is worthy of you. And don't be turnin' away from it. Your mind must stay open even if your heart's still a'hurtin'. It'll be your lifelong regret if you don't. Think of your mamm and daett, of your family, and of your children yet to come. You don't want to get old all alone in that big house of yours with no man to ever comfort your heart. *Da Hah* has plans for you," Arlene said, her voice now gentle.

"It's just so hard," Ella choked.

"I know it is. But you must not think you know best," Arlene chided. "It's better to walk the road one is given by *Da Hah*."

Surprise gripped her at Arlene's words. She knew they were true but hadn't expected to hear them. The visit had been to talk with Arlene about Daniel, not about her and Aden.

"Life has a lot of hurtin' in it, but the angels came to help us. Did they not come when Aden died? It shows *Da Hah* is firmly in control."

"I will try" was all Ella could say.

"Be thinkin' about it," Arlene said, squeezing her hand. "But I'm thinkin' I've spoken too many words already, seein' I've never walked your road. You will forgive me for my boldness?"

"There's nothing to forgive," Ella said through her tears. "I will try to make wise choices in the days ahead."

"Then I'd best get back to my wash," Arlene said, letting her hand drop and bending over to pick up the empty hamper.

"And I'd best be getting back to my duties."

Ella walked toward the buggy, glancing back once, but Arlene had disappeared into the washroom. Nelson and Mervin must have heard her walk on the gravel because they came out of the barn with a shout. Ella's horse jumped but quieted down under the brush of her hand.

"Sorry," Nelson said, stopping Mervin with his hand. "We didn't mean to scare your horse. Is he a new one?"

"New to me," she said, forcing a smile.

"Those are the skittish ones," Nelson said as if he knew all about horses. "Once you get to know them real well, they become much better."

"You're a horseman already," Ella said with a laugh, untying the horse as the boys moved back toward the barn. This much they already knew, one did not stand too close when a buggy took off.

As she left, she waved at the two little bodies with their hands in their pockets and mischief in their eyes.

On the drive home, the conversation with Arlene kept playing in her head. *Do I really keep my eyes on the stars and not on the road in front of me? Am I really supposed to consider the bishop's offer? Can love rise up from the earth to reach the heavens instead of coming down from the sky? Life was to be lived with my hand in Aden's hand. Another man's hand is simply unacceptable.*

FOURTEEN

The house on the corner of Chapman Road came into view. The white walls almost reached out, invited her in, and drew her to itself. Of course, no house made of wood and block could do that — even her own — but the emotion felt good. She was almost home. How quickly this had happened. Surely *Da Hah* had blessed her already with a refuge.

The troubling thoughts that had followed her from the conversation with Arlene fell away like dandelion fluff in the wind, floating away into nothing. She would think more about Arlene's words later.

Ella eagerly unhitched the horse and turned him out to the pasture. He seemed glad to be back, kicking up his heels and tearing around the fence line. Ella watched him run. When the horse got to the back pasture, she went inside. With the front door shut behind her, the feeling of refuge now mixed with a sense of loneliness as she confronted the great silence in the rooms.

These rooms should be full of people; full of laughter and joy. These walls should be home to more than just one person. It's too large, too beautiful, and too majestic to be lived in alone. Somehow I will fill it. Ronda and Joe are a good start. Beyond that it doesn't matter. Today the answer came, and tomorrow I will receive the grace I will need for the future.

There were bags to be unpacked. Ella wrestled with the suitcase as she dragged it upstairs. *How much easier things would be if Eli or Monroe were here to help.* With a final wrestle, she made it to the top. She picked the bedroom at the right with its open view of Chapman Road. The room would also look toward the sunrise. *What better way to begin each day of the new life before me?*

Ella unpacked, deciding the bedroom across the hall would serve as her improvised kitchen since she still wasn't convinced of Ronda's basement-living suggestion. Still, to permanently fasten cabinets on these new walls seemed a shame. Instead she would place them on the floor, simply set up along the wall.

Buckets of water could be brought up the stairs and carried back down in the slop container. An occasional splash of dishwater tossed out the window was not beyond reason, especially at night when no one would see her. Ella wondered how many people threw dishwater out of their upstairs windows. She smiled at the thought. It didn't seem very civilized.

Ella finished unpacking and went back downstairs. There was still time to do a load of wash since it was not yet one o'clock. If she hurried, the clothes would dry by dark. The wash line was strung up from the back porch to the windmill, which stood high in the air. Its tall blade turned slowly in the wind, creaking as water was pulled up and dumped into the holding tank. The horse drank from there. The rest of the water spilled onto the ground and could be diverted in summers to a rain-starved garden. An inch-wide black pipe ran underground to an outside spigot by the house. From there a bucket could be filled in spurts as the windmill turned and gravity carried the water toward the house.

Ella started the washing machine with two jerks of the starter rope. She added the soap once she found it in the grocery bags her mom had sent along in the move. An hour later, her wash was clipped to the line and flapping in the breeze. It would easily be dry before dusk.

As evening approached, Ella's sense of loneliness increased again. All afternoon she had heard no noise, joined in no human conversation, nor seen another human face, and, besides the wash, she had completed no chores. With this strange silence came the memory of what Arlene had said. *Do I really have my eyes on the stars, thus missing the road at my feet?* Ella turned the question over all afternoon and was still considering it when she brought the wash in just as the last of the sun's rays hung in the sky.

She ironed most of the pile of clothes as darkness fell. She lit the kerosene lamp, went to get the casserole from the basement, and heated it in the oven. While it warmed she added the jam, butter, and bread to the sparse table setting. Satisfied, Ella sat down to eat, bowing her head in silent prayer. Chewing slowly, she jumped when she heard the sound of buggy wheels suddenly rattling in the gravel outside and a horse blowing its nose loudly.

Surely Daniel has not returned to try his foolish love talk again. He had better sense than that. She walked slowly to the front door, fear gripping her. *Is this the bishop? This soon? Come for his answer?* He was the last person she wished to see. What with Eli, her parents' wishes, and now what Arlene had said, she couldn't think straight enough to face the blaze of his blue eyes. Her legs were like water just thinking about it.

The firm knock came at the door, and Ella forced herself to answer. She opened it slowly but was unable to make out the face in the darkness. She saw just the shadow of a lengthy beard. *So, no, it isn't Daniel.* With her heart heavy, she weakly said, "Come in."

"Danki," the familiar voice said. *No, it's not the bishop either.* It was the voice from Aden's funeral — the voice that had thundered condemnation against mankind's sin, roared against youthful folly, and came from the one who was ready and able to use even the death of a good man for his own purposes.

"I'm alone," Ella said, surprised she would say such a thing. Perhaps she responded to the man's stance. He stood so vigilant against even the appearance of evil but was now ready to walk into a home alone with a woman who wasn't his wife.

"Am I botherin' you?" he asked, not moving from the porch.

"I was in the middle of supper," she said.

"Then I'm sorry. I'll come back later."

"No," she said, "there's no need for that."

What he wanted, Ella couldn't imagine. *Surely Preacher Stutzman didn't come with a marriage proposal.* The thought almost made her laugh, but she caught herself in time. He was, after all, Preacher Stutzman and not a man to bring laughter to a woman's soul.

With his hat turning in his hand, he nodded and stepped shyly inside. Ella had a hard time with the change in the man. *He hardly seems to be the same person whose sermon had thundered at Aden's funeral.*

"I won't keep you long," he said with a glance toward the food on the table. "Your supper will be gettin' cold."

"How are the girls?" Ella asked, wanting to place him at ease. Perhaps what had been said about him was true, that he was a man broken by his wife's death. *If so, he must have loved her a great deal,* she thought with a twinge of compassion.

"They're doin' okay," he said with some hesitation. "Sister Susanna helps out when she can. But it's not the same since Lois passed. Nothin's quite the same." He stroked his beard gently. Ella noticed for the first time that his eyes were as blue as the bishop's. Somehow during his preaching, his voice had always overshadowed any other part of him, particularly his eyes.

"I would think so," she said, still wondering what could be the reason for his visit.

"The girls —" he said. "The other night when Mary had her earache spell, I was thinkin' that something would have to be done about their continued care. Susanna already has her hands full, and I have my work on the farm. It's more than enough to keep one man busy, and I can't exactly afford to hire farm help. Yet the girls need watchin' during the day and sometimes a visit to the clinic like Mary did for her ear."

Ella felt her whole body stiffen. *So this is going to be another marriage proposal delivered like his sermons, like they were utterances from on high — straight, cold, and to the point.* The thought chilled her to her toes. *What does Preacher Stutzman think? That I will rush to my wedding day with him because his girls need a mother?*

His voice continued. "I got to thinkin' that perhaps there would be a way out for me, one that would please both my girls and you." He glanced at her face but didn't seem to see the anger rising in her eyes.

"See, I can afford to pay for their care but not farm-help wages. I suppose you think me a cheapskate." A smile played on his face, his eyes remained focused on the floor, and his voice sounded apologetic. "But if I am, then I am. I cannot help it. But it would do my girls good to be taken care of by you.

You are a responsible girl. You're well brought up in our people's ways. And I could trust them with you. Perhaps Monday through Friday? Just for a short time or until I can make other arrangements?"

The smile played on his face again, sad this time.

Ella's mind raced to understand. *Preacher Stutzman wants me to care for his daughters, and he will pay for the service. He isn't speaking of marriage.* Ella almost let out a sigh of relief.

"Would you consider it?" he asked in a voice just above a whisper.

"I . . . Well . . . Yah," she replied, finding her voice, "it might be just what I am looking for."

"Oh?"

"Ach, surely you know I'm needing to support myself. And I do have this big house."

"I see," he said, looking relieved.

"Oh," Ella said, remembering, "I should tell you that Ronda and Joe are moving into the first floor after their wedding. I'll be upstairs or in the basement. But perhaps that would even work better since Ronda could help with the girls sometimes."

His face brightened. "That does look like *Da Hah*'s hand, and I'm pleased. So you can start next week?"

"Next week?" Ella asked. Her mind started spinning as she considered this new direction. "Of course. There's no reason why not."

"I will bring them Monday mornin', then. And I hope your supper isn't cold." He nodded, reached for the knob behind him, and backed out of the room, shutting the door after himself.

Ella stood still, staring after him. *Amazing.*

FIFTEEN

Ella allowed the memory of Preacher Stutzman's girls at their mother's funeral to swim before her eyes. They seemed to be lost in a haze of incomprehension. She sat down at the kitchen table, but her uneaten food had lost its appeal. The casserole would be long cold now, but it didn't matter. Her mind was no longer on food. Before her the small faces of the girls refused to fade. She was to care for them. *Is this an answer to prayer, an answer to my need?*

The empty house was quiet again, but if the girls were to come to her, that silence would soon be a thing of the past. *By next week this house will be full of people, life, energy, and children — as it is meant to be. Who would have thought of such a thing?* She nibbled at the casserole, oblivious to how cold it was.

Ella got up from the table, washed the dishes, and drained the water into the bucket below the sink when she was finished. She carried the bucket outside and behind the house, where the garden would be planted next spring, and dumped the contents into the darkness. *How* Da Hah *continues to supply my needs! I am very unworthy of such grace.*

In her room Ella found her tablet by the light of the kerosene lamp. It was hidden under the wedding dress and in the safest place she could think of. It was a place her family hadn't been tempted to look. The crisp white pages and blue handwritten words comforted her. They were a connection between her past and her present.

Dear Journal,

You have become as familiar and as comforting to me as a friend or perhaps even a husband, but that doesn't seem possible. Aden is the only one I can imagine as my husband, and he certainly was a whole lot better than you are. He was not like you at all, but real, alive, and so in love with me. Yet this is what I am left with. But I am thankful for anything to dull the pain from where the love has been torn from my heart.

I'm alone tonight in my big house, but I won't be for long. Preacher Stutzman —

of all people — called on me tonight, and I am to take care of his girls during the weekdays. Who would have thought the fierce preacher would ever make contact with me, or that I would take the care of his children? I guess death and sorrow changes a lot of things.

His three girls will be the first additions to my big house — and so quickly. Ronda and Joe move in after their wedding. I think the house will be more than full then, and I feel much more satisfied already.

I had thought I would live here alone or perhaps with Eli if he got in trouble with his Englisha girl, who he now has. Surprise, surprise. But Daett said today that Eli could stay at home. Daett is wise. Eli's better off at home. Daett will be more understanding of him there. And now it turns out I wouldn't have room here anyway. How like God, I guess, to help out in ways one doesn't expect.

I suppose I should be bitter with Aden gone. I admit there were times I was, especially in those first weeks, but one doesn't question God for long. It does little good anyway. It only eats at one's heart. Our preachers would take care of the problem anyway. It's hard to question God for long and listen to them preach. They firmly believe God controls all things for the best.

I now have Ronda and Joe and the Stutzman girls to supply income for me. I think there's one more thing I'd like to do. I wonder if I could possibly have a quilt shop in the basement? That would be just the thing and would work, I believe, even with little girls under my feet. They won't be that different from my younger sisters.

Clara could do some of the creative drawing. We could even start out with a duplicate of my wedding quilt with this house as the centerpiece. It could be sort of a specialty item, related to the house. We could try one at least and put out the sign. I'm not going to sell the one I already made, that's for sure. It has too many memories; sad memories, yes, but precious too. I could at least use it as a sample to sell from. Don't you think that would be a good idea, dear Journal?

Isn't that strange? Now I'm talking to a journal. I must be muddled in my head like Daniel and Eli. I hope not, but I wouldn't be surprised one bit with all that's been going on. The house is so quiet tonight, as if it's afraid to breathe. Don't houses always make some kind of noise? Ours always did at home, and if you listened long enough, something somewhere would squeak. I've been listening for a long time now, and not a squeak can be heard anywhere. Perhaps it's the newness of the house.

Well, Journal, my friend, I really need to get to bed even if I have no chores to get up for. There is no way I will allow myself to get soft and spoiled. I grew up as a farm girl, and a farm girl I will always be.

The temptation to get soft will be great. Thankfully I will have things to do. There's the bishop to think about, and I must say I'm worried. He's a decent man, otherwise he wouldn't be a bishop. Mamm and Daett think the world of him, and yet I can't accept him.

I expect he could come back for his visit anytime now, and I will have to have an answer for him. That answer must be, "No." But I must also ask him if he can help out with Eli to please Daett. Surely the bishop will be understanding about my refusal.

Why, then, am I troubled, dear Journal? Do you feel my hand tremble? You might not, but the letters of blue ink aren't quite as well written right at this moment. I feel like a cloud hangs over me. It may be off in the distance, but it's a thick black one, full of rain and lightning.

Daett would say it's all female emotions and that I'm worrying about nothing. I know he would tell me so. He would tease me, but I still long to hear his voice, his laughter, and his prayers. I'd love to hear him say the words even if I don't agree with them. He'd say, "You need a husband like the bishop."

The bishop will come soon to say what he has to say, and I will say what I have to say. Then it will be over with, and life will go on. Now I really need to get some sleep.

Ella set down the pen, folded the tablet, and went into the bedroom to place it under the dress in the cedar chest. The faint light of the kerosene lamp filled the room. She knelt to pray beside the bed. Her lips moved, but no words came out. Longings rose in her heart to speak the words out loud, but she didn't dare.

Suddenly she got to her feet, grabbed her coat, and went outside. Perhaps if she were outside, she could breathe the words in her heart. How that could be, she had no idea. It was just that way.

Above her the starry Milky Way swept across the summer sky, almost reaching from horizon to horizon. The great clusters of stars bunched together till they couldn't be numbered.

"Dear God in heaven," she prayed, "would You please help me? I thank You for all the help You've given already — for Ronda and Joe, who are planning to move in, and for the little Stutzman girls. Yet I'm still afraid of what lies ahead. I don't want to choose my own way like Eli is doing. Mamm and Daett think I should marry the bishop. You know how hard it will be to stand up to them and go against their wishes, especially when I have no other man to love.

"I had Aden, but You took him from me. I can't ask to have Aden back, and there isn't anyone else like him. There never can be. So please help me with the bishop, God. He plans to marry me. He almost said so, and I can feel it. I'm just little me, against all that. It doesn't feel like my refusal will mean a whole lot."

Ella paused and let her eyes search the sky. *Have I been too bold to talk to God like this? Does He mind or even hear? Does He have plans for me? What could they be? How am I to know?*

Her hand trembled on her chest, and the stars swam before her teary eyes. Above her the heavens remained silent. She remembered where she was and that it was late. Sleep was necessary for the day ahead.

Ella wrapped the coat tightly around her and forced herself to go back inside. She turned the wick down low on the lamp and blew out the flame. Climbing under the covers, she pulled them tight under her chin and closed her eyes.

Moments later, she saw herself — as clear as day — in a buggy, driving along the road with other buggies. A long line of buggies stretched out over the familiar valley roads, but she didn't know where she was headed. Up ahead, buggies slowed down and then pulled into a big field. People climbed out. Many women were dressed in light-colored dresses, so this couldn't be a funeral. It must be a wedding. Enough men stood outside the barn to represent at least five or six districts. Instead of joy, fear stabbed her heart. Who was getting married? She had heard of no one from this area being published.

Ella struggled to see inside the house and get past all the seated people but couldn't seem to make much headway. She caught herself in a cry of alarm. It seemed desperately important to see the young couple sitting in front of the row of preachers. Struggle as she might, all she could see were the backs of the six people all lined up in the straight-backed chairs.

In desperation, Ella ran into the house through a side door. It seemed like her legs would hardly move, and her breath came in labored gasps. Finally, she was close enough to break through the crowd to get her first look at the couple in the center. To her shock, she saw herself — Ella Yoder — and Bishop on the center chairs.

She awoke with a cry and sat bolt upright in bed. Her chest pounded so hard it hurt.

"It was a dream," she cried into the darkness. "It's just a dream!"

SIXTEEN

Susanna opened the front door of the *dawdy haus* when Preacher Stutzman knocked.

"Yah?" she said with a puzzled look on her face.

He tried to keep his eyes on her face but quickly dropped his head. "I've decided to visit the widow Weaver tomorrow," he said, "and see what she has to say. Could you take care of the girls?"

"It's about time that you're gettin' around to it. You should have asked for that woman's help a long time ago. Now why don't you ask her to marry you? She's just sittin' over there by herself waitin'."

"I have my plans," he said, ruffled that she pushed him. "Till then, Ella Yoder will be taking care of the girls, starting Monday morning."

"Ah," Susanna replied as a smile lighted up her face, "Ella Yoder. Well, good for you."

"Goodnight," he said, turning to go.

"It's a wise thing to do," she called after him.

He fixed supper for the girls and settled them down for the night. Mary wrapped her arms around his neck in the upstairs bedroom and hugged him.

"I'm taking you to someone's house next week," he said, stroking her hair. "She's a really nice woman, and she'll be taking care of you and your sisters."

"Will she be our new mamm?" Mary asked.

"Nee," he said, shaking his head, "she's just taking care of you."

Mary settled back on the bed, clutching the covers tightly.

"I'd like a mamm sometime, then," she said. "A real one like we used to have."

Sarah nodded sleepily beside her.

"Well, someone will take care of you now," he said, trying to smile. He blew out the kerosene lamp and in the darkness found his way downstairs where he sat alone in the stillness of the house, listening. Baby Barbara made no noise in the bedroom. She should be soundly asleep for the night.

Tomorrow holds another hard day of farmwork, and I really should be in bed. Ivan felt the shame run through him. He had thought for all these years that the Word of God and the work of God were his highest goals. But now he realized he had never noticed how much he had loved a woman — perhaps even more than *Da Hah* Himself.

He missed Lois. He missed her until the pain ached all the way down to his feet. *How can a person be so lonely? How can a man with three small children, a hundred tasks to do, and all the comforts a man could want in this life seem so utterly without purpose?*

He had mowed his hay today and wondered why he even cut the stuff. *What is wrong with me?* Now the thought pressed in on him, grabbing him by the throat. Since he had seen Ella Yoder again, he couldn't get away from the thought. *This is a woman I could love.*

Shame filled him again. Hopefully none of this had shown on his face when he spoke with Ella. He had been so careful to show nothing even as his heart lurched inside him. *Am I to fall in love again?*

The desire wouldn't go away and served only to increase his shame. He wanted a woman to love, one who would love him as Lois had. He didn't want marriage to the widow Weaver. Ella was the one he truly wanted. She knew how to love, care for a man, and fill the emptiness inside his heart.

Next to Ella, Nancy Weaver looked like a pale weed and a noble attempt to fill the needs of his daughters, but she left his own heart untouched.

Ivan stood to his feet and rebuked himself. *No, Ella cannot be mine.* Da Hah *has spoken — roughly, yes, with the death of Lois — but He is* Da Hah, *and who am I to question His ways? Lois has been taken from me and for a reason. Perhaps through this I will be able to see the condition of my own heart. What a presumptuous fool I would be to walk into the arms of another woman I loved.*

The idea caused his hands to shake as he blew out the kerosene lamp. In the darkness, he felt better. Surrounded by its embrace, his shame was at least hidden in the shadows. He sighed as relief came. When exhaustion gripped him, he was thankful. The labors of farm life overcame even a man's loneliness, his reluctance to sleep, his unwillingness to eat, and his disappointments living life without a woman to love and care for.

Ivan lowered himself wearily into bed. Tomorrow morning would come soon enough. Things could be faced then. He closed his eyes and moments later heard the familiar cry of the baby from her crib. In a haze he tried to get out of bed, but then the crying ebbed, and he drifted off again.

Again baby Barbara cried, this time more insistently. Ivan slid slowly out of bed and walked over to the crib. Little Barbara hollered loudly right into his face, even as he tried to calm her. Strange how she didn't know when he was right there. His fingers tested under the diaper. Yah, she needed a change.

Sleepily he moved the baby to the dresser, found a match, lit the kerosene lamp, and changed the diaper. As he laid her back in her crib, she showed no intentions of sleep, and so with one arm, he carried her on his shoulder out to the kitchen. He set her on the floor beside the oven, then lit the fire, and waited while the milk warmed. When it was ready, he took the bottle and the whimpering baby into the living room where he settled in the rocker and held the bottle up to the baby's searching mouth.

Images faded in and out of his mind as he resisted sleep. *What do women have that men don't? Do they have some special strength that* Da Hah *gives them, unique only to them? Lois had always taken care of these middle of the night feedings and yet still got up with me at the same time each morning and had breakfast ready when I came in from the chores. She worked all day like I did and went to bed around the same time. How ever did she do it?*

The arrangement with Ella Yoder will do until the widow Weaver and I can be married. It's what I have to do, and that's all there is to it. Tomorrow I will make my visit to the widow and set things in motion. Now he was drained; had given up in a way that was hard to explain. *What is will just have to be. What once was can never be again. That is as clear as day.*

The rocker squeaked steadily under him.

That he didn't want to visit the widow was beside the point now. The man in him who wanted what he could not have must stay hidden. Ivan watched the scene in his mind with bated breath. In the barn he would have waved his hand and swatted at the problem till it moved away. In church he would have thundered, quoted the Scriptures, and looked across the room of the assembled with a stern eye. Here, with a hungry baby in his arms, he was reduced to silence over what could not be swatted away.

Yes, tomorrow I will go visit the widow. The hickory rocker squeaked again under him as if in agreement, and the baby continued to softly swallow the warm milk. *The widow will say yes, and we will begin to make plans at once. We will say the sacred vows, and my*

154

life will become what it must become. Temptation to hope for more will be gone.

"I will do it," he spoke aloud into the quiet house.

The baby started, and her face became a mass of fright in the faint flickering lamplight.

"Hush, hush," he whispered quickly as he rocked the chair and jabbed the bottle around in search of the baby's mouth. The baby bawled louder, refusing and turning her head sideways so that the nipple slid along her cheek.

"Hush now," he whispered, rocking and hushing until silence came. Gently he offered the bottle again, and she accepted, burping a few minutes later. He laid her on his chest and patted her back. Enough sleep had already been lost. He got up from the rocker and headed back to the crib, carrying the kerosene lamp in one hand and the infant in the other arm. Setting the light on the dresser, he lowered the baby slowly to the blanket.

She whimpered but made no more sound. He waited and then climbed back into bed. Sleep wouldn't come, though. Wild thoughts raced through his head — thoughts of Ella Yoder, how she would care for his three girls, and of how many women would do such a thing.

She will get paid, he told himself, but that didn't help much. *What I really want is for her to care for me, for my place, for this house, and, yes, for my children. But I don't want her taking care of them at her house. I want her here at mine.* He almost spoke his objections aloud again but held back the sound and pulled the covers up over his head like a little boy when the night dreams troubled the soul.

SEVENTEEN

With the sun just above the horizon, Ivan knocked gently on the front door of the *dawdy haus*. He held baby Barbara in his arms, and his two older girls stood behind him.

"Ah," he began and then stopped when he saw the look on her face.

"Your hay isn't dry yet," Susanna said, "and I got the wash to do this morning. Couldn't you have done this yesterday when Mamm and Daett's night was a little better?"

Although Susanna looked weary, he plunged ahead. "I'm doing it today. I'm going to ask her right now."

Susanna paused and wiped her brow. "Well, the sooner the better. I can't do this much more, what with the hard nights Mamm and Daett are having. It's getting worse all the time. You need a wife for yourself and a mother for these girls real soon."

"That's why I'm going to the widow Weaver's today."

"I suppose I'll figure some way to take care of the girls. Things like this do need to be done, and I'm willin' to carry my share of the load."

"You carry more than your share . . . much more than your share."

"We all must do our duty," she said, smiling weakly. "*Da Hah* gives grace somehow."

She shamed him with her righteous life. *What would she think if she knew of my struggle last night, of the secret desires in my heart, or that my life doesn't measure up to what I expect of myself?*

"Well, don't leave them on the front porch," Susanna said, bending over to lift Mary into her arms. "Have you given them breakfast yet?"

"Daett gave us oatmeal," Mary said, "with brown sugar and cream."

"You do need a woman," Susanna said over Mary's shoulder. "You know that isn't good for them."

"Am I getting a new mamm?" Mary asked.

"Oh, hush now," Susanna said, hugging her. "You'll find out soon enough."

"We're going to Ella's house next week. Is

she going to be our new mamm?" Mary asked.

"No," Susanna said, "but she'll take good care of you until you have a new mamm."

"I'll be back as soon as I can," Ivan said, stepping off the porch and turning quickly toward the barn.

"I hope I like Ella," Mary said in a faint voice behind him.

So do I, although there is little doubt in my mind about it. Ella is that kind of girl. She will be a good wife for the man who marries her.

Ivan called the horse in from the barnyard, harnessed him quickly for the task ahead. He could do no less than hurry since Susanna had been kind enough to care for his girls. *Yes, hurry I must with this wedding proposal. There are no needs for romantic notions. The widow likely has similar sentiments. We are in a different world now and might as well accept it. No longer is the youth group, with its dreams of love and romance, a part of our lives. When death broke in on both of us, life took on a practical reality.*

He threw on the harness, and the horse held still for him this morning. Driving out the driveway, he wondered if the horse knew his mission this morning. *Is that why he behaves so readily? Perhaps this is a small sign that* Da Hah *approves of my mission.*

159

Ivan drove south and then west for a mile before he turned onto Nancy Weaver's road. She kept the farm herself since her husband's death some years ago. He wondered how long it had been but could only reason that Nancy had lived without her husband much longer than he had lived without Lois. The length of time before remarrying was often different for men and women. A man simply isn't cut out to take care of children on his own.

How does Nancy keep the farm in operation without a man around? Her boys are several years older than my girls, but even so, they could not contribute enough to manage the place. From somewhere there had been talk Nancy had a hired hand to help milk and manage the farm. *She is a remarkable woman, no doubt, and one worthy of asking for her hand in marriage.*

Ivan slapped the reins and drove faster. They would make a good family together; her three boys and his three girls. A little large, the family would be, and a full house, but that couldn't be helped. With more children still likely to come, the family would be even larger, but that was as it should be. This was the way *Da Hah* had made things, and they were not to be ashamed of His ways.

The widow's house lay just over the next hill, and his horse slowed down to make the ascent. Above him the early morning sky was open, cloudless, and seemed to stretch out forever. Ivan let the horse take his time and noticed his own hands on the reins. *Why are they clenched so tightly?* He could feel the sweat under his collar even as the cool morning breezes blew in through the open buggy door and ruffled his shirt.

Surely I'm not in the midst of youthful jitters! Yet he knew the answer before the question had come. Truth be known, he didn't want to ask Nancy Weaver for her hand in marriage. And then an even more startling realization struck him. The question he readied for the widow Weaver, he really wanted to place before Ella Yoder. The thought shamed him, but his resolve drove him on. *I will not give in now, just when I am so close.*

Before him he saw the crest of hill. He was still hidden, and his buggy remained unseen by those on the other side. Once he crossed the crest, he might be noticed, and there really would be no turning back. Surely his intentions would be known to all. What other reason did he have for this early morning visit down this particular road?

His fingers dug into the leather of the

buggy lines, and he set his teeth firmly together. There was no way he would turn back now. *Have I not thundered often in my sermons about choosing the correct path?* And yet with a cry, he found himself turning the buggy around in the middle of the road. The wheels screeched on the turn bars.

He let the horse have its head as if he was mad with youth and on his way home from a Sunday night hymn sing. The horse raced as if he understood the close call.

What will Susanna say about this? No matter, it's too late to worry about an answer now. He took the little one-lane bridge by the river so fast the buggy wheels left the ground for a moment, clattering loudly as they bit into the gravel.

He pulled back on the reins and slowed down. *It's not too late to change my mind yet again.* He almost turned the horse around, but the memory of Ella's face rose up before him. His nerves were raw as she seemed to be smiling at him. Surely he had gone entirely mad from the stress he was under. Yet he wanted a wife like the one he used to have. He wanted to love a woman with all his heart again, passionately and without reserve. And he knew in turning from the widow Weaver, he had chosen to not let that desire go so easily. *Is it possible to be happy again?*

What does Da Hah *have to say about this? And what of Susanna?* He trembled at the rebuke that lay ahead. Still he released the reins again, giving the horse his head, and the buggy sped along the back roads. All the while he considered his plight. *Perhaps I should stay silent about my hidden desires. If my resolve is strong enough, maybe I will be spared punishment from on high.*

An atonement might help, but how do I atone for what I haven't committed? Perhaps I can atone by preaching. I can strongly condemn and rebuke the hidden passions of the weak human heart. My conscience will permit that because I would, first of all, be preaching to myself. Is that not the first order of good preaching? Then, after many years of living in holiness, perhaps my heart will cease betraying me.

Pulling into Susanna's driveway, Ivan's hands shook as he unhitched the sweaty horse, whose breath came in great heaves. He calmed himself by reaching for hope deep inside of himself. He hoped his resolution would bear fruit. To lessen his guilt, he filled the bucket of oats to the brim, poured the whole thing into the feed trough, and left the horse to drink and munch away.

"You get her answer, yah? And so quickly," Susanna asked, standing on the front porch and holding a hamper full of wet wash. "*Da Hah* must have been with you."

"I turned back . . . before I got there," he said, his eyes staring at the ground.

"She surely didn't turn you down. I can't imagine that Nancy Weaver would turn you down."

"No," Ivan said, shaking his head. "I said I turned back. I never asked her."

"You never asked her?"

"I'll try again later," Ivan said, meeting her eyes.

"I helped you out this morning . . . so you could waste both our time. Ivan, you're not a young blushin' man. You've already been married. What's wrong with you?"

Ivan turned away.

Susanna sighed and then said in a soft voice that surprised Ivan, "Well, then, I reckon it hasn't been that long since Lois passed. You're still missing her. I guess it won't do to rush you."

"I loved her," Ivan said in a voice that suddenly broke. As he tried to collect himself, he said, "Let me help with the wash at least. My hay's not ready yet."

"That would help," Susanna said, handing him the basket. "You poor man."

I'm not poor, he wanted to say. *I'm full of wrong desires.* But he kept silent as he took the hamper from Susanna.

"Thank you," she said.

He nodded and walked over to the wash line. One by one he snapped the pieces on, spun the wheel slowly, and sent the line off into the air. If anyone drove by and saw him doing woman's work, they would think he really did need a wife. Well, he did, but there were some things a man simply couldn't speak of to anyone.

EIGHTEEN

Ella sat in church, squeezed between the other single girls on the hard bench. Preacher Stutzman's stirring sermon gripped her full attention. He was that sort of man, especially when in full cry. His voice filled the house this morning, his hands stretched outward for long moments at a time and then folded on his chest, and his beard jerked at the end of each full breath he expelled with great force.

How did one reconcile the gentle man who came to her door the other night with this morning's firebrand who could spew forth volumes of Scripture from memory? He thundered like a summer eve's lightning storm, and the thunder was just beginning.

Preacher Stutzman seemed hardly the father of the little girl who sat on the preacher's bench behind him. With her head now resting in her hands, four-year-old Mary had been in his lap before he got up to preach and would return there when he was done. That scene didn't make sense either.

"Our spiritual father Abraham," Preacher Ivan roared, stretching one hand high in the air, "stood on the top of the mountain with his son Isaac. He was there by the command of God and was told to sacrifice his only son. In our own lives, we find ourselves commanded to the mountaintop by God Himself. Abraham went because he knew how to obey, as all of us must learn to obey. Abraham was there to be tested, as all of us will be tested.

"Sacrifice your only son, *Da Hah* had commanded three days earlier. Abraham went to the mountain, lifted his knife to obey, and do what he could not believe humanly could be done. Abraham was there to fulfill a command he thought was unjust, and yet he was ready to obey — if *Da Hah* said so."

Preacher Stutzman's voice dropped a few decibels. "Yet *Da Hah* stopped Abraham at the last moment. He stilled Abraham's hand because Abraham's heart was right. Abraham was, as we all must be, ready to place *Da Hah* first in his life. He was ready even when the cost was the life of his own precious son. *Da Hah* sent a lamb that day, but we must think ourselves as holy as Abraham

167

was. Abraham lifted his eyes and saw a sheep caught by the horns in the bushes. We, though, often lift our eyes and still have to sacrifice what *Da Hah* wants. The world, the devil, and our own lusts must be sacrificed if we are to be a holy people."

There was silence in the room for long moments. Preacher Stutzman's gaze swept from one side of the room to the other. Ella felt chills up and down her spine. There was definitely more coming. The hand was up again, and Preacher Stutzman called out, "Are we worthy of the faith of Abraham? He was willing to sacrifice everything. Can the same be said of us? Do we place *Da Hah* first in our lives? Are His commandments more precious to us than our sons, our daughters, our wives, our farms, or our possessions?"

Ella took a deep breath. She had heard Preacher Stutzman before, most memorably at Aden's funeral, and his tone of voice, even then, had made an impact on her. *It's puzzling that one man can be so different. And yet tomorrow the care of his three girls will be on my shoulders. Will Preacher Stutzman use this tone at my house? I certainly won't consent to it.* Troubled thoughts stirred in her. *Did I make the wrong decision by agreeing to care for the girls?*

She recognized the answer, just as plain as day. Right before her eyes, Mary sat with her face in her hands. Her face revealed no sign of any troubled thoughts. Mary looked as contented and relaxed as any well-cared-for child should. Her sisters sat behind Ella with Preacher Stutzman's sister, Susanna. If she turned around, she would see that they both had the same look about them. They were loved. True, they were motherless — but loved.

Ella took another deep breath and relaxed. The girl beside her glanced sideways and gave her a puzzled look. Ella gave her a quick smile. *I had best get control of my reactions. Besides, he has never raised his voice after church, even on the Sundays Aden and I visited here. If he did, I would have heard him when the men gathered in the yard on summer afternoons after the Sunday meal or in the house on winter days. There is no way to hide that voice.*

Comforted, she settled down. It was time to listen to the rest of the sermon. *Perhaps some good can still be had. I sure need something to give me direction for the many decisions lying ahead. Likely it won't come from this man, but I reckon it's still the Word of God, thundered or not.*

Preacher Stutzman stood in the living

room doorway. His hands were at his sides, and his voice was soft now, almost weary. "The faithful servant went as his master Abraham had told him to, traveling off to a far country to obtain a wife for Abraham's son. Now, how many of us could trust our parents the way Isaac must have trusted his? I ask our young people that today. Can we still follow the holy Scriptures as Isaac did? He trusted *Da Hah* to bring him the wife he should have.

"The world tells us to choose by the lust of our eyes and pick our life's companion from what pleases us. We make our decision because of our tastes and the beauty we see on the outside, but Isaac did not. He trusted his father to choose his wife, and yet Abraham didn't even take the task upon himself. He sent his servant. Still, Isaac didn't complain. Can we say the same for ourselves? I speak to our own shame. I must confess myself — the greatest transgressor in this matter — yet should we not be the same as Isaac?"

Preacher Stutzman's eyes swept up and down the row of young boys.

"Listen to your parents," he said. "They know what is best. They know what a life of marriage is like and what kind of wife you will need. Do not listen to the world.

Abraham's faithful servant arrived in the foreign land and appealed to *Da Hah* for a blessing on his task. In the same way, your parents beg and plead with *Da Hah* in prayer for you. I know they do because they are godly parents. *Da Hah* will answer them as *Da Hah* answered Abraham's servant.

"The young maiden Rebecca came down to draw water for the camels." Ella knew the story, and for the next few minutes, she listened absently but grasped the preacher's point. Finally she heard him say, "It is time to close now, but remember to obey God and trust your parents. Perhaps others can say the same thing better than I can, but that is the best my poor tongue can do by way of finding words to express the Word of God. I hope it has been in accordance to *Da Hah*'s holy will and in line with the sacred Scriptures. You, brethren, will now be the judge as I take my seat and ask that you give testimony to what has been spoken."

Preacher Stutzman called out three names — the bishop, another minister, and one of the older men from the congregation. He then took his seat beside Mary, who leaned her head into his lap.

"I heard nothing against the word of God today," the first of the witnesses began.

Moments later the second witness said, "We are so blessed to hear from *Da Ha* today."

The third closed with an equally flattering review, "Today, once again, we can see why we are so blessed to not only be among the people of God but to be so privileged that heaven still speaks to us. Our young people should listen with their ears open all the way."

Preacher Stutzman's sermons always received good testimony, if for no other reason than their fierceness.

The song leader gave out the number, and the singing began. The clock on the kitchen wall showed the time as a little past twelve. With the last stanza finished, Ella got up with the other girls and followed them into the kitchen. Behind her the men had already set up the tables in the living room, and the married women began to sit down.

She might not attend the youth functions anymore, but she was still a single girl and would be expected to act like one. *Until forever,* she thought. The image of a wrinkled old maid who still waited on the Sunday tables rose in her mind. That idea was a little impossible. Surely somewhere in the future, she would sit and be served but not now.

Ella would have chosen the women's table to wait on, but that was taken, as was the boys'. With no choice in the matter, she waited until prayer was completed and then walked over to the men's table, carrying the water pitcher. They had already started to eat, dipping their knives into the peanut butter and reaching for the pickle bowls. She waited a few moments and then moved in closer to the broad shoulders and beards. Glasses were lifted up to her. Most of the men smiled a greeting to her. One of them was the face of Preacher Stutzman, but his face was not smiling. That didn't bother Ella, and yet it did. *He knows I will take over the care of his girls tomorrow, and he could at least act friendly toward me.*

When the first bowl was down to the last pickle, she brought in a fresh one while carrying a bowl of peanut butter in her other hand. As Ella approached the table, Preacher Stutzman was spreading butter on a piece of bread for Mary, who sat beside him. His knife reached for the peanut butter bowl, but it was empty.

"It's all gone," he said in a low voice.

"She's got more," Mary said, whispering and peeking over his shoulder.

Preacher Stutzman turned to her, but to Ella he didn't seem like Preacher Stutzman

173

anymore. He was the other man with the cautious blue eyes; the man who had called on her to watch his girls.

"Well, it looks like she got here just in time," he said with a gentle smile to Mary.

The little girl nodded and turned her beaming face toward Ella. Ella leaned across the table to exchange the bowls.

"Mary, this is Ella Yoder," Preacher Stutzman said, whispering again. "You're stayin' at her place all next week, startin' tomorrow."

Little Mary's eyes got big but didn't leave Ella's face.

"You'll like her house," Preacher Stutzman said softly. "It's a nice house and really big."

"Will Sarah and the baby come?" Mary asked.

Preacher Stutzman nodded.

"I'll like it, then," Mary said, still beaming.

"I'm sure you will," Preacher Stutzman said, drawing Mary tight against him and apparently forgetting Ella for the moment.

She turned to go as he finished preparing Mary's peanut butter sandwich. The bowls were empty at the other end of the table, and concerned, bearded faces turned in Ella's direction. She dashed off to the kitchen for refills.

"I hear you're takin' in Joe and Ronda after their weddin'," her cousin Susie whispered in the kitchen, "and Preacher Stutzman's girls. What a handful that will be. I guess you never do things halfway."

Ella smiled with effort, grabbed the bowls she needed, and whispered back, "They're waitin'."

"You need any help at the house?" Susie asked. "Mamm said I could come over once in a while."

"I'll let you know," Ella said, turning to go, "but I'm tryin' to keep things down to where I can handle them."

"Well, don't be shy to speak up if you get in too deep," Susie said to her retreating back.

Susie meant well, but her words meant the whole community knew of her plans and had opinions on the matter — opinions that might not be as friendly as Susie and her mother's had been and might be about what an unmarried woman ought or ought not do.

Marry, that's what they would say. Ella leaned between two broad shoulders to replace the bowls. *They probably think I should get a man like one of these men, a man who would take proper care of me. He would keep the house the way a house ought to be kept — with a man's authority. Was that, perhaps, Preacher Stutzman's hidden message — a sermon on the proper attitude a girl should have? Does Preacher Stutzman know about my father's wish that I take Bishop Miller as a husband? Was he reminded of how I live when he stopped by to make arrangements for his girls' keep? Not likely . . . and yet possible.* She pushed the thoughts aside and walked back to the kitchen for bread this time.

"The whole table needs bread," she whispered to Susie. "I need help."

"Sure," Susie said, grabbing two of the plates of bread and following Ella back into the living room. They exchanged the bread plates, careful that no crumbs spilled onto the men's laps. Ella felt the back of her neck grow warm. There was no doubt about it. Preacher Stutzman had been staring at her.

NINETEEN

Ella stood against the living room wall. The first meal was almost over, and the bishop looked ready to call the prayer out.

"If we have eaten, let us now pray," the bishop announced in a voice that reached the recesses of the house.

All heads bowed, and silence settled quickly. Ella folded her arms and focused her eyes on the floor.

"And now our great and mighty God," the bishop prayed, "we give You thanks for the food we have received. May Your grace be over us in the days ahead as You have guided us in the past with Your mighty hand. Bless now all who are here today and Your children everywhere. Amen."

Ella waited as the murmur of voices resumed and the tables emptied. A few of the married men moved slowly outside. Toothpicks hung from their mouths as they murmured in low voices to those nearby. At

177

the single boys' table in the other room, they jumped up as one, heading for the door in a long line and spilling out into the yard.

Ella followed one particular figure until the boy turned sideways. It was Daniel. He purposely looked away from her during the service and the meal. Now, with a good look at him, Ella thought that he looked happy. Perhaps Arlene had spoken to him with success. Ella sighed with relief. At least there was one less thing to weigh on her mind.

Several of the married women came from the kitchen table and shooed the menfolk farther away, out toward the yard. They grinned meekly over their toothpicks, tucked their beards in, and complied. Several grabbed loose benches and took them along outside, setting them up in uneven lines under the oak trees.

Ella helped clear the tables in preparation for the hungry young people to fill up even before the utensils could be cleaned. The other young girls took seats, and she followed. Out of the corner of her eye, she saw Daniel's buggy leave. He was alone but turned south at the road, heading toward Arlene's house.

She had to stop worrying about him even if he seemed like a brother to her.

"You'll be at the singin' tonight?" Susie

asked, making Ella jump.

Waiting until prayer was done again, Ella whispered back, "I'm going over to Mamm's for the afternoon, and I have to get home early after that."

"Hidin' away are we?" Susie spread butter on her bread. "And why did you jump when I spoke? Are you nervous about something or watching someone?"

"Not really," Ella said, trying in vain to smile. *Why does guilt plague me even when I'm not guilty?* She had no plans to mention Daniel's name.

"You know, Ella, *Da Hah* has someone for you," Susie said, bending toward her, "even if your heart's been broken. I don't blame you for thinking of whoever it was you were thinking about." At that, Susie smiled a knowing smile.

"I expect I'll just be an old maid with a house full of people and children," Ella said quietly, hoping none of the girls around them would join the conversation.

"That's what they all say," Susie said, spreading the peanut butter on thick before she added a piece of cheese.

Not me, Ella almost said but changed it to, "What about you?" hoping the conversation would take another direction.

Susie's cheeks colored slightly.

"Well, it's about time," Ella teased, glad the tactic had worked.

Susie paid close attention to her sandwich.

"This fall or spring?" Ella guessed. "It's been over three years, right?"

"Quiet," Susie whispered out of the corner of her mouth while she focused her eyes straight ahead.

"You started it."

"I guess I did," Susie said, relaxing a bit and letting her shoulders fall a bit. "I can't wait though! It seems like forever already, but it's only been four years."

Ella reasoned that Susie likely had her wedding dress material picked out, and the dress might even be almost made by now. Susie's joy would be equal to what her own had been, and her expectations would grow higher as the day drew closer. Only Susie's hopes wouldn't be dashed to the ground like stones thrown from the hay field.

Thankfully Susie turned to speak to the girl beside her. Ella listened to the soft fall and rise of their conversation. She ate in silence and was glad that the discussion of weddings had been cut short.

When the meal was ending, prayer was announced, and they all bowed their heads. Ella then rose to help with the last round of table clearing. Afterward, she left the house and walked toward the barn, which turned the heads of several boys still in the yard who knew their duty to help her.

Not that she needed the help. At home the women worked in the barns and fields as freely as the men did, but on Sundays, a woman who had to hitch her own horse made the menfolk — even the young ones — fidgety. Someone would feel obligated to offer his help and retrieve her horse from the crowded barn stalls.

Thankfully she saw Susie's boyfriend, Fred, out of the corner of her eye, getting up from his bench and coming toward the barn. He might or might not be ready to leave himself, but Susie would have no objection if he helped.

"You don't have to help," Ella said, just inside the barn door.

"Someone has to," he said with a smile. "We can't have a good-looking girl hitching her own buggy, now can we?"

"Watch your mouth," she said.

Fred laughed and went to get her horse. He stopped the horse outside the barn, took the bridle she held out for him, and put it on the horse. Together they walked toward her buggy, aware that half the folks gathered in the yard were looking their way.

"Susie almost spilled the beans today,"

she said, teasing and holding the shafts high in her hands.

"What? That her mother won't let me see her anymore?" he said with a straight face.

"Fred," Ella said but had to laugh. "You know what I mean."

"Birdies fly, and birdies land, and I expect everything happens eventually."

"I expect they do," she said, getting into the buggy.

"You have a good ride," he said, slapping the horse on the neck and letting go of the bridle.

Ella drove south toward her parents' place, half expecting no one to be at home. Instead, Clara raced out the door when her buggy wheels had no more than turned in the driveway.

"We're all home," she said, dancing around in front of the buggy. "Eli and Monroe are sittin' around in the living room."

That sounded like a good sign. Eli must not be too out of sorts if he hung around downstairs on a Sunday afternoon instead of in his own room.

"So why are you out here helping me unhitch instead of the big boys?"

"I told them to stay put and that I wanted to help you," Clara said, smiling from ear to ear. "I saw you come from way down the hill."

"That's awful nice of you," Ella said, getting out while Clara pulled the tugs off her side.

"Are you settled in your big house yet? I want to come over again, but Mamm won't let me. There's too much work around here," Clara said, disappointed.

"I expected that's how it would go with me gone. But maybe you can come sometime later."

"Now you'll have Preacher Stutzman's girls, and I could help with that. Your big house needs me an awful lot, I think."

Ella laughed. "It sounds like you have more plans than I do or time to do them in."

"They all need to be done at your place. That's the problem."

"Tell you what," Ella said, unhitching her side and leading the horse forward while Clara held the shafts. "I know something you can do for me, something that can be done right here."

"Something Mamm will let me do?"

"Yah, I'm sure. See, I have had an idea. I think a quilt shop in my basement would be a real nice business to start up."

"But how can I help since that's over at

183

your house?" Clara asked, wrinkling her face.

"I'm not finished yet," Ella said, holding up her hand. "See, you can draw some more pictures for things I can use on the quilts."

"Really?" Clara's said. Her face instantly lit up. "I could even do that at school when I'm done with my lessons."

"See?" Ella said, smiling and holding the horse's bridle. "If Teacher Katie asked you why, you can tell her. Say that it's for my quilt shop, and she won't mind at all."

"That's wonderful," Clara said, dancing again and causing little pieces of gravel to spin off and hit the buggy wheels. "Then I can make lots of drawings, and you can use what you like."

"See, things do work out," Ella said, leading the horse into the barn and finding a stall for him.

As the two turned to walk toward the house, Clara said, "Bishop Miller was here."

Clara's words struck Ella like a stroke of lightning from the clear blue sky. "Here?" she gasped.

"Yah," Clara said, nodding soberly, "he talked with Eli a long, long time, and Mamm cried after he left. Daett looked happy, though."

"What did he say?"

"They didn't tell me. They are awful secretive about it. The Bishop took Eli down to the basement for the talk. You don't think Eli's getting excommunicated do you?"

"No," Ella said, feeling rattled. *How did Bishop Miller know Daett wanted him to speak with Eli? Did Daett and Mamm tell him?* Her mind swam with the rushed thoughts, and any answers only seemed to cause more problems than they solved. Clara held the door open for her, chattering away, seemingly unaware of the discomfort her words had caused.

"Hi," Dora said and then glanced at Mamm.

They looked pleased, as if they shared a secret too good to mention. Ella wanted to grab Dora by the arm, march her upstairs, and demand an answer.

"You have a good Sunday at the new district?" Her dad's voice boomed across the room.

"It was Aden's district, so I knew most of the people," Ella said, attempting a smile.

"Sit down, then, and have a bowl of popcorn. Mamm can make some more. I have to do something for the occasion of my daughter's return to the old home place," Noah laughed, motioning toward the popcorn bowl. *What in the world has put*

185

Daett in such good spirits? It wasn't hard to guess, and Ella felt her heart pound with the tension.

"Noah," Lizzie said, but her voice had a tease in it.

"Well, she's come home again. Isn't that an occasion?"

"Yes, it is," Lizzie said, but she didn't look in Ella's direction.

Ella glanced at her dad's face. He definitely had a twinkle in his eyes; more than what would be associated with her visit. Clearly her family was up to something.

"I want to know what goes," Ella said. "You people are up to something. The popcorn will just have to wait."

"You mean you don't know?" Dora asked, gasping.

Ella shook her head.

"She doesn't," Dora said, rising from the couch. "Then I'll tell her right now. She has to know what's going on."

"No, you won't," Mamm said, standing to face Dora. "You sit right back down, Dora. I'll tell her the news."

"I don't think I like this," Ella said in a voice barely above a whisper.

"There are so many secrets around here," Clara protested. "The bishop visits Eli, and now Ella doesn't know. What next?"

186

"You just keep your little head to yourself," Dora said, shaking her finger at her. "Some things are just for grown-up ears."

"Then why do they happen in front of me?" Clara said, sounding rebellious.

"You'll have to ask *Da Hah* that," Mamm said with her hand on the upstairs doorknob.

"I think I'll look to the chores," Eli said, getting up.

"It's not time yet," Clara said. "Why so soon?"

"Then I'll look to lookin' after them. They'll come soon enough," Eli said, heading toward the front door.

"You'll do nothing of the sort," Daett said. "Now sit back down until chore time. Your Mamm will tell the story to Ella upstairs, and you'll be just fine in here. *Da Hah* is doin' great things for our family, and you don't need to be runnin' away from them."

"Yah," Eli said, calmly sitting back down.

Ella couldn't believe her eyes. Her stubborn brother had just obeyed without protest. She turned to silently follow her mom up the steps.

TWENTY

Lizzie had a look of deep contentment on her face as she sat down on Ella's old bed, motioning with her hand for Ella to be seated.

"What's this all about, Mamm?" Ella asked, trying to relax.

"I guess we could have spoken downstairs, seein' this is all good news. But I guess I'm still a little old-fashioned about such things. Some things were just not meant by *Da Hah* to be publicly said, such as the doin's of a man with the woman he loves."

"I don't know what you mean," Ella said, meeting her mom's eyes.

Mamm smiled mysteriously. "You don't?"

"No, I really don't."

"Then why do you think Bishop Miller was over here speakin' with Eli?"

"I don't know that either. Really."

"You are tellin' me the truth?"

"I don't lie, Mamm, especially about

somethin' like this. The bishop could tell on me."

"Then he didn't speak with you? Perhaps at your house? And you didn't tell him about Eli needin' his talking-to?"

"He didn't come by the house, so I couldn't have told him anything of the sort."

"Well," Lizzie said, frowning for a moment and then relaxing, "then this is a wonder indeed, perhaps even more than we had thought."

Ella clutched the side of the bed and tightened her grip on the familiar quilt. It brought little comfort as questions whirled through her mind.

"Mamm, maybe you'd best tell me about the bishop and what he wanted with Eli."

"Yah, maybe," Lizzie said, seeming to ponder the whole experience for a moment. "He came the other night and said he had heard some things about Eli and the *Englisha* girl. Of course, he told all that to Daett in private first and then spoke with Eli for more than an hour."

"How did he know about Eli? I sure didn't tell him."

"He must have heard somewhere, which doesn't surprise me. Eli should have known these things can't be kept quiet."

"Eli seems to have taken this well," Ella

189

said. "He doesn't seem nearly as stubborn."

"*Da Hah* has been good to us," Lizzie said and then lowered her voice. "Daett thought the bishop could do him good, and he was right, as usual. But that still leaves you. We thought you had given the bishop a good word . . . about your relationship with him . . . before he came."

"I didn't," Ella said firmly. "How could I? He didn't stop by."

"But you will when he does come by, won't you? Especially now? Especially now that the bishop came on his own free will? Think what that means. He came to speak with Eli without being asked. What a heart he must have for our family. Surely he must already consider the matter with you almost a done deal. He must care an awful lot about you, Ella, to take up Eli's matter on his own. How can you turn him down now?"

Ella heard Preacher Stutzman's words from the Sunday preaching so loud she could hardly hear her mom's question. "At the well, the servant found a woman who was worthy of Isaac. She drew the buckets of water — she and her servants — for all the camels. The servant knew then his master Abraham's desire had been answered. It was the sign that a bride for his son Isaac had been found."

"Ella," Lizzie said, touching her hand, "what are you thinkin'?"

"What Preacher Stutzman said today," she whispered.

"In church?"

Ella nodded.

"Then *Da Hah* has already spoken to you? In the sermon?"

"It seems so," Ella said through dry lips. The memory of her dream and her fear rose strong, but she kept her hands still, gripping the quilt. Before her the road seemed blocked in all directions, and only one path lay open. That path led straight into the bishop's arms as his wife.

"You cannot know what joy is in our hearts . . . your daett and mine," her mom said. "Not only has Eli received help, but he is like a changed boy since the bishop spoke with him. We find this such an honor — that such a worthy husband should turn up for you. After what *Da Hah* has torn from your heart, it now seems He has given back even more than He took. You must open your heart, Ella, and see what *Da Hah* is doing. This is so plain for the rest of us to see."

"I loved Aden," she whispered. "It has not been long yet."

"Yah, I know," Mamm said, stroking her arm. "Our little girl is all grown up now. I thought you had been asked to carry more than your heart could take. But now I see *Da Hah* does know what He's doin'. It was just my earthly eyes unable to see this all the time. *Da Hah* has taken Aden, who you loved, and He has given you back much more. Almost like Job of old."

"Mamm," Ella said, her voice barely rising to a whisper. Lizzie didn't seem to hear.

Mamm looked at the alarm clock on the dresser. "It's about chore time. Are you stayin' for supper?"

"I can't stay long because I have to get back before dark. The Stutzman girls come tomorrow morning already."

"I guess you do have your own house to keep. Perhaps I can send some supper back with you."

"You don't have to," Ella said, standing on her wobbly legs. "I'll help chore, though. I don't mind doing that."

"I'm sure the girls would appreciate it," Lizzie said as she reached for the doorknob. "I'm so thankful for your good sense, Ella. You always did have a good head on you. This will be hard for a while, I suppose. I don't know because I've never been through this exactly. But the bishop's a *gut* man. He'll make a right *gut* husband for you. Don't expect the feelings to be exactly the same for a while, not like they were for Aden. They can't be, but you'll love Bishop for what he is, especially by the time of your weddin'."

"I don't know," Ella said, stepping toward the door. She suddenly felt dizzy. *There really is little use in further discussion. How has this all happened, and so fast? I love my faith, my parents, my place in their world, and now they all seem to point in one direction, toward the image of Rebecca — submissive and meek before the will of those around her.*

"You have suffered so much," her mother said, embracing her in a long hug. "Daett and I are so glad for what has come your way. We can rest in peace at night now . . . even with you alone over there in that big house of yours. Now that we know the bishop will keep his eye on you and someday soon take your hand in marriage. You are so blessed, Ella. You really are."

"He hasn't come by yet," Ella said. Her voice was weak, but a faint hope started to rise in her chest. *Perhaps he won't come.*

"He's not stayin' away for long," Lizzie said, knowingly. Ella tried to breathe as they walked downstairs. She tried to keep a smile on her face as everyone prepared for chores.

"You can borrow one of my chore dresses," Dora said, and Ella followed her back upstairs. Alone in the room, Dora turned quickly toward her.

"So what goes? It seems some sort of mix-up happened between you and the bishop."

"You can say that," Ella said, giving Dora the story.

"You're still not for him, then?"

"Not really."

"Then why go along with it?"

"Several things," Ella said, not feeling up to a lot of details. Dora might not understand anyway. "Mamm and Daett are really for it."

"I am too, if that means anything," Dora said with a sheepish smile. "I guess I always was. Now that I saw the bishop with Eli the other night, I'm even more so. He's a real *gut* man. All the things we've ever heard about him are true. All of them, Ella. Eli told me a little about the bishop's talk after he left. He really made Eli see what all was at stake. The bishop told the story of our forefathers and what they stood for. Eli said he had never heard things quite like that before. The bishop told Eli how he must not let even the love of a woman draw him away from his heritage. He even told him a story from the *Martyrs Mirror.* Eli had never heard of the story before, but we looked it up in Daett's copy. It was about this young man who left his wife and two small children to give his life for the faith. Those are *our* people Ella, and how can any of us ever think to turn our backs on them?"

"I'm glad he helped Eli," Ella managed.

"You have a lot to be thankful for," Dora said, handing her a dress from the closet. "We all do."

"That's something, coming from you."

"Oh, I could be all blue about it, I suppose."

"Oh?" Ella said, sitting down on the bed. The chores could wait a few minutes.

"I guess I'm pretty down about my own prospects, is all. You seem to get all the really wonderful men. Aden and now Bishop comes callin' for you. Why don't I attract that sort of attention?"

"You can have the bishop," Ella said, but she knew Dora didn't hear the words or the attempted tease in her voice. Dora had walked over to the window, where she was looking out across the fields.

"I still haven't given Norman his answer," Dora said as her mood darkened. "He said he might not come back again."

"He's not serious, surely," Ella said, walking over to Dora and putting her arm around her shoulder.

"I'm afraid so. He's got his eye on some-one else, I think."

"But he asked you, didn't he? Who said there was another girl?"

"He didn't have to. I know it already. No one wants me, Ella."

"So why not tell him yes? You like him, and you could be married after you're twenty-one. Perhaps he'll be back soon, and you can tell him then."

"Not in a blue moon, he won't. He's gone. That's why I think you should be thankful, Ella — *really* thankful for the men *Da Hah* keeps sendin' to you."

"You shouldn't be saying things like this," Ella said as her heart sank again, "but I guess we'd better get to the chores."

"Always duty callin'," Dora said, turning away from the window. "And when do I get my turn at joy?"

"It will come," Ella said, but Dora didn't look convinced.

"You do believe that?"

"Yah, if you stop being so dark about everything."

"Yah," Dora said, nodding, "I guess I'd best get out of my dumps and get about my duty. That's what you'd do. And I do want to make the hymn singin' tonight. You comin'?"

Ella shook her head.

"That's right. You have the bishop now," Dora said, holding the door open for her.

They walked out to the barn together. The familiarity of it all — the impertinent rush of the cows, the sound of milk in metal pails, and the lift of one's spirits that always came when choring with her family — brought tears to Ella's eyes. Surprising herself, she consented to stay for supper afterward.

"I'll get your horse for you," Eli said after supper was over.

"I'll come over when Mamm lets me," Clara said, standing at the front door.

"You do that," Ella said, stepping outside. She waited while Eli brought the horse from the barn, and then she held the shafts up for him.

"I want to thank you for sendin' the bishop over," Eli said, holding the horse bridle in his hand. "You do a lot of people good with your life."

"I didn't send him, Eli."

"He came because of you. That much I know."

"I suppose so," Ella said, fastening the tugs on her side. "I'm just glad you've gotten some sense into that thick head of yours."

"Now if it stays in," he said with a broad smile.

"It had better," she said with a stern voice as she climbed into the buggy.

He let go and slapped the horse across the backside as it went by.

TWENTY-ONE

Ella drove toward the big house on Chapman Road, letting the horse have his time. The morning would come soon enough, bringing with it Preacher Stutzman's children. How early, it was hard to tell, but his arrival surely wouldn't be long after dawn. She imagined the moment when the three girls would be alone with her. *Will they be frightened? Should they have been told more? Has Preacher Stutzman taken the time to explain properly where they will be left?*

How like a man to not even offer an introduction beforehand. He will probably just drive in and drop his children off with me — in the care of a strange woman. She slapped the reins sharply, and the horse jumped, jerked his head, and instantly increased his pace. He turned his head toward her for a brief moment as if he thought she had lost her mind.

"Got to get home," she said in explanation.

Her hands tensed on the reins. *How smooth it had been of the bishop to call on my parents without my knowledge. Yet, perhaps he had gone simply out of the goodness of his heart, moved by compassion for Eli. Is the man not highly esteemed by Daett and Mamm, and aren't they usually right? They had been about Aden. Never have I heard a complaint come out of their mouths about my choice of a husband.*

On the last corner, just before the hill rose enough to see the house, she caught a glimpse of her driveway and the waiting buggy. The horse was standing at the hitching post. She had never seen the bishop's buggy in the daylight, but Ella knew that Bishop Miller had come to call.

For a moment she considered turning around on the road, rushing back down the hill, dashing into her parents' place for the night. The reason could be easily explained that she simply wanted to spend the night at home. Ella hesitated as her hands tightly clutched the reins.

The matter was decided before she could make up her mind. The bishop climbed out of his buggy and produced a rope from behind the seat. He glanced down the hill in her direction. He had seen her. There was no way to turn back now. With tight lips, she willed herself forward, even slapping the reins to cover for her nervousness.

"This could be worse," she said quietly to herself. "You'll just have to learn to like him since he's a *gut,* solid, and kind man. He wouldn't have talked to Eli for any other reason."

"Good evening," the bishop said when she pulled up. He reached for the bridle and guided the buggy to a halt in front of her barn. She wanted to tell him she normally parked on the other side but didn't dare.

"Good evening," she said, trying to smile.

"I hope I'm not catching you at a bad time," he said, patting the horse on its head and beginning to unhitch.

There was little choice but to dismount and help on the other side.

"Well, I wasn't exactly expectin' you. I didn't know when you'd come."

He nodded. His expression was one of understanding, and his blue eyes were bright in the last light of the summer sky. "I don't need to stay long if you have things to do."

"No," she said with resolve. "I have some things to get ready for tomorrow, but please come in."

Ella felt herself relax a little. Her smile strengthened, and she held the buggy shafts while he took the horse forward. She then led the way to the barn, and he followed with the horse in tow.

She almost told him what she wanted done for the horse — how much grain to give — but it didn't seem appropriate for some reason. The bishop's manner squelched that sort of exchange. He led the horse to the water and then slapped the horse's backside, watching him trot out to the enclosed field.

She held the front door of the house open for him, and he walked inside and removed his hat, holding it till she motioned toward the table. He walked over and left his hat there.

"Not quite unpacked yet," she said, smiling. She was not certain he could see her in the semidarkness. He waited while she found a lantern and began to pump the air handle.

"I can light that," he said softly, and she let him.

She went into the bedroom to leave her bonnet and shawl. Behind her, Ella heard the lantern catch with a soft pop, and light flooded the living room. "I'm not really ready for company, but Mamm fed me supper tonight. I still don't have much in the house in the line of food," she said, motioning for him to take a seat beside her on the couch.

The pain shot all the way through her body. This was how she had faced Aden those hundreds of times over the years — on the couch at home. But this wasn't Aden. The emptiness almost choked her.

"That's fine . . . about the food," he said with warmth and confidence. "I didn't come to eat. I had supper at home."

Ella tried to breathe. *My parents like this man, he has an impeccable reputation, and I will heal with time.*

"I could make popcorn," Ella said, getting up from the couch.

"Nee," his said, waving his hand in the smallest of motions, "it's good just to speak with you."

Ella sat down and waited in the silence, feeling as if her body would never move again.

"Since we spoke last at your parents' place, have you given thought to the question we left each other with? I know it was a little early then, and perhaps it still is now. That's why I was a little hesitant to return, but I had said six months. I didn't wish for you to think I had forgotten you."

"You were over to speak with Eli?" she asked. This subject felt much safer.

"Yah, I heard talk of his *Englisha* girlfriend, and I thought at once of what this would do to your parents and the heartache his actions would cause. I know our young people often do things out of emotions and passion, things which can lead to much error. I hope I was not out of order in speaking with him. I know I wasn't asked, but my heart was stirred in concern for your brother."

"Eli seems much better," she said because this was true and she was thankful. "He seems a lot less stubborn about the girl than when I and *Daett* spoke with him."

"That's how those things go," he said, smiling broadly. "Many times it's hardest to take things from those closest to us. Sometimes when one hears from the outside — from others not so close — the hearing gets better. I guess we all are like that, not just Eli."

"I suppose so," Ella said, thinking of Preacher Stutzman and his sermon. She had heard the same things said by her parents but had finally listened today. She had come to her senses, her dad would say. "I guess it goes that way for me too."

"All of us are human," the bishop said with his blue eyes turned in her direction. "Eli's a good boy."

"He could have done a lot of damage to himself," Ella said. "It might not have been stopped in time if you hadn't spoken to him."

"The girl will forget before long," the bishop said. "Eli's a *gut*-looking boy. I think he'll stay true to the faith till his dying day, especially with one of our *gut* girls at his side."

Ella smiled at the image. The bishop was so natural about the subject. "We are all thankful," Ella said with a slight blush. He was so close to her, almost as close as Aden used to sit.

"I really didn't do much, plus that's what I'm called to do . . . to help our people in their time of trouble."

Silence settled between them for a long moment.

"You sure you don't want popcorn?" Ella asked, starting to rise again.

He shook his head, cleared his throat, and motioned with his hand for her to be seated. "I really want to come over . . . quite often and see more of you."

Ella paused. *What is there to say?* "My door is open to you," she said with a voice that trembled.

"Have you thought about — what we talked about?"

"Yah, I have."

"Perhaps I rushed a little too fast by asking for your hand in marriage the first time I came."

"Yah," Ella said with some relief. *The truth is good, and I might as well speak it. Of what worth is a marriage if truth cannot be spoken?* "Your question — so soon — troubled me a lot. The pain was still great then. It still is, I guess. Sometimes I don't know whether I can ever love again, at least like that. I suppose it's best to tell you that now."

"I am clumsy sometimes, Ella. I know I am. I've never been married. Yet the Lord has given me grace. I see now why. The reason I waited so long was so my heart could love you. I hope I don't speak too plainly. I have just never felt like this before."

She shook her head. "No, your words are fine. It's just —"

While Ella paused, the bishop took up the opportunity. "I am sorry again for my haste. Yet perhaps it was best that way. By approaching you that early, your heart has been given a better time in which to begin healing. Sometimes wounds are that way. If they are left alone, they only fester, but with the proper care, they can begin to heal."

"I can't promise to marry you. Not yet," she said plainly, meeting his eyes, which were so blue they startled her. *But they aren't Aden's eyes.* "It must be enough for you if you just come over . . . whenever you wish."

"You are a woman of great courage, and — yah — honesty. In this *Da Hah* has given me a great gift. I hope in time to be worthy of your love. I love you, Ella," he said, reaching out and taking her hand.

Ella didn't resist. This was his right. She had just told him he could come to visit, and a touch of affection would perhaps help. With a deep breath, she smiled and laid her other hand on top of his. He squeezed her hand and laughed softly. His laugh was melodious and deep, but this wasn't the laughter that she had so long loved. The emptiness was an echo that roared in her ear.

"So tell me what you plan to do with this great big house of yours."

Ella leaned against the back of the couch and folded her hands on her lap. "Well, Preacher Stutzman's children come tomorrow, and I plan to care for them during the week, for a while anyway. Between you and me, Preacher Stutzman has paid — or soon will be paying — someone a call. A wedding is well on the way, I think. Also I have Joe and Ronda renting this floor of the house. They are moving in after they marry next week. The house should be quite full then, I think, and I sure can use the money."

"Ivan," he said in a tone that was still soft but with an edge on it. "You are taking care of his children?"

Ella turned to meet his eyes and laughed. "He hasn't called on you, has he?"

She laughed again. "Preacher Stutzman?"

He seemed to relax against the couch. "You never know."

Ella wanted to tell him he ought to go thank Preacher Stutzman personally for his sermon. For that reason, she was more willing to accept his visits. She almost laughed again at the look he would get on his face if he knew.

"Well, I really don't mean to hold you up," he said, getting up. "So I'm welcome to come back when I wish?"

"Anytime," she said. Her smile was a little weak, but she was just thankful she had a smile to give.

"Let's not leave like this, though, without a solid plan. How about I come on Saturday nights? I've never courted before, you know. Is that how it's done?"

The pain shot through her again. Surely her distress didn't show too much. "Saturdays will be fine," she said, glad he hadn't chosen Aden's schedule.

"It has been good to see you," he said as he put his hat on, quietly motioning for her to remain seated. He opened and shut the front door quickly. She sat still on the couch for a full five minutes, until the sound of his buggy wheels had completely disappeared.

TWENTY-TWO

Ella had set the alarm clock but awoke well before its jangle shook the early morning air. Fragmented thoughts from last night returned. The bishop had been here, and she had consented to his return. She had slept soundly — no dreams — so perhaps she had already begun to accept the inevitable. The bishop's wife would be her fate before all was said and done.

She swung her feet out of the bed and onto the floor. *Who really cares? Without Aden, what difference does this make — or matter? Little, really. I will never care for another man anyway. If everyone else is happy with this arrangement, they should all leave me in peace.*

Perhaps I'm being rebellious like Eli this morning. Well, so be it. At least I have my house for now, work I want to do, and hopefully the quilt shop to start up.

She dressed quickly and went downstairs.

After lighting the lantern, she prepared a cold cereal breakfast and ate by herself. Cold cereal couldn't always be for breakfast — not with three little girls to care for. The thought of food preparation startled her. There was no stove upstairs or in the basement. The chimney wasn't designed to work with another stove on the second floor, and it couldn't safely be adjusted now. How like a woman, to forget something like this.

Yet there must be a way around this problem. Ella's mind spun. *Ronda will simply have to share the stove for food preparation. The girls can eat later, after Joe leaves for work, and the food can be stored upstairs or in the basement. Will Ronda need to be told about this before she moves in? No, likely not. Ronda is a sensible girl.*

Buggy wheels rattled in the driveway, and Ella jumped up. Preacher Stutzman was early. The girls would likely be bundled up against the morning chill and surely have at least one suitcase full of clothes and diapers. Ella rushed to the front door to help, forgetting her own coat that hung in the closet.

The knock sounded before she got there. *How did Preacher Stutzman get to the front door with three small girls so quickly? Maybe he left them alone in the buggy. But he doesn't seem to be that sort of man.*

"Yah," she said, opening the door.

His figure was surrounded by the early morning rolling fog. "I thought I'd come and tell you myself, so you won't worry."

"Yah?" she said, repeating herself, completely puzzled.

He clutched the brim of his hat as the fog swept around him. "The children won't be coming after all. I suppose Susanna and I can handle them."

"Did I . . . do something?" She asked the burning question and wondered, *What did he see in me yesterday to cause this decision?*

"No," he said, looking at the ground. "The young Bishop Miller stopped by last night. He thinks this arrangement might not be appropriate because he's seein' you now."

"The bishop?" Ella said as her hand flew to her mouth. "He came to speak with you last night?"

"Yah, I really didn't know anything was going on between the two of you. I wasn't tryin' to cause problems — for you or for him. If I have, I am most sorry. I'm kind of clumsy since Lois passed. Perhaps before that, I was too, and she was just good enough not to tell me."

"He really told you that?" Ella asked, still trying to absorb the news.

"Yah, well I'd best be going. I have more than enough work to do already, and now I'm starting a bit late."

"Wait," Ella said, causing him to turn back to face her. "I will speak with the bishop about this. I will be by later for the girls."

"You will speak with the bishop?" he asked with a look of astonishment on his face. The question hung in the air.

"It's not right," she said, surprised at her own boldness. "The bishop told me nothing about this, and I didn't know he would say this to you. I am the one who is sorry for his actions."

"You are sorry for the bishop?" Preacher Stutzman asked and then laughed roughly as if he didn't believe she had been so bold.

"Yes, I am," Ella said, feeling a sense of resolve surge in her heart. "I will be down at your place soon to pick up the girls. That is if it's still okay with you."

"You — but how will you do this?" Preacher Stutzman asked while holding his hat in his hand. "He is Bishop Miller, not just any bishop. But perhaps I should not speak so . . . of your promised one. He is a *gut* man."

"Whatever he is, he is wrong on this," Ella said. "If you don't object, I will be down later."

"You will speak with the bishop first surely?"

"Yah, I will speak with him first."

"You will tell him that I told you the girls could not come here and that I did not encourage you?"

"Yah, I will speak only for myself."

"Then I would be more than glad if we could continue with our plan. I really don't know what I'll do otherwise. Susanna is already burdened with the girls' care, and I have the summer farm tasks to care for."

"I will come, then."

"I hope you do," he said and then was gone, swallowed quickly by the morning fog. Only the sound of buggy wheels lingered as Ella stood with one hand still on the open door.

"Well," she said, "what nerve the *gut* bishop has."

Then she took stock of her words and wondered at her boldness. *What have I just proposed to do? I — Ella Yoder — will speak with Bishop Miller and plan to change his mind.* Her spine tingled. *No wonder Preacher Stutzman had looked so astonished, standing on my front porch!*

Courage returned quickly. *I really do have the upper hand. The bishop will, no doubt, realize this, and I will quickly gain his approval for the care of Preacher Stutzman's girls. I'll go at once.* Breakfast was already eaten. With a glance toward the road, she saw the problem, but the fog could be overcome. Preacher Stutzman was out riding the roads, and so could she.

The horse greeted her with a whinny and stuck his nose into her face, causing her to push him away. "I don't like you that much," she said.

He bobbed his head violently.

With haste she threw on the harness and led him outside. She swung him under the shafts, fastened the tugs, and tied the horse to the hitching post. In the rush, she had forgotten her bonnet and shawl and went back to the house to get them. That was not a good sign, especially for a trip to the bishop, but she really needed to do this, good sign or not.

Once on the road, the fog seemed to clear up some. She thought of Preacher Stutzman's three girls, and a swell of emotion rose in her chest, driving her on and strengthening her courage. *They had looked so lost and so young on the day of their mother's funeral. Why had sorrow come for them so early in their life?* Da Hah *must have his reasons, hidden though they were from human eyes.*

A car and then another one passed her. Both pulled out in plenty of time to avoid her and then slowly passed by. Thankfully she had remembered to keep her buggy battery charged. The blinker on the buggy frame sent its bright flash into the mist in either direction.

The rays of the sun soon came through in spots, enough to where the fog didn't seem to cause any further danger. As she approached the bishop's house, Ella saw a light still on, and she pulled in the driveway. This early in the morning, the bishop was likely still in the barn and in the middle of chores.

Ella didn't knock on the barn door but simply opened it and walked right in, straight into the glow of the lantern hanging from the ceiling. The bishop had fewer cows than she was used to, but they lined the stanchions as usual. The looks on their morning faces were quite familiar.

"Good morning! What a surprise," the bishop said, getting up from beside a cow and causing his stool to scoot noisily on the floor. "You are the last person I expected to see."

"I can leave if you want me to," Ella said, surprised by her own boldness.

"Now, now," the bishop said, laughing but

quickly catching her mood, "I wouldn't be saying something like that at all, not when you obviously have something important bothering you badly enough to rush over this early in morning — and in the fog. Did I say a wrong word last night? I certainly didn't mean to."

Ella caught her breath and calmed herself. Now that she was here, things did look a little different.

"Preacher Stutzman came by and said he wasn't bringing the girls over as we'd planned. He said you had spoken with him last night and convinced him to drop the arrangement. I don't think that's right. He really needs someone to care for his girls. I'm about the only one available, and I need the money."

"He's not paying you that much, is he?"

"Forty dollars a week." This obviously was now part of the bishop's business.

"Like I said — not too much."

"The amount isn't the matter. I don't think it was right . . . what you said. Preacher Stutzman really needs someone to care for his girls while he works."

"I am concerned about how this will look when the word comes out that I'm seeing you, that's all."

"He has never asked me for anything else

or done anything untoward. Nor has he implied it."

"I know that now," the bishop said, smiling warmly. "Perhaps I was a little hasty with my actions. I know I can be that way. See, I also spoke with Susanna after I saw Ivan. Perhaps I should have gone back and talked to Ivan again after Susanna told me Ivan is about to ask for one of our women's hand in marriage. But I didn't."

"I told you that last night," Ella said, "and the woman he's askin' isn't me."

"Yah, that I know. Susanna didn't tell me who this woman is, but if it was you, she would have said so."

"Then I can take care of his girls?"

"I guess it will be okay," he said, smiling again, "since you have your heart so set on it. I guess no harm could come of it."

"I *do* want to," Ella said forcefully. There was no sense in leaving any doubt in the bishop's mind. He might as well get used to her.

"You are a woman of courage, I must say, yet tempered as a godly woman should be," the bishop said, reaching for his three-legged stool on the concrete floor. "I see more and more why *Da Hah* had me wait for you. I have never met a woman among our people I can value more."

Ella felt the heat creep up her neck. He spoke so plainly.

"I hope I do not disappoint you," she said, meeting his eyes.

"You will not. And you will be what *Da Hah* intended a woman to be — a *gut* helpmeet for me."

"I really must go," Ella said, finding her voice.

"It will be a long week till Saturday," he said just when she reached the door.

Ella managed a smile, stepped outside, and closed the door behind her. The fog had rolled in again and rose in great billows around the buggy. She could hardly see the outline of the horse. For a moment she thought to ask the bishop if she could stay until the sun had cleared the clouds but thought better of it. Inside the buggy, she got the horse turned around and out on the road. His hoofbeats cut a hollow sound in the morning air, and a chill rose around her, creeping through her shawl and making her eyes burn with tears.

TWENTY-THREE

Ivan stood inside the house. His mind was in turmoil. *How can I feel this way with my sermon on Sunday? Has my soul learned so little even after such a vigorous application of God's Word? What chores can be done or have already been done? The girls are dressed, breakfast is over with, and the baby's diaper is changed. Now the fields absolutely need to be tended. The farm can't be neglected any longer.*

He carried the baby and two-year-old Sarah and urged Mary to follow behind with her slow steps. *Susanna will need persuading if she hasn't already figured out my predicament. What am I to tell her — that the bishop forbids me to take my girls to Ella?* The answer brought a blush to his face behind his beard. This was shame twice over and then some.

He didn't knock on the door. He was too tired for such formalities. Susanna was his sister, after all. When he was just inside the front door, hoofbeats sounded from the road, and he grabbed the screen door again, opening it so violently his fingers slipped on the wood frame and bent the screen outward.

Did Ella arrive already? Such hope rushed through him, causing his face to burn with shame again. *The girl does not belong to me, nor would she ever. Ella is promised to the bishop.*

Ivan's eyes caught sight of the buggy. Although it appeared fuzzy in the fog, he knew it wasn't Ella's. Wearily he turned back into the house as disappointment flooded through him.

No, she won't come because surely the bishop won't let her. The screen door slipped from his hand and slammed on his fingers. The pain felt good, like it cleaned his soul for a moment and purged him of this forbidden desire.

"That was an ouchy," Mary said with wide eyes. "Does it hurt bad?"

"I'm bigger," he said, smiling through his clenched teeth. "My fingers are thicker than yours."

"Mamm's were too," Mary said. "Do you think they still are, up there in heaven where she is?"

"I think so," he said, wondering what the young bishop would say of such theology. Thankfully he wasn't here to venture an opinion.

"So you're back?" Susanna said, coming out of the bedroom. "Thankfully Daett had a good night." Seeing the girls, Susanna continued, "I thought you were taking the girls to Ella for the week."

"I'm sorry," he mumbled. "Something's come up."

"Something?" she asked, raising her eyebrows. "I'm afraid you'll have to explain better than that."

Ivan gave a quick nod toward the girls.

"Why don't you go up to the playroom?" Susanna said, bending over to smile at Mary. "You can take Sarah along since you've had breakfast." She gave Ivan a quick glance, and he gave her a grateful look.

"We had eggs," Mary said, "and bread with the eggs."

"You go play for awhile," Susanna said, holding open the door while they scrambled up the steps. Ivan set the baby on the couch that was pushed tight against the living room wall. It formed a protective corner and passed for a crib in the *dawdy haus*. A rocker stood beside it in the only place where there was room, the silhouette framed the front of the window.

"So what have you done now?" Susanna asked. "Surely you didn't preach one of your sermons to her? Did she chase you out of the house?"

Ivan avoided her eyes. "The young bishop forbids this," he said in a voice barely above a whisper.

"The *bishop?*"

"Yah, I guess he was seein' her, but I didn't know."

"Bishop Miller is seeing Ella?"

"Yah, I guess."

"What has that got to do with takin' care of your girls?"

"He doesn't think it's fittin'."

Susanna's eyes never left his face. "Did you also ask for her hand in marriage? I can't believe you'd do something like that."

"I did not," Ivan said but knew his face blushed deeply under his beard.

"So the two of you are fightin' over the same girl. Now I've heard everything. You preachers ought to be ashamed of yourselves."

"I am not," Ivan said. His voice was higher now, but his gaze remained on the floor.

"I told you last week to get the deal done with the widow Weaver. If you had done that, you wouldn't be in this mess. Is that why you couldn't ask her — why you're going around and around with the matter? You really want to ask Ella for her hand, is that it?"

"I'm an honorable man," Ivan protested, but he knew his struggle was all over his face.

"I didn't say you weren't. You have as much right to her as the bishop does. Whatever you want to do, just get off your high horse and do something about it."

"It's not right. You know that."

"Takin' a wife isn't right? Of course it is. You're needin' one bad."

"Ella," he said, sensing the name almost choking him, "she is not right for me."

"Now I've heard everything," she said. "What will come of this, I wouldn't know."

"Nothin' will come of it," he said firmly. "The bishop told me I can't take my girls to her, and I'll listen."

Susanna laughed. "I told him last night you were looking at some other option. So that's why he was so interested in the matter."

"You did?" he asked, meeting her eyes.

"Yah, so what?"

"I don't know," he said, suddenly glum again. *What good is it? Even Ella — the* gut *woman that she is — can't persuade the*

224

bishop or change his mind. He is known to be firmly set in his ways. "It's not right. That's all I can say."

"Well, you two will get it figured out, I suppose. In the meantime, us womenfolk have to carry the load. I hope the young bishop doesn't mind a piece of my mind the next time I see him. He can win his own battles without me carryin' a share of the load."

"You best not be speakin' to him. Ella's already gone over to try to change his mind. At least she said she would."

"About this matter?"

"Yah."

"You told her to speak with the young bishop?"

"I didn't," Ivan said, shaking his head.

Susanna put her hands on her hips. "So what will you do if Ella does come for the girls?"

"What is that question supposed to mean?"

"If you don't know, then why should I tell you? Look, if the girl fights to care for your children — now that's material for a wife, if I ever saw any."

"It's not right," Ivan repeated and moved toward the door. "The bishop is seein' her."

"Why did the Lord wait till the last day of

225

creation to make man?" Susanna said, throwing her hands up in the air. "He should have done so on the first day and given Himself some more time to straighten out the mess."

Ivan let the screen door slam, making sure his fingers stayed out of the way this time. Outside in the yard he heard a horse's hoofbeats on the pavement again, this time coming from the north, from the direction of Ella's house. With an effort he didn't look around. Once inside the barn, he couldn't help himself and peered out through the cracks in the barn door. His beard was so close to the boards, the hairs caught in the cracks. He winced from the pain of the plucked hairs and watched to see who had come up the drive.

Outside, the hoofbeats had ceased, and Ivan saw why. The buggy had stopped, and Ella was climbing out. His heart pounded in his chest. *So she did go to speak with the bishop. Did she obtain his permission? Does this mean what Susanna thinks it does?*

He remained at the barn door. Duties in the hay field, his chores, horses, and wheat fields all seemed but dim realities beside what was about to unfold before his eyes. Ella had taken upon herself the care of his girls. Clearly it was an action far above the call of simple duty.

Ivan watched from his post. Ella knocked at the front door, and a welcoming Susanna opened it. He couldn't hear what they said, but the screen door slapped behind them. He watched the spring on the screen door vibrate from the slam and then settle into its normal sag. He stood there motionless for a long moment, in which the world seemed to hang still, and waited for something to happen.

A fly buzzed past his nose and landed on his arm, and still he didn't move. Behind him came the noise of the cattle in the barnyard. He heard their halfhearted, low moans and the slurps of mud as they walked through the muck, but still he waited. His heart beat hard in his chest.

The door at the *dawdy haus* opened again, and Mary came out first. Her little hands held open the screen door as Sarah followed, barely able to walk because of the bag she carried in her arms. He could see Ella next as she stepped out onto the porch, laughing and reaching for the bag in Sarah's hands.

Sarah laughed then. Her face puckered up with sheer joy, showing her pleasure in every action. Behind them Susanna's form appeared, holding the screen while Mary marched down the steps. With the baby in one arm, the bag in the other, and Sarah's hands holding tightly to a fold of her dress, Ella came across the yard.

Ivan choked on his breath, and a gasp rose from his lips. He stilled the sound with force. This was the bishop's girl and not his to think of, even if *Da Hah* would have no objections. He tore himself away and then stopped at the sound of Mary's voice. "Are we going to your house?"

"Yah," he heard Ella reply, "to my big house."

"Are you are my mamm now?"

Ivan strained to hear the answer even though he knew only one answer could be given. Ella's laughter filled the air. "I'm just takin' care of you, dear, for the days during the week as long as your father wants me to. He's probably lookin' for a mamm for you right now."

"I don't want another mamm." Mary's voice rose higher. "I want you."

What Ella said, he couldn't hear. Her voice was too low. She lifted the baby into the buggy first and then attended to the two girls. Carefully she untied the horse, her hands only off the lines for a moment as she climbed in. The buggy moved quickly out to the road and then vanished around the bend. With great horror, Ivan realized his hands were white as they clutched the barn door handle.

TWENTY-FOUR

Ivan drove the hay cutter. The click of the blade was loud in his ears. His three horses pulled steadily as streams of sweat ran off their bodies. He knew the time had come to give them a rest, but he drove on. He was distracted. *Why didn't my intentions work? Will God hold me accountable for this breach, this affection for Ella?*

It seems there is but one thing to do. I must move on whether I want to or not. I must force myself to the act, even though my courage failed me last time. Today when the hay is done, it will be time for another attempt — another trip to ask for the widow Weaver's hand in marriage. Ella has the girls, so there will be no need to tell Susanna. I can make the trip over to the widow's place, return, and still be home in plenty of time for chores.

He was resolved to do this even though his heart sank. *This will be a good marriage. Our children will get along well. They'll be a perfect match — three girls and three boys. Nancy Weaver will make just the right kind of wife for me, a preacher. She is steady, sure, and* gut. *No, my heart won't pound in her presence, nor will my hands grip barn door handles till they are white, but I will find a measure of joy with her.*

The sweat streaks on the horses came into focus so suddenly he almost fell off the mower seat, jerking the lines so hard. One of the horse's sides already quivered. *What is wrong with me? Am I a man outside the will of* Da Hah? *No mistake about it. A loss of one of the Belgians would simply be too hard to bear, a sure smiting from on high, even if it is my own fault. The horses will have to be saved at all cost.*

With great haste he unhitched the traces and walked the horses back to the barn. He left them to drink in the shade and ran to find a five-gallon bucket to dump water repeatedly over their backs. The one whose side had quivered, he paid extra attention to.

Ten minutes later, he was satisfied he had saved them, but what was to be done with the rest of the day? Now that he had over-heated them, the horses would need more time to rest. There was danger in taking them out again. Yet the hay field needed to be cut today. Ivan's mind raced for options. Two of the horses could probably work the rest of the day. The third, whose side still flinched at intervals, was out of the question. The horse could probably work tomorrow, but not today.

Perhaps I should leave now and call on the widow and finish the hay when I return. But that won't help much, and a man ought to care for his farm duty first. Things like the search for a wife should come afterward.

The young colt was in the barn, not quite trained yet, but perhaps he could work with the colt. Quickly he pulled the harness off the troublesome horse, led him into the barn, and released him to his stall. The colt jumped when Ivan brought him out and let the leather straps fall across his back. He soon calmed down. To help things along, Ivan placed him between the two larger Belgians. The body movements of the two would guide him and keep mischief down.

Ivan drove up and down the field, allowing the horses to rest as soon as any sign of distress showed. The time taken was worth it because the only other option would be worse — dead horses. By two o'clock he was done, and there was still time left to make the trip to see the widow. He trotted the horses to the barn, pulled the harnesses off, and turned them out into the yard. In a rush, he caught the buggy horse and had him ready moments later.

Ivan climbed into the buggy, got the horse on the road, and attempted to collect his thoughts. *Do I really want to do this?* The question presented itself again. *There still seems to be no other answer except yes. Given the circumstances, it has to be.* He slapped the reins lest his courage fail him again.

Nancy is a wonderful woman. I should feel fortunate to obtain such a wife. That is, of course, if she will have me. We are both older and have been married before. He considered that his desire for Ella would fade from his memory soon enough as life moved on. Yet his heart hurt inside. He drove on, ignoring the pain.

The widow's place lay bathed in the warm afternoon sunlight as he topped the hill and turned in the driveway. He couldn't help notice that every board on the unpainted barn showed wear and every mud hole in the barnyard looked deep. Several thin cows turned to look at him, chewing their cud slowly. Clearly the widow tried to keep the farm in good shape, but the attempt must be hard with her boys still so young.

They could use each other, Nancy Weaver

and Preacher Stutzman. Already the names sounded right together, and the young bishop surely would be happy to hear of his plan. With a deep breath, he climbed out, tied his horse, and walked up to the front door.

He knocked and waited. No one came, so he knocked again. The sound of little patters of feet came from inside, and the door opened. One of the boys, whose name he didn't know, stood looking at him.

"Good afternoon," he said, seeing the boy had questions in his eyes. "Is your mamm home?" he asked, trying for a warm smile.

The youngster nodded but offered no more.

"I'm Ivan Stutzman," he said, hoping the boy would recognize the name.

"I will get Mamm," the boy finally said, leaving the door open and disappearing into the house.

Ivan saw her coming to the door. She was a tall woman with an open face, much as he had remembered her. Her apron was dusted with flour, her hands had crumbs still on them, and her feet were bare on the hardwood floor.

"Oh, I didn't hear anyone drive in," she said, smiling a welcome but not offering her hand. "I hope James didn't give you any trouble. He doesn't talk much since his father passed." She looked to the floor for a moment.

"I'm sorry," he said, feeling the rightness of her pain. They were truly two souls caught in a common sorrow. "My girls are a little young yet, but I'm sure they remember as well. Lois is much missed at our house."

She nodded. "But *Da Hah* knows best even when we don't think he does."

Behind her, James appeared and leaned against his mother's side. She wrapped her arm around him and pulled him close. *How is the rest of the conversation to proceed with the child around?* He searched for words to say. "You still keep your farm fairly well?"

"We have to since someone has to support the boys — and myself, as far as that goes. Daett helps when he can. Next spring Amos should be old enough to work the fields. He'll be eleven by then. It seems like a lot on a small boy's shoulders, but *Da Hah* will give strength to bear the load, as he does for all of us."

Ivan cleared his throat. He really needed to get back to his chores. He felt no emotion as he had with Lois, or as he would, he supposed, had this been Ella in front of him. Still, feelings or not, this was no time for doubts.

"Could I speak with you?" he asked with a slight motion of his head toward James, hoping she would understand.

"Go outside to the barn for a bit," she said softly, and James immediately left. That much was good. The boy had been taught to obey.

The silence hung between them, and Ivan kept his gaze on the hardwood floor.

"It's been some time now since Lois passed. Not too long, I guess, but soon enough. I have given this much thought. I know it's not the first time for either of us, but *Da Hah* must have had His own plans."

He glanced up to meet her eyes. "I thought perhaps . . . I could see you on Sunday night. Perhaps in the afternoon? I don't know . . . since we're not youngsters anymore. It's not like we don't know what this means or like we need a lot of time to make up our minds. Yet we should take some time — a short courtin' time, perhaps."

She smiled a weary smile, which summed up the situation. They were about their duty, and they both understood each other.

"I would be glad to say yes," she said, her voice slowly wrapping around each word, "but I have already agreed to another man's request for a visit. No, it's more than that. Mose Troyer spoke to me almost a year ago, and I asked for some time . . . for a woman's heart heals slowly when she's loved and lost a man. Mose kindly agreed and came back last week." She suddenly looked so very tired to Ivan. "And I told him yes."

"You are promised?" Ivan asked, hearing the sound of his own voice off in the distance.

"I am," she said.

"But Mose," he managed as the image of the older farmer became clear in his mind.

"I know," she said, meeting his eyes. "It's hard either way, but *Da Hah* will give grace. A woman can learn to love any man with time, I suppose. Is that not our people's belief?"

He cleared his throat, noticing that his heart beat wildly. "That's what they say. I guess I've never experienced it."

"The boys need a father, and Mose is a good man. I've known him for years . . . even before his wife passed away ten years ago. I think he loved her deeply, and I trust there are no hard feelings between us."

"There are none," he said, suddenly feeling an unexpected joy. "May *Da Hah* give His blessin's to the two of you."

"And may He meet your need," she said, smiling her weary smile again.

Ivan nodded and reached behind to find

the door. In the yard, James had come back from the barn, and Ivan stopped to speak with him. "Sounds like you will have a daett again soon."

"Shhh." James said, placing his finger on his lips. "Mamm told us, but no one else is to know."

"I guess not," Ivan said, ruffling his hair. "I'm glad to hear it, though, but I won't tell." He walked toward his buggy. His feet seemed to almost float on the ground.

James still stood where he left him, watching him leave. The little fellow would grow up to be a *gut* little man. Ivan could still see him when he reached the top of the hill.

So she said no. Could this possibly mean that Ella could be mine? It was an awful forbidden thought and one he should immediately chase away. He took a deep breath, letting the emotion of it run all the way through him.

At least he had done his duty and was now free. *Da Hah* could have opened this door to the widow if that had been His will. Since He hadn't, his desire to see Ella was no longer completely his fault.

The road stretched out in front of him. And then he remembered the bishop was still interested in Ella. For a moment there had been only Ella and him left in the whole world.

His head ached. *Ella, too, is already spoken for. Why did I not visit the widow last week as planned? Perhaps her answer would have been different then. Instead I turned around like a sinner. Now I — Ivan Stutzman — am leaving for home empty handed. What a clumsy man I am when it comes to love, and surely* Da Hah *will punish me for the pursuit of my carnal desires.*

TWENTY-FIVE

Ella fixed the girls a supper of mashed potatoes, gravy, corn, and green beans in small quantities. It was a supper like she would prepare for real company. They *were* real company, even if they were only two small children and a baby.

"Baby Barbara only takes the bottle," Mary said, pronouncing the words slowly. "She can't eat the big stuff."

"Maybe she'd like to taste it," Ella said, taking the spoon and touching the tiny offering to the baby's lips. She opened her mouth and then puckered up her face while her jaws toothlessly chewed.

"She's never had that before," Mary said, astonished. "She likes it!"

"I think she does," Ella agreed, unable to keep the catch out of her voice. *How sweet this little one is, and she's been left totally in my care.*

"Daett always gave her the bottle," Mary

said. Beside her Sarah nodded her head.

Ella laughed. Sarah didn't have the slightest idea what was just said. Her head just went up and down. Her little white head covering had already slipped off for the night, and her long baby hair hung down over her shoulders.

"What about Susanna?" Ella asked.

Mary shook her head. "She didn't."

"Maybe I shouldn't have either." Ella said, stricken with the thought. *What is the correct age to start babies on real food? Is it eight or nine months or more like a year?*

"She likes it," Mary said, interrupting her thoughts.

Obviously this is true, but is it safe? I certainly don't want a sick baby — or worse — on my hands! But baby Barbara had now replaced the puckered look with one of enjoyment. Her mouth was open again. Ella took a deep breath, stuck the spoon in the mashed potatoes, touched it to the gravy, and then slipped the spoonful into the waiting open mouth.

Mary threw her head back and laughed. Sarah imitated the motion and let her own laugh bubble out of her throat. Ella finally joined in. She felt bold, alive, and deeply moved by these three, and the emotion startled her. *Is this what it's like to be a*

241

mother and have children like Aden would have given me?

Quickly she wiped baby Barbara's mouth. *I can't get too attached. They go back home soon and will eventually live with the woman Preacher Stutzman will marry.*

"Shall we help with the dishes?" Mary asked.

"You're a little young," Ella said.

"Sometimes we help Daett. We really do."

"You help Daett?" Ella asked and left the rest unsaid. *It is simply impossible to imagine — the sight of Preacher Stutzman with his hands in the dishwater bowl and a little girl on a chair beside him. Is the man from Sunday's fiery sermon really capable of such a task?*

Mary nodded. "Sarah wants to help, but she's too small."

"I guess she is," Ella's said with another catch in her voice.

"I'm not," Sarah said loudly. "I'm big!"

"Why don't you both help, then?" Ella said, seeking compromise. Neither would be of much help, but the gesture was what mattered.

Ella heated the water on the stove and transferred the dirty dishes to the counter. She set the baby on a blanket on the kitchen floor. She kicked her feet, raised her hands into the air, and watched Ella's every move.

Mary was already dragging a chair across the floor, and Ella completed the task by grabbing another one for Sarah. Ella helped little Sarah up while Mary made the jump onto her own.

"Do this first," Ella said, demonstrating by scraping the first dish.

"I already know how," Mary said, taking the next plate.

"It still doesn't hurt to show you again," Ella said. "You scrape the dishes, I'll wash and rinse them, and Sarah can dry them."

Sarah clutched the cloth in both hands. Ella expected her to get bored quickly and quit, even with the few dishes they had to do. But as she washed, both girls stayed on the chairs and worked alongside her. The baby stuck her finger in her mouth, rolled onto her side, and rather seemed to enjoy the whole thing.

"Now we're done," Ella said, holding the last dish up in triumph.

"I want more to wash," Mary said. "Can we eat again, so there's more?"

Ella laughed and shook her head. Her voice was not to be trusted at the moment. *These are not only little girls without a mother, they are incredibly sweet little girls.*

"You are both such dears," Ella said, giving them both a hug at the same time, one in each arm. "Do you help like this at home?"

"Yah," Mary said, "but not like you just let us. This is more fun."

Ella's throat was tight with emotion, but she quickly found her voice to ask, "Not even with your Aunt Susanna? Isn't it fun to wash dishes for her?"

"She just works," Mary said. "Big work, and we can't help with big work."

"Well, it's time you started. Now off to bed, all three of you."

"I'm going to like it here," Mary said, and Sarah nodded vigorously beside her.

"That's good," Ella said, smiling. "We'll all sleep downstairs for the first few nights. Then we have to move upstairs. I have some more people comin'. They're a young couple who are just gettin' married."

"Will you get more little girls so we can play with them?" Mary asked while her eyes searched Ella's face.

"No, just you," Ella said, smiling through the tears that stung her eyes. Her breath caught at the aloneness and the lost look she saw in Mary's face. She gathered both girls in her arms, pulled them to the couch beside her, and quickly brushed the tears from her eyes. "Shall I read you a story?"

They both nodded, nestling tight against

her. On the floor, the baby rolled toward them and came to rest on the blanket.

"What story?" Mary asked.

"I don't know. I don't really have any storybooks here. Mamm and Daett have lots of them at home."

"Then you can tell us one," Mary said with confidence.

"I suppose so," Ella said, searching for an appropriate subject. There were stories from her schooldays, still vivid in her mind. "I know what. I'll tell you the story of a little boy's midnight test."

"What is midnight?" Mary asked.

"It's the middle of the night."

"When it's really dark?"

"Yah," Ella said, suddenly unsure this was an appropriate story because it was set in the darkest of nighttime. But Mary was leaning against her and didn't seem alarmed. Ella glanced at Sarah and then drew a long breath. She would have to keep her eyes open for the first signs of discomfort.

"There were these school boys. They were a lot bigger than you but not really big yet. They had a tree house where they got together on Saturday afternoons. They played games, had fun, and talked. One day they formed a club. It was supposed to be a brave group, and no other boys could join unless they passed the test — a test that had to be done at midnight."

"What's a test?" Mary asked, moving against Ella's side.

Ella ran her fingers over Mary's cheeks. "When you get to school, you'll learn. There they give tests to you on paper, and you have to write down the correct answers. If you get enough of them correct, you pass. But this was not to be a paper test. This test had just one question: Are you brave enough? You had to pass the test with a perfect grade."

"Yah," Mary said, seeming to understand.

"Soon another boy wanted to join. His name was Mark. He grew up on his parents' farm where his father milked cows. He had grown strong from all the hard work. Mark was a big boy and very brave. In school he heard about the tree house, the club, and the test that had to be passed in order to join. He went to the boys one Saturday and asked them if he could take the midnight test.

"The other boys told him what he had to do — at midnight, of course — and Mark said that was no problem. He had done other things just as scary and hadn't been afraid. The boys smiled at each other and told him the story of Roman Miller. Big, strong Roman Miller was from the other church district and had tried last week to pass the test. He had failed. Did Mark think he was better than Roman Miller? Mark hung his head at the news but still showed up on that specific night as planned. No moon shone that night, making it really dark, just as the boys had intended. Mark was allowed to find his way with a little flashlight but wondered what they were up to. Surely they wouldn't scare him with the dark."

"I would have been scared too," Mary said, pressing her head tight against Ella's shoulder.

"Me too," Ella said, glancing at both girls. They didn't seem overly alarmed, just observant.

"This was what Mark was told to do. He was supposed to take a kitten into the woods — the Miller's deep dark woods. There, a little ways across the field, he was to leave the little kitten at a cabin they all knew about. The boys had tied a white flag with a note on the door of the cabin. Mark was to bring the flag and note back. The kitten had to stay there. The boys said this was very important. Mark couldn't bring back a note he had written himself because he didn't know what the note said. The test was to see if Mark could go into the dark woods all by himself.

"So he started out with the kitten under his arm. Then he put the little animal into his coat pocket to keep safe. The night was really black, but Mark wasn't scared. He walked bravely right into the woods. An owl hooted above him, but Mark wasn't afraid and kept on.

"He finally found the cabin with the flag hanging on the doorknob. Mark pulled the kitten out of his coat pocket and set the little guy on the ground. The kitten mewed at him, making a quiet little sound among the big tall trees. Mark petted the kitten and explained what he had to do. He told the kitten that this was a test and that someone would surely come along soon. The flag and the note had to be taken back to the tree house.

"As Mark started to leave, he looked back one more time. The little kitten stood by the door, mewed loudly, and tried to follow him. He ran quickly into the trees, so the kitten couldn't follow, but then he stopped. Mark suddenly knew he couldn't do this. This was very wrong to leave the kitten out here in the dark woods all alone. By the morning, the kitten would have walked far away from the cabin and gotten lost.

"But what about the test? Mark so wanted to pass the test. After school he wanted to go with the other boys to the tree house, talk with them, play their games, and be part of their club. 'I have to pass the test,' Mark told himself and turned away again. He had taken only a few steps when he stopped again. He just couldn't leave the kitten alone in the woods.

"Mark almost cried when he ran back, grabbed the kitten again, and tucked the little thing back into his coat pocket. The little kitten mewed, but Mark didn't think long about that. He had failed the test. Now the other boys would think he wasn't good enough and that he hadn't been brave enough to leave the kitten there, even when he came back with the flag and note. Mark said, 'Well, I'll show them. They can just have their old tree house if they want it. I'm not going to leave a kitten out there even if it means I can never join the boys' club.'

"Out of the woods Mark ran, quickly finding his way back to the other boys. He showed them the note and the flag . . . and then he pulled the kitten from his pocket and said, 'You can have your tree house. Anyone who would leave a kitten alone in the woods is not a good friend to have anyway.'

"To Mark's surprise, the boys began to cheer. They slapped him on the back and shook his hand. 'You have passed!' they said.

" 'But I didn't leave the kitten,' Mark said, feeling very puzzled.

" 'That was the test,' said all of them at the same time. 'We don't want any boys to join us who can leave kittens in the woods at night — even to pass a test. You are a brave boy, indeed.'

" 'You mean I really passed?' Mark asked, still unable to believe it.

" 'You have,' they said, slapping him on the back some more. 'Now you're one of us.'

" 'Wow!' Mark said, feeling like he would cry right then and there. 'What a strange test that was.'

" 'But a good one,' they said, and Mark had to agree. It really was a good test."

"I want a kitten," Mary said in a sleepy voice. "A nice kitten like that."

"Don't you have any in the barn?" Ella asked. "Every barn has some cats."

"I don't know," Mary said, leaning her head against Ella's shoulder.

"I think you'd best go to bed now. Sarah's already asleep." Ella said, standing up and lifting Sarah into her arms. Mary followed her into the bedroom where Ella tucked them both in. Back in the living room, the baby kicked her legs, still wide awake. Ella changed her, warmed the bottle, and rocked her gently. Her eyes soon closed, and Ella gently lowered her into the crib. Thankfully she didn't stay awake all night. *This evening is, at least, a good start, even if much trouble lay ahead. With children, trouble always comes at some point, doesn't it?*

Ella stood, looking at the sleeping baby. *Why is the world so full of trouble?*

TWENTY-SIX

Ella checked around the house one last time and turned off the gas lantern hanging from the kitchen ceiling. The light from the kerosene lamp in the bedroom flickered faintly. Its beams reached just outside the doorway. *Why do I feel so tense, as if danger is around somewhere? It's probably just the extra responsibility of the girls' care.*

With one last check around the room, Ella turned the lamp in the bedroom on low, as far down as the wick would go before it smoked. She took a deep breath, climbed into bed, and fell into a fitful sleep.

With a start she awoke in the darkness. *What time is it?* The alarm clock was out of reach and turned away from her. The lamp still flickered on the dresser. Neither of the girls made any noise in the bed beside her, and the baby was quiet in the crib.

It had been a dream — but even more

vivid than usual. Buggies were parked in the wide field behind the barn. She had hoped the outcome would be different this time, but this dream ended the same way her other dreams had ended. When she could finally see the faces of the bride and groom, they were of the bishop and herself.

Ella clutched the quilt and struggled to breathe. *Why does marriage to the bishop so frighten me? Have I not made peace in my heart that this is* Da Hah*'s will? My parents approve. Can they really be so wrong? Is the sermon by Preacher Stutzman not from God?*

The flickering light cast crazy shadows on the bedroom walls. *Somehow I have to make peace with this. Love can't be so filled with fear, grip my heart with such terror, and come for no reason whatsoever. Perhaps others can live so, but I cannot. My heart will never allow this.*

"Dear God," she whispered, pushing the covers back, "please help me."

Careful not to awaken the girls, she crept into the living room. The night was so dark that only the faint outlines of the house windows could be seen. *Like the bedtime story about Mark who had set out to be brave and pass the test, is this my test? Has* Da Hah *moved on me to tell the story so I can learn from its lessons and move through my fears?*

"Oh God," she prayed. "I am not brave, and I don't know what to do." She considered kneeling for such a formal petition but then thought maybe comfort would come from the stars, from the open heavens above her as she prayed. There was no one to see if she walked outside in her night clothes, and so Ella stepped out the door, past the porch roof to a view of the clear night sky, and then farther on down to the gravel drive.

Here it would be safe to speak with the Almighty, even if she had no husband to guide her. *Oh, if Daett or Eli — even with his stubbornness — were in the house behind me. How their presence would comfort and soothe my nerves.*

The gravel slid under her slippers, and the stars blazed gloriously over her head. She turned and looked back to the house — her house. This was where she belonged — in this house. That much was certain. With that certainty, her fears began slipping away.

"Aden," she whispered. Tears formed and felt cool on her cheeks in the slight breeze. "You are with God, now that you left me. You were called away from this earth. Why? I don't know, but it must have been for a good reason. Is heaven up there somewhere? Can you see me now? Could the angel that took you to God come back to help me out? Would that be possible?"

Ella trembled. The blaze of stars above her looked as if they were ready to answer. They appeared to be producing a being clothed in white who, perhaps, was ready to take her away like Elijah of old in a chariot of fire. She barely dared breathe as she waited. *Will I see Aden again?* Great happiness swelled up in her heart. Laughter was ready to come out of her mouth. *Am I about to see heaven?*

Great ages had passed since she had seen Aden, sensed his joy, or felt the warmth of his arms around her. Was this now to be again? Ella lifted her arms skyward as if they moved all on their own. Heaven was more possible in that moment than it ever had been.

Ella waited. The stars twinkled but her arms grew suddenly weary. No, there would be no chariot of fire, no angel, and no Aden to snatch her away. She must remain simple Ella, caught up in her troubles on the earth, alone outside her house in her night clothes, and anyone who drove by would surely think she had lost her mind.

"I'm not brave," she whispered. The tears

came, and the sobs racked her chest. "I can't face this dark world alone. How am I to go on with life — even if it's lived in *Da Hah*'s will? How am I ever to marry the bishop?"

Long moments passed, and Ella quieted her sobs. *Surely it isn't right to make such a fuss. Others have lost their loved ones, and they go on with life. They also marry again, some sooner than others, but almost all do eventually.*

The bishop is a good man, and he needs a wife. Deep down, I need a husband. She wanted one with all her heart, but the one she wanted was Aden, who was no longer here. *I need to just make the most out of this situation. A sensible and brave woman would do that.*

Ella turned to go back inside. If nothing else, she needed to get some sleep. Life really would continue on whether she wanted it to or not. But now, suddenly she knew. Marriage to the bishop would include a consequence she hadn't thought of before. *I will have to leave the three girls alone and uncared for if I married the young bishop.*

Surely someone else will take care of them until Preacher Stutzman marries. And he is already making such plans. The bishop had been confident of this, yet hadn't Mark thought *the same thing about the kitten — that it would be safe if he abandoned it? Will the girls be safe with someone else until Preacher Stutzman marries?* She remembered the light touch of their heads against her side while they sat together on the couch.

"I can't," she whispered. "It wouldn't be right until I know for sure."

She felt better now with some resolution reached. This night's excursion hadn't been entirely in vain.

Ella walked back inside the house, but sleep was far away even though the alarm clock showed the time was past one o'clock. The very thought of dropping off to sleep was beyond her reach now. Sleepless nights must be part of the care of a mother, something that happened whether one wanted it or not.

Carefully she opened the cedar chest, extracted her journal, and took the lamp out to the kitchen table. If she wrote, perhaps sleep would come.

Dear Journal,

I had the dream again tonight. The bishop and I were about to get married, and I have no idea why that frightens me so. He's a gut man, and Mamm and Daett think so too. Yet my nerves fail me. Why one should go by nerves, I don't know. I never thought of myself as such a person.

I went outside to pray and to see the stars, and I thought surely I would be taken up into heaven, so real was the experience. I actually saw Aden's face — in my mind, of course — but it all seemed so real. I guess it just shows how mixed up I am. How I do miss Aden. He must be so happy in heaven, and I am left alone down here. How can I ever marry another man? The very thought is simply beyond me.

Yet other women do. I know they do because I have seen them, and they are women who have been married before. Perhaps that's what makes the difference. Maybe this would all be different if Aden and I had been married and if I had borne his children.

One thing I do know for sure is that Preacher Stutzman's girls have already made for themselves a warm place in my heart. I will not abandon them before he marries again.

It's strange how complicated a man Ivan Stutzman is. On Sundays he thunders in his sermons, and then when he talks to me alone the next day, he can hardly keep from staring at the floor. And the way he nervously turns his hat around in his hands, it's like nothing the bishop does. Now there is a confident man.

I suppose most girls would fall all over themselves to just get a date with him, let alone a marriage proposal. What makes me so different? I guess I've always been different; at least that's what Aden used to say.

I have plenty of work to do. Joe and Ronda will be here soon, and the house will be more than full, which is the way it should be. Hopefully having all these people here will help me move past my sorrow and provide support at the same time. I'd like to start on the quilt shop idea as soon as possible.

I wish God would just tell me what kind of life lies ahead of me instead of surprising me with all these unexpected turns. But then He wouldn't be God, would He?

Ella shut the journal softly, picked up the lamp, went back to the bedroom, and set both on the dresser. Tomorrow the journal could be put away. Pulling the covers over her, sleep came quickly, and she slept soundly with no dreams.

TWENTY-SEVEN

With the white cloth base firmly attached, Ella stretched the quilt frame taut. It was a maneuver she often performed at home with Mamm. This was the first time she had tried it by herself. It was more difficult than expected, like the rest of her recent challenges, but somehow she would manage. She simply had to.

Beside her the baby wrinkled her face as if ready to burst into tears. Ella stopped stretching the frame but kept a hold of it. "Mary, talk to your baby sister," Ella said, motioning with her chin.

Mary went over to her sister and after a moment reported, "She doesn't want anything. She's fine."

"That's good," Ella said, giving the quilt another pull. The peg slipped into the hole on the frame, causing the quilt to stay taut, and she let go with a relieved sigh.

"Just keep talkin' to her," Ella said,

"especially if she acts as if she'll start crying."

"I will," Mary said, patting the baby's cheeks.

She was such a darling — all three of them were — and they were all so easy to take care of. Perhaps this came from being tossed back and forth between Preacher Stutzman's home and his sister's home. Although such an experience could have hardened them to life, on the contrary, it seemed to make them the sweet children they were, and how quickly the three had taken their place in her heart.

The basement was cool, even for a summer's day. The large room really was the perfect spot for her quilt shop. Though she had only the one sample quilt finished, she felt compelled to open the shop and see what would happen. Hopefully, she would be able to sell customers on the idea of made-to-order quilts once they saw her handiwork.

Yesterday Ella had painted and hung her little sign, *Ella's Quilt Shop.* The brush strokes had come easy, and the effect was pleasing, sort of personal, intimate, and reflecting her love of quilts.

As she considered what to do next, she heard the sound of an *Englisha* car crunch its tires on the gravel outside.

Already? A customer? Surely not! She walked over to the basement window for a quick glance outside, confirming there really was a car parked in front of the house.

Scarcely able to breathe at the idea of her first customer, Ella waited until she heard the knock on the upstairs door. She rushed upstairs, wondering how she should act in front of *Englisha* customers. She really hadn't given it much thought. *Will I really sell a quilt? Me? Ella Yoder? Take a deep breath. If I keep my hopes small, they won't be dashed to the ground.*

"Good morning," Ella said, opening the door with a slight tremble. "Can I help you?"

The woman smiled broadly. "Your quilt shop. I saw the sign. Are you Ella?"

"I am. I'm just barely open. My shop is in the basement."

"This is a lovely house," the woman said. "It looks new. I left my husband down at one of your people's furniture stores. We saw your sign earlier, but he didn't want to stop in with me. Anyway, I'm Marie, and I'm from Maryland. We drove up yesterday and got the travel brochure the county puts out. It has all of the Amish businesses on it, but I didn't see yours. You must be very new."

"I am," Ella said. "Let me take you down to the basement. We can just go down these outside steps, or I can take you through the house."

"The stairs are fine, dear. All of you Amish are such wonderful folks. I just have to look at the quilts, and I'd love to take one home with me."

"Well, I don't really have much," Ella said, holding the basement door open. "In fact, I just have a sample. If you like my work, I can make your quilt to order."

"Then I'll look at that," Marie said, moving inside, sounding slightly disappointed.

"Here it is," Ella said, motioning with her hand to her wedding quilt, now hanging on the wall.

"Oh, it's lovely!" the woman said. She then saw the girls and said, "And your children, how adorable they are! My goodness, you don't look old enough — and three already. You people really are the salt of the earth. I wish we had more children. We only had the two, and now I regret I didn't have a dozen. Old age does change your thoughts on the matter, and my husband agrees too, mind you."

She then took a corner of the quilt and

held it up. She released it and backed away to get a fuller view. After a moment, she said, "This really is quite good. I was so hoping to take a quilt home with me, but if you can make one close to this design, I'd be willing to wait and have you ship it to me when it's finished."

"Yes, that would be fine," Ella said. "That's what I'm hoping to do for my first customers. It will take me a while to have several quilts ready to offer. In fact, yours will take a little time. We made the sample quilt in our spare time. My sisters and mom helped." Ella cleared her throat. *Should I say something about the girls? The woman thinks they are my own. Should I correct her?*

"Is this a picture of the house? This house?" The woman said as she took a closer look at Clara's picture, now beautifully incorporated into the quilt.

Ella nodded, and the moment to say something about the children passed quickly.

"I thought so. What a lovely idea."

"Actually my sister drew it. Clara is quite the little artist."

"I would say so. Yes, this is just grand. I do want you to make one for me. Can you do something with some red and gold tones? That will match our bedroom nicely."

"Yes, but," Ella said, pausing, "I haven't mentioned a price yet."

"Oh, I assumed all the Amish shops charged about the same. The one I visited yesterday was very reasonable — around four hundred and fifty dollars, I think. Yours is nicer, though. Would that be a fair price?"

"Oh, yah, that is more than enough."

"There would be shipping, of course?"

"Yah, I guess so. You'll have to excuse me. This is my first sale, and I don't know how to think of such things."

"You'll be just fine, dear, and I'll take it," Marie said, carefully running her hands over the quilt one more time.

Ella found her new bill book and said, "If you'll fill out your address here, I can then ship the quilt when it's done."

Marie wrote in large letters, filling out the information on the page. "How long do you think it will take, dear?"

"A few months." Ella said, hoping she wasn't disappointing the woman. "Three months? Is that too long?"

"That will be fine," Marie said, taking out her checkbook. "May I give you a deposit now and pay the rest when the quilt is finished?"

"Yes, of course," Ella said, not having thought through the process. After all, this was her first sale, and so soon. Surely *Da Hah* was looking out for her.

Marie looked again at the sample quilt. "That drawing of the house is so nice. It seems very few of you Amish folks do any artwork. Has your sister done other drawings or even sketches? I would love to look at some and possibly buy one for my home."

"Oh, yah, Clara is good at that."

"You ought to have her draw some more. You could put her art up for sale here in your quilt shop. I know I'd buy some if you had them ready. I expect others also might. I don't think I've seen any sketches in any of the places we stopped at so far."

"We can't draw pictures of people," Ella said. "Any image of humans is strictly forbidden. It's a very strict rule in our beliefs. We are not to show pride in the human person. That is an honor that belongs only to *Da Hah* Himself."

"I know that, dear," Marie said with a warm smile. "I meant of farm life, of course. Scenes. Why don't you think about that?"

"I'll tell Clara," Ella said. "My sister does love to draw."

"No sense squandering the gift God has given, that's what I say. Now, I really must go," Marie said, stooping down and stroking Mary gently on the cheek. "You girls are very sweet. You haven't made a peep all the time I've been here." Then turning to Ella, she continued, "My husband probably wonders where I got to. He should know better, though. Hah, once I get around quilts I'm lost, that's for sure. It's a good thing you only started up, or I'd be here all day."

"Thank you," Ella said, offering her hand. "I'll get this made as soon as I can."

Ella opened the basement door and listened to the retreating steps. She let out a sigh of relief. *My first sale!* She didn't dare move until the tires crunched again on the gravel. Sitting down in a chair, Ella pondered what had just happened. *Did I really just sell my first quilt or is this a dream? Did I promise too much? Can I make the quilt in the time I allowed?*

Surely I can. This is for a customer, a person who paid me money — money I can hold in my hand and money to deposit in the bank in Randolph. I am on my way. I really can do this! Best of all, Da Hah *approves. Why else would He bless my efforts so quickly?*

"Who was that?" Mary asked, pulling on her dress sleeve.

"A nice lady who just bought the first quilt I'll have to make."

"She smiled at me," Mary said, seeming

pleased. Beside her Sarah smiled as she watched her sister's every move.

Across the room the baby wailed, and Ella rushed over to pick her up. She grabbed the bottle on the table, and the baby quickly nestled against her, emitting the happy sounds of satisfied slurps.

"Just think," Ella said out loud, "I just sold a quilt."

From outside, the sound of disturbed gravel came again. But this time it clearly wasn't from *Englisha* car tires. A horse and buggy had pulled in.

"Visitors again," Ella said, but Mary was busy on the floor, her attention on her game with Sarah. They piled wooden blocks so high that the last one teetered on the edge and balanced by the merest chance against the pull of gravity.

"Don't touch," Mary said to Sarah as Ella went to the basement window again. She saw both Dora and Clara coming up the sidewalk and jerked open the basement door. Baby Barbara was still in her arms, but the bottle was left behind on the kitchen table.

"You have come to visit?" she hollered. "What about your choring?"

"Look at you," Dora said, ignoring Ella's question. "You look like a mother, I do declare, but then you always did."

Ella pretended to groan but actually took delight in Dora's comment. "And you, Clara, I'm so glad you could come."

"We can't stay for long," Clara said. "Mamm consented to let us come, but we have to get back and do our work."

"I think Mamm let us come so we could check up on you," Dora said. "She pretends like she doesn't worry about you, but I think she does."

"Oh, that's just Mamm. It's not been that long yet," Ella said. "Do come in. Come see my little quilt shop. And can you believe it? I just made my first sale!"

TWENTY-EIGHT

"What sold?" Clara asked, glancing around. She saw the quilt hanging against the wall. "You sold *that* one? You sold your weddin' quilt?"

"No, of course not," Ella said quickly, "but it was one just like it, only with reds and golds in it. The woman will wait till it's made, and then I'll ship it to her. Isn't that something?"

Dora eyed Ella and said, "For someone who is having troubles, you're doing awfully fine."

"It's not quite like it seems," Ella said with a weary smile creeping across her face. "Do you really want my troubles? Do you want to trade places with me?"

"No, she doesn't," Clara said. "Besides, she has good news." Then Clara realized it was news she had only overheard between Dora and Mamm. "I think it was something I wasn't supposed to hear," she said apologetically to Dora.

"You are the naughty one!" Dora said. "I see it's best not to speak of any news at our house, what with all the people who hear it."

"Then why'd you tell Mamm?" Clara said, sticking up for herself.

"What is it?" Ella asked. "And don't be so gloomy. Clara said it's good news."

Dora's face lit up. "Well, Norman talked to me after the singin' Sunday night, and I told him yes — that I'd accept his offer."

"She actually did say that," Clara said, confirming her sister. "I heard her tell Mamm. Can you imagine that? I would have taken him right away, the first time he asked."

"Oh, what do you know about boys?" Dora said. "See, us grownups know better. You shouldn't act too eager in front of a boy, especially if he acts nice to you."

"If he's nice, then what's wrong with that?" Clara asked.

Ella laughed. "Isn't your plan a little risky, Dora? What if he didn't come back and ask again?"

"I only took two weeks," Dora said. "I think it was about the right amount of time to keep him waiting."

"That's not bad, I guess," Ella said, picking up Sarah, who was pulling on her dress with both hands. Ella sat down with two girls in her arms now. "You do have good sense, I know, and I trust the way you handle Norman."

"See there?" Dora said, turning her nose in Clara's direction.

Clara glared back.

"You two aren't getting on well since I'm not there to straighten you out, are you?" Ella asked.

"I don't know about Clara, but the house just isn't the same," Dora said.

"Yah, and Dora's too bossy," Clara added. "She thinks she has to run things."

"Someone has to," Dora said. "It's not like you're old enough yet."

Ella laughed again. "So when do you have to be back home? I'd keep you here all day and night if I could."

"Just after twelve," Dora said, taking Sarah from Ella's arm. "Now tell us what we can do. We didn't come over just to argue with each other."

"Yah, we can do that at home," Clara said with an impish smile.

Ella thought a moment. "Well, you can help me move upstairs. I thought I'd have to wait till Joe and Ronda arrived, but as long as you're here, we might as well do it now. Ronda stopped by yesterday and made the final plans. They are coming for sure. She offered to help then, but this would be even better."

"Then busy we'll be," Dora said. "Just point the way."

"My bed first," Ella said, making sure Mary followed them up the stairs, the baby still in her other arm. "Strip off the covers while I get Barbara settled on the blanket. Then we'll heave together."

"This was easier when Eli and Monroe helped," Dora said as she and Ella wrestled the mattress on the stairs.

"That's why I thought it might be better to wait for Joe."

"We can do this," Dora said, pushing harder and grunting. "Maybe we need Clara's help. I think the girls can watch themselves for a moment."

Ella shook her head and then made a sudden rush for the top of the stairs, pushing the mattress for all she was worth. Dora did her part as best she could, and the two girls collapsed against the upstairs wall and laughed heartily.

"See? We did it!" Dora said. "Now if we could just fix some other problems this easily."

"Other problems?" Ella asked. *What don't*

I know about?

"Eli saw the *Englisha* girl again," Dora whispered.

"No."

Dora nodded. "I haven't told anyone. Not even Mamm."

"But you must," Ella said. "That was our mistake last time. Mamm and Daett have to be told. That is, if you're really sure. Are you?"

"Well, I didn't see them together. But, yes, I just know."

"Then you really must tell. Today. Right away when you get home."

"What will this do for you and the bishop?"

"It's Eli I'm concerned about," Ella said, not thinking too long.

"Perhaps you should think about yourself for a change. You can't lose him, Ella, and you know the bishop won't like this."

Ella stood still, remembering the words he spoke to her, *I see more and more why* Da Hah *had me wait. I have never met a woman among our people I can value more.* Red crept up her neck.

"Have you already promised him?" Dora asked, gripping Ella's hand. The mattress leaned against the wall, forgotten. "Oh, I can't believe this! You really are going to marry the bishop."

Ella shook her head.

"Ach, please don't say so. If you're already promised, then this wouldn't mean anything. The bishop wouldn't go back on his word."

"It's Eli we should be concerned about," Ella said, finding her voice. The bishop's words still rang loudly in her mind. *Did he really mean them, or were they just words? Is his love real?* Her stomach ached. Aden was the only man she ever asked such a question of. The tears began to form.

"So, you *do* care for the bishop. I never would have thought it from how you were actin' earlier. But, Ella, oh I'm so glad for you, even if you're not promised to him yet. He'll ask you soon enough. He's a *gut* man, and we really must keep Eli's actions secret — at least until the bishop asks. Do tell him, Ella. Let him see that you care for him, like you are showing it right now."

Ella shook her head, but Dora was looking out the window with a gleam in her eyes.

"Eli will help out with this. I know he will. He's as interested as we are in keepin' this a hush. He'll not spill the beans. He won't if I don't tell on him. The bishop thinks the problem's solved, and Mamm and Daett do too."

"No, I can't," Ella said, mouthing the words carefully.

"But you *must*. For once, think of yourself. You can't just lose the bishop like that. He's much too great a catch."

"I don't want the bishop, at least not for those reasons," Ella said.

Dora turned to face her sister, her hands on her hips. "For once I have to tell you what is right. Ella, this is right. Eli's problems stay Eli's problems. It's not right that he affect your life. This is too important. You'll never find another man as right for you as the bishop."

"I had Aden," she said. The words came out as a cry and were accompanied by the tears on her cheeks.

Dora relented. "Your heart must be pure gold, Ella. If I had a chance like this, I'd take it, no questions asked. It's all that simple to me. I'd tell Eli to keep his *Englisha* girl hidden until after the weddin' or else. And he would too, believe me. But then I'm not you. I guess that's why I get a boyfriend like Norman, and you get the bishop."

"Would you quit it?" Ella said. "It's not like that. I can't explain everything, but it's complicated." *Should I explain further and tell Dora about the dreams? But the words seem so distant, impossible to find at the moment, as if saying them makes less sense than silence.*

She turned from Dora and looked out the window. "Just give me a minute," Ella whispered.

She looked into the distance and then to the road. For a moment she could almost see Aden in his buggy — driving down the road, holding the lines taut in his hands, smiling that joyful smile he always gave her — but the seat beside him was empty. She opened her mouth to call out to him. That seat beside him was meant for her. She belonged with him. How many times had she sat there, felt the strength in those arms simply because they were near, and sensed the depth of his love for her, his desire that she be with him. *Aden, wait for me!* She was uncertain whether she whispered the words out loud or not and didn't care.

The buggy turned the corner, the horse's legs made long, even strides, and Aden's smile only widened. But now the smile wasn't turned toward the empty seat beside him. It was turned up to the sky, as if he saw a great thing above him, a sight that drew him with great fascination. Never had she seen such delight on his face, and then he was gone. Just like that, she was back in the room with Dora. The mattress was still leaning against the wall.

"I loved him so much," she whispered.

Dora met her eyes and then gave her a hug. "I understand."

"I thought I just saw him," Ella whispered. "He was driving his buggy, but I wasn't with him. You should have seen the look on his face. His eyes were on the sky, Dora."

"The angel took him," Dora whispered. "Remember, *Da Hah* does what He wishes. But you must not scorn the gift He has left you in the bishop, Ella. You really mustn't."

"I won't hide things from the bishop," Ella said, determined. "I won't hide something like Eli's actions from him."

"Whatever you say," Dora sighed. "That's the way you are, I guess. I just wish I was half as good as you are."

"You shouldn't say that, and it's very prideful and not true. I'm just a girl like all the others."

"Whatever you say, Ella. At least I tried," Dora said. "Now let's get the rest of these things upstairs before Clara thinks something happened to us."

They pushed the mattress into the bedroom and set it on the frame. Together they walked downstairs where Clara was waiting with a questioning look on her face. Ella wondered if she should try to explain about her tears and red face. *Should I say the words, "I'm to be the bishop's wife, and Eli is being naughty again"? How can I explain such things to a younger sister?*

Dora took the lead and said, "It's just grownup stuff."

"I figured," Clara said. "That's what I thought when the two of you didn't come down for so long. Dora's telling her secrets there, where I can't hear them."

"Let's just hope you don't have to go through the sorts of things that must be spoken of in the shadows," Ella said, laying her hand on Clara's shoulder. "Aden's passin' still hurts me."

"Oh," Clara said, "I see. I guess I should mind my own business. Anyway, the baby's fussin'."

"I'll fix a bottle," Ella said, bending over to give Clara a hug.

"We have to go soon," Dora said, glancing at the clock.

"Then we'll eat first." Ella decided that on the spot and immediately started fixing sandwiches while Dora carried small items upstairs. They sat down to eat together but first bowed their heads in silent prayer.

After the table was cleared, Dora said, "We really have to go. Mamm won't let us come again if we stay past our time."

"Go, go," Ella said, shooing them out the door. She walked to the living room window and watched the buggy disappear over the knoll.

Twenty-Nine

At the last minute, Ella thought long and hard about whether to attend Joe and Ronda's wedding. *I have an invitation, and the event would be a welcome diversion. There would, of course, be the pain associated with a wedding, but then there is also the wonder of the moment when two people become united as one. Those few seconds in time when the couple's lives are changed forever is so wonderful.*

Few things in life are quite like the promise someone gives to another to honor, to love, and to hold alone in the heart until death separates them. Few things are held in higher esteem or are more sacred than the words spoken at a wedding. Heaven or earth or the will of man or woman are never to break them. Only the vows said on one's knees at baptism held greater weight. The wedding is today. If I am to go, the time to decide is now.

Finally Ella simply said out loud, "I will go."

Mary looked up from her play.

"Go where?"

"To Ronda's wedding. Do you want to go?"

"Yah," Mary said, easily excited.

"Come then. We have to get ready."

Mary got up and grabbed Sarah's hand. She ran, partly dragging her sister toward the bedroom and laughing as she went. Baby Barbara giggled from her blanket on the floor, waving her arms and feet around.

Ella took their Sunday dresses out of the closet. Her eyes softened at the sight of their cheerful faces, and she decided once again that she would never abandon Preacher Stutzman's girls, even with Eli and his troubles with the *Englisha* girl. Both subjects would have to be brought up with the bishop on Saturday. She would tell him everything. That was just the way things had to be.

She pulled the girls' dresses up over their heads and slipped their Sunday ones on. They giggled as she fastened the buttons in place. *What kind of woman will Preacher Stutzman choose as his wife? Will she be like his Sunday preaching — strong and fierce — or will she fit the rest of his life — timid and tender? Will the new mother have children of her own? Will they take up all her time and care, so that she neglects the girls?*

What troubling thoughts and really none of my business. Surely once the vows are spoken between Ivan and his future wife, all things will fall into their proper place, and the three girls will be loved.

Ella quickly dressed herself and gathered up the three girls. Mary and Sarah ran beside her to the buggy as their little black shawls flapped in the slight morning breeze. Ella carried the baby and the satchel in her arms.

Ella left all three in the buggy while she harnessed the horse. He came willingly out of the stall, neighing and rubbing his nose against her arm. She threw the harness on, fastened the straps, and led him outside. Mary acted like she was driving down the road and repeated, "Horsey, getup!" while Ella hitched the horse to the buggy. Mary used her father's Sunday preaching voice, catching Ella by surprise. It sounded so strange, yet cute, coming from such a little body. The resemblance was unmistakable.

"You'd better stop calling out to the horse like that," Ella said, holding the reins and making ready to climb in the buggy. "He could take off before we're ready."

"Oh," Mary said, falling silent.

Ella pulled herself up, placed one arm around both Mary and Sarah, and slapped the reins with the other.

Both girls laughed in delight as the buggy rattled out the driveway. It was really *gut* to hear their joy and feel the brisk morning air on her face. It made one's spirits soar. It had definitely been the right decision to attend the wedding, even if just to behold the girls' enjoyment of the ride.

As they passed the river, the mist still hung along the water's edge. A cardinal sang with such vigor that Ella could clearly hear it above the clip of the horse's hooves on the blacktop. Only the gurgle of the water at the bridge threatened to drown the sound out, but the two sounds seemed to blend together, almost becoming one. A smile filled Ella's face. It had been a long time since she had heard such lovely music.

"I forgot where we're going," Mary said with a voice sounding like a musical wind chime.

"To Ronda's wedding," Ella said, hoping her mixed emotions didn't come through. She certainly couldn't explain to a child how her joy was mingling with the regret of going to a wedding without Aden. She didn't even understand herself how she could be feeling such joy.

"When will we see Daett again?" Mary asked.

Her mind spun. It hadn't occurred to her that perhaps Preacher Stutzman would be there today. *How will this look if he is? I will be there with his three daughters, and he will be sitting on the preacher's bench. Will everyone know that I have been hired for their care? Sunday care had not been in the bargain.*

"He's comin' for you on Friday night," she said, hoping that would suffice.

"When is that?" Mary asked.

"Soon," she said, "in just a few more days."

"Is he at church today?"

"I don't know," Ella said. *Hopefully Preacher Stutzman isn't going to be there. It would make the day so much better if his district hasn't been invited. Surely they haven't been! They can't invite that many people.*

Ella drove out of the river bottom, and gazed at the vista of the countryside before her. In the early morning light, the roll of the land to the south stretched out before her. The beauty of this part of the state never ceased to stir her. In the east and toward the lake, one could see the low mountains, but today they were obscured by the low morning clouds. They were dark, and their movements rapid. That was not surprising. These sudden summer showers weren't unusual, but this was Ronda's wedding day. No doubt Ronda was in a tizzy right now. Rain on a wedding day didn't reflect well on the bride. Of course that was all nonsense, but it still would be a disappointment.

When it came, it came quickly. The lash of the sudden rain brought with it a wind strong enough to stir the tree branches. Ella quickly shut the side doors and pulled the waterproof buggy blanket out from under the seat. Mary laughed out loud. Sarah didn't look too sure of herself but finally joined in. With the blanket firmly wrapped around their waists, the girl's laughter pealed out into the rainstorm. Baby Barbara just blinked her eyes in the wet wind.

The horse shook its head but gamely plowed on. He really was a *gut* horse. A horse that didn't slow down in the rain was a horse to be thankful for. She remembered a driving horse from her youth that, despite her dad's urgings, had always stopped beside the road and refused to continue until the hard shower ceased.

It had rained at Aden's funeral. On that day too, the mountains had given their quick offering. Only then, it had been like a sign of God's concern as the heavens let loose her tears. Today was a wedding day, and again the heavens were weeping. *Were the old women correct? Is this really a bad sign?* Ella shook her head. *This is just foolishness. Ronda will be the perfect bride, and Joe will be the perfect husband. Soon the sun will break through the clouds.*

Ahead of her, she caught the first sight of the farm where the wedding would be held. Buggies were already parked all over the grounds. Ella slapped the lines. No doubt she was late. Thankfully the men were still in a long line out by the barn, so there was yet time.

As she came closer to the farm, her mind reeled in shock. *This farm is the place in my dreams. This is the farm where the bishop and I get married.* Ella clutched the lines in sweating palms. *What does this mean? Surely the dreams are only a ridiculous figment of my wild imagination. Now that I see that Ronda's wedding is here, it shows the foolishness of the dream, a monstrosity born of my own fears and ungrounded in reality.*

Ella pulled hard on the reins and turned right into the driveway. The horse shook his head as if he objected. In front of the barn, she pulled to a stop. Two boys, wearing their black hats low on their heads, separated themselves from the line of men. Ella couldn't see who they were and held her breath. Hopefully they were boys she knew and wouldn't ask too many questions.

"Good morning," they said together, stopping on each side of the buggy.

"Good morning," she said, climbing down. One of the boys was her cousin from the district. He would know why she had Preacher Stutzman's girls with her.

"Thanks," she said, reaching back inside the buggy for Sarah's hand.

"Stutzman's girls behavin'?" her cousin asked.

"They're angels," she said, setting Sarah on the ground.

"Preacher Stutzman?" the other boy said, raising his eyebrows.

"Yah," she said. *Why should I explain further? He can ask my cousin.*

She walked slowly up the sidewalk with both her hands full and hoped again Preacher Stutzman wouldn't be there.

THIRTY

The song leader announced the first song, and Ella drew in a deep breath. She had just glanced quickly around the room and noticed that Preacher Stutzman wasn't seated on the preacher's bench. He had every right to be here — if he had been invited — but his absence did make things so much easier.

The ministers got to their feet and were led by the young Bishop Wayne Miller upstairs for the young couple's prenuptial counseling. That the bishop was here was no surprise. He might even marry Joe and Ronda. At least he knew she took care of the Stutzman girls.

Ella watched as Joe and then Ronda got up to follow the preachers. *What is it like to get up in front of all these people and know that they are all turning to look at you?* Ronda's face was almost white as she took the steps one by one. Joe, his figure sharp in his new black suit, looked more relaxed.

With a full breath, the song leader led out on the second line, his voice rich and rising and whirling in a triumphant sound. Ella gave herself to the moment and joined in the joyous sound as the congregation added their voices. A wedding day was surely one of the highest experiences her people participated in. Even the songs on days like this were special. Most of them were sung only for the occasion and were so filled with joyous emotion.

The whole room rose and fell with sound as even the very walls seemed to join in the emotion. It was good that she had decided to come. The last line was sung twenty minutes later, and then another song number was given out.

Joe's shoes appeared before the song started. He stepped quickly and quietly down the stairs and was followed by Ronda's much quieter footsteps. Both of their faces were sober. *What counsel have they been given? Were they warned about calamity and of the duty of faithfulness to each other through the trials of life? Perhaps they were told of children to come — loved then lost — or of parents who would need support in their old age.*

At least they have each other. Ella

squirmed on the bench. She had lost Aden without a wedding, yet what God did should not be questioned. She swallowed hard against her tight throat. There was a reason for everything, even if it couldn't be seen with human eyes.

Joe and Ronda settled quickly back into their seats as the song leader cleared his throat. Ella waited, but no sound came. The bishop's black shoes appeared on the first step above them.

The whole house perked up as the ministers came downstairs and found their seats. Feet scraped on the floor, and a preacher Ella didn't recognize got up slowly. He looked around the room and then began to speak.

"Our dearly beloved brothers and sisters, we are gathered here today for a special occasion — to give a brother and sister in holy marriage, as has been instituted by *Da Hah* Himself. In the garden He made man and soon saw that it was not good for man to be alone. The same still holds true for us today. It is not good that a man dwell alone, without a wife, without children, without a real home.

"Our brother and sister have found each other in the *Villa Gottes,* and we are here to honor and recognize their desires. They are

291

a *gut* example for all of us to follow."

Ella held baby Barbara as the service continued. She squirmed and looked as if she were ready to cry but then quieted down.

"I hope," a second preacher said, "that you, as a young couple, will draw valuable lessons from the example of Jesus. Whatever the circumstances you experience in your married life, even in the seemingly impossible ones, there are simple deeds you can do for each other and turn them into acts of love. Miracles can be made out of the most common things. Jesus did this when He turned the water into wine. In the same way, you can meet the needs of each other."

Ella snuck a quick glance at Ronda and Joe. They were intently watching the preacher. *What is it like to receive such gut advice on a wedding day? What must it be like to be getting married?* Ella let her eyes find the preacher's bench. The young bishop was listening intently. *What is he thinking? Is he imagining himself seated on the chair up front with me sitting across from him? Why am I so afraid? He is a gut man.*

The second preacher finished and sat down, motioning with his hands toward the home bishop. He got to his feet slowly, coming to stand in front of Joe and Ronda.

Ella felt the tears sting again. They were about to be married.

"If it is still the desire of the brother and sister to be joined in holy marriage, will they please stand to their feet?"

Joe got up first, and then Ronda stood next to him. Ella was sure she saw Ronda's dress tremble.

"Does the brother believe that by the will of God, he has been given sister Ronda to be his lawful wedded wife?"

"Yah," Joe said firmly.

"Does the sister believe by the will of God she has been given brother Joe to be her lawful wedded husband?"

"Yah," Ronda said, looking down at the floor.

The questions continued, and then the bishop reached first for Joe's hand and then Ronda's. "I now give these two into the bonds of marriage from which no man can ever part them. You are now husband and wife in the sight of God and man."

Joe and Ronda sat back down. From the back of the room, the song announcer bellowed out the number. It was an explosion of sound in the solemn silence. Ella joined wholeheartedly in the singing. *How* gut *it is that I came! This does my soul so much good to see love still alive and well even if it is in other's lives and not my own.*

The song ended, and Joe and Ronda got slowly to their feet and walked out. The two couples seated beside them followed. What a beautiful sight the six of them made, walking side-by-side, the boys in black suits and the girls in dark blue dresses. Ronda had an amazing ability to turn even common colors to her favor. *Perhaps Ronda can help me in the quilt shop, even design for me. That is if she has time. There can't be that much to do as a young married woman.*

Ella rose when her bench of women moved toward the kitchen. A few of the ladies shook her hand and smiled at the girls. *Apparently everyone is comfortable with the situation. That is something to be thankful for because it would take too much energy to do all the explaining.*

Ella followed the line out to the pole barn, where long lines of tables had been set up. Directed by the ushers, she ended up at a table near a wall. Multiple couples, most of them only paired for the day and clad in identical outfits, rushed about. The boy and the girl were always close together, and their arms were full of plates heaped with food.

Ella gasped when Eli came out of the makeshift kitchen where the cooks toiled behind temporary curtains. Behind him came Amos Hershberger's Miriam. Her eyes were more intent on Eli than on the plate balanced on her long slender fingers.

"Why didn't you tell me you were a table waiter?" she whispered as he walked by.

"They had someone back out," Eli said, laughing at her expression.

Eli is so confident and full of life. Miriam is perfect for him. The sight of them together almost took Ella's breath away. *Oh, why doesn't Eli see what's in front of him? How can the boy be so stubborn?*

Eli, with Miriam in tow, left the plates at the table he was in charge of at the far end of the pole barn. On the way back, he teased Ella by whispering loudly, "You're a mamm already, I see. Three of them. And no husband!"

"Ach!" She gasped and glared at him.

Watching Eli's face, Miriam laughed, obviously impressed by the wisecrack.

Does she know about the Englisha *girl? Likely not, and just as likely she would drop Eli like a hot potato fresh from the coals when she finds out. If a good shake would do any good, I would stand up and give Eli one right here and now.*

"Who was that?" Mary asked.

"Just my brother," Ella said quietly. "He's not as fierce as he looks." *Why can't Eli just*

be decent? It would make things so much bet-
ter for everyone.

Young Bishop Miller got to his feet at the other end of the pole barn. "We are all gathered together for the meal now. Let us pray."

They all bowed their heads, and the sound of the bishop's prayer bounced off the sides of the metal building. *If he made as* gut *a husband as he prayed, then Mamm and Daett certainly are correct.*

The waiters passed the food quickly from one end of each table, and the guests sent the heavy plates down each side. Ella helped the girls with what they wanted, keeping the portions small. She might be acting like their mamm, but eating leftover food off their plates would be taking things too far.

After the last bite had been eaten, Sharon, Ronda's mom, worked her way toward Ella.

"I'm so glad you could come," she gushed.

"I almost didn't, what with the three girls."

"Just because you're taking care of Stutzman's girls is no reason to stay away," she said, shaking Ella's hand. "So why don't you stay for the youth supper tonight?"

"Oh, but the girls need naps," Ella said.

"You can use one of the bedrooms upstairs," Sharon said quickly. "They'll sleep as well there as any place."

Ella considered the invitation and said, "I suppose that is true. I'll stay, then."

"That's a *gut* decision," Sharon said, patting her on the shoulder. "And I think it's so nice of you to give Ronda and Joe a place to stay — and at such a reasonable price. That will give them a real nice start in their married life. Ronda was quite mixed-up and didn't know what to do when the other plans fell through."

"I'll be glad to have them," Ella said.

She hadn't known how much she missed the young folk gatherings. Somehow this felt right. With the wedding, no boys would be asking girls home afterward.

"Let me know if you need anything," Sharon said. "I suspect Ronda's got her mind on someone else today."

"I would think so," Ella said, laughing.

"Yah, and we are so happy for them," Sharon said, glancing toward the center table. A tear sprang to her eye. "Ronda's got herself a *gut* man."

"They do make a nice couple," Ella said.

Sharon lowered her voice and said, "Ronda says the young Bishop Miller's callin' on you. I'm so glad to hear it. We were all so shocked at Aden's passin'."

"I guess life must go on," Ella said, wishing the subject hadn't come up.

"*Da Hah* will heal your heart. He's about that kind of business," Sharon said, squeezing Ella's shoulder and moving on.

All around Ella, people had risen from the tables and moved to speak with friends and relatives. The noise in the metal-clad pole barn was at a high volume.

"Come," she said, taking Sarah by the hand and the baby in her other arm. "Let's go inside the house. All of you could use naps, I think."

The yard was full of people, and a few nodded as she passed. Upstairs, the bedroom was almost empty. One baby lay on the bed with blankets spread around on the floor. Ella got Mary and Sarah to fall asleep easily enough, but the baby objected. After fifteen minutes, Ella gave up and headed downstairs with Barbara in her arms. There she spread a blanket out on the floor and remained within earshot of the upstairs bedroom door.

Here she was like a real mamm, taking care of her girls, but no one looked at her strangely. The flow of women and girls in and out of the house was constant.

"Hi, Ella," the girls her age would say as they passed through the room on some sort of business in the house, but few stopped to talk long. Mary and Sarah awakened an hour later, and the rest of the afternoon passed along pleasantly enough. By five thirty long lines of buggies again filled the driveway. Almost all of them were filled with young people coming back for the evening supper.

At six, Ella joined in with the line of girls moving out to the pole barn.

"I'll take care of the girls," Sharon whispered, coming up to her. Ella looked at Mary and Sarah and raised her eyebrows to ask the unspoken question.

Mary smiled, and Sarah nodded vigorously.

"I guess," Ella said, handing baby Barbara over to her. "This is so nice of you."

"Don't worry about it," Sharon said. "Go enjoy yourself while you're still young."

Ella thanked her again and found a seat between Naomi Schrock and Esther Hochstetler. Across from them the benches filled up with the boys.

"How are you doing, Ella?" one of the boys asked.

"Okay," she answered with a smile. "I don't think I know you."

"Amos Troyer. I knew Aden, but I live in one of the north districts — way up," he said, waving his arm in that direction. "Aden was a good friend and a good man."

"I know," Ella said. "I still miss him."

"I suppose you do," Amos said.

Ella saw Naomi out of the corner of her eye give a sharp glance in Amos's direction.

Amos picked up on it and said, "I'm sorry I brought it up. I just thought about him when I saw you."

"It's okay," Ella said with a weak smile. "Time heals. Is that not what they say?"

"Well, I wish you the best," Amos said, nodding and then turning to the boy beside him.

The singing started at seven thirty, and Ella abandoned herself to the music. No one gave out selections half the time. They just started the song when one had ended. These were her people, and she had actually dared to attend a singing again. If Aden were here, he would be seated across the bench from her now. She could almost see him, blending in among the white shirts and black vests. *How he loved to sing, raising his voice with the best of them. Soon the singing will be finished, and Aden will pull his buggy up to the walk outside. I'll dash out to meet him, and my heart will be full of love and happiness.*

Her voice caught in the midst of a line, and Ella glanced down quickly. Naomi kept her eyes on the song book in front of her.

Hopefully she hadn't noticed. Ella gathered her emotions in check and joined in again.

Eli sat across the room with his back to her. Miriam was still beside him. Ella saw their heads turned toward each other, and the songbook laying on the table. When the song ended, they whispered together, and Eli laughed softly. *Can this be? Has Eli come to his senses?*

As soon as the last song was over, Ella found Sharon near the pole barn door, collected her girls, and waited — at Sharon's insistence — while Sharon sent her husband to get Ella's horse.

"You shouldn't," Ella said but to no avail. Her buggy was soon delivered to the front of the pole barn.

On the drive home, only the stars were out. The last rays of summer's light had gone, and the girls sat sleepily beside her. When she reached home, she tied the horse and took the girls inside, making sure they were settled in upstairs before she went out to unhitch the horse. The harness was heavy in her hands as she pulled it off. She managed to lift and hang the leather straps on the barn hooks in one swoop. She slapped the horse on the rump, and he raced out through the outside stall door with a whinny. Outside the stars hung close above her head, seemingly drawn even closer by the darkness.

Ella somehow felt pressed down and heavy. *But why? The day has been a joy. Is it because life must be faced again? Perhaps it's because the bishop is coming over on Saturday night, and I really don't want to see him. Mamm and Daett think the bishop is perfect for me. A lot of other people obviously do too. How can I be so wrong?*

Ella lingered, gazing long at the sweep of the heavens, and then walked to the house, pushing the dark thoughts away.

THIRTY-ONE

"They got married," Mary said, bubbling with excitement at the breakfast table. "They got married yesterday."

Has this little four-year-old just absorbed the information? She didn't express any of this excitement on the way home last night. "Yah, they did," Ella said, nodding, "and Ronda will come to live with us soon. Perhaps today. Do you think you'll like that?"

"I'll like it a lot," Mary said. "She's nice."

"What about you?" Ella asked Sarah, but she was already nodding and trying hard to put her spoon to her mouth without missing the target. Her older sister knew how to handle her spoon without spilling, but Sarah hadn't quite mastered the task yet.

"Like this," Ella said, holding the spoon with Sarah's little fingers wrapped under hers. "Slowly . . . and then in there."

Sarah smiled, but as soon as the spoon left her mouth, the contents spilled out. Ella saw it coming and quickly spooned the oatmeal back into Sarah's mouth. The girl chewed a few bites and puckered her face and started to bawl. The oatmeal, once again, poured down her chin.

"She's messy," Mary said with disapproval.

"Sarah's just a little girl," Ella said. "She has to learn just like everyone else."

"I don't have a bib," Mary said, showing her pleasure.

"That's because you've already learned," Ella said. "Sarah will too in time." The rest was best left unsaid. *You, Mary, had a mother at Sarah's age while Sarah doesn't. Surely Preacher Stutzman will have a wife soon — a decent one willing to care for children who aren't her own — and these girls will then receive the proper care they need.*

Who will Preacher Stutzman ask to be his wife? Ella ran through the list of available widows in the community and came up with only a few names.

Ben Kaufman died three years ago. His widow, Lovina, would be a little older than Preacher Stutzman, and she had seven children of her own. Ella frowned. *Susie Miller, from one of the north districts was younger, had four children, and was widowed two years ago. Her oldest boy was at the wedding yesterday with one of his aunts.* Ella glanced quickly toward Mary. *The boy would surely pinch Mary's ears if he ever had access to her. Perhaps he'd even snap her cheeks and other such torments when no one was watching. I'm certain he would.*

That leaves Nancy Weaver, from the southern district, and her three boys. The girls would be safe with her at least. Surely Preacher Stutzman would have enough sense to ask her. She's available, although one never knows for sure. There could always be something in the works with someone else. Even in the second time around, such things are kept secret, although my date with the bishop certainly hasn't been.

"Can I have more?" Mary asked. "I'm still hungry."

"Sure. Do you like the oatmeal?"

Mary grinned. "It's good. I like it."

Ella placed a small dab in Mary's bowl and added the sugar and milk.

"I want to stir," Mary said, reaching for her spoon.

"That's good, but just don't spill. Stir real slow," Ella said, keeping her eye on the girl.

Mary beamed. *Does anyone ever praise this child? It is hard to imagine the rough Preacher Stutzman with words of honey in his mouth. How dare the man not speak kind*

305

words to such darling girls! Perhaps I should remind him of his duties on Friday night when he picks them up.

With a start, Ella jumped to her feet. *I really must stop interfering in Preacher Stutzman's business.*

"We have to get ready for Ronda and Joe," Ella said. "Are you girls going to help me?"

The girls both nodded. "We'll help with the breakfast dishes," Mary said. Baby Barbara lay cooing beside the table.

"That's a *gut* plan," Ella said, putting the chairs in place around the sink. It might actually take a little longer this way, but working with the girls was more important.

Before they were finished, buggy wheels could be heard rattling in the driveway.

"Sounds like they're here already," Ella said, rushing to clear the last of the dishes from the kitchen table. Ronda would understand the late breakfast with the three girls to care for, but Joe might not. It seemed important to make the best impression possible on the first morning.

Both Mary and Sarah ran to the living room window to look out as Ella set the last of the dishes in the sink. At the knock on the door, Ella left the sink full of dishes. Joe would just have to think what he wanted to think.

"Good morning," Ronda said when Ella opened the door. How chipper she sounded. Beside her, Joe grinned broadly. "Hope we're not too early."

"I'm still finishing up the dishes," Ella said, holding the door wide open, "but come on in."

"This is so wonderful of you," Ronda said. "You don't know how much this means to us."

"It's really nothing," Ella said. "I'm the one who needs people in the house."

"It is large," Joe said, glancing around, "and well built. I was here for one day of the work frolic."

"Daniel did a good job," Ella said, wishing at once she hadn't mentioned Daniel.

Ronda walked over to the window where Mary and Sarah sat.

"Hello, girls," she said.

They both smiled, and the baby kicked her feet on the blanket.

"I think they like me," Ronda whispered to Ella.

"Of course they do," Ella said quietly. "You're a nice person."

"Yah, she is," Joe said with a laugh.

"You haven't lived with me very long," Ronda said, coming up to stand beside Joe and putting her arm around his waist.

"Well," Joe said, "you'll get sweeter every day, I'm sure."

"Can I show you both around?" Ella asked, ready to move the conversation past the newlyweds' cooing.

After the quick tour, Joe said, "The house is even better than I expected. There's plenty of room for three families. Shall we start to unload our things?"

"Yes, put them anywhere you like," Ella said. "As you can see, I've already moved my belongings upstairs."

Minutes later they had completed the third trip, and Ronda said, "This is all that could fit on the wagon. The living room couch, kitchen table, and chairs all come on another load." After a moment, it occurred to Ronda to ask, "Ella, other than upstairs, where are you staying?"

"Well, I guess just upstairs. That's what seems best."

"What about a kitchen?" Ronda asked with concern. "I hope you plan to use the one down here. I won't mind at all."

"Two of us in the same kitchen?" Ella said with a laugh. "Really, I hadn't thought things through completely, but I know that won't work. I plan to make do somehow."

"With the girls? You're the one who needs the main floor. Why don't we move upstairs?" Ronda said, turning to look at Joe.

"It's no problem with me," he said. "Up or down, it's all the same, just so long as you're there."

"I wouldn't even think of it," Ella said, interrupting their loving gaze at each other. "I'm either upstairs or in the basement because that's where my little quilt shop is."

"I really would feel better if we didn't put you on the short end of things," Joe said.

"I tell you what," Ella said, having a sudden inspiration. "What if there was a stove hookup in the basement? Joe, would you know how to install a stove down there?"

Joe thought for a moment. "I think there's a hookup there already. I remember seeing it the day I was here for the work frolic. Whoever laid the chimney put it in. They would have known that an extra woodstove usually goes in the basement."

"Really," Ella said, relief flooding her. "It would solve our problem if I could have my kitchen downstairs. I could even live there all the time and just go upstairs on the weekends."

"I'll go down and look just to be sure," Joe said, moving toward the basement door. "Do you have an extra stove, then?'

"No," Ella said, "but maybe Daett would know where I could find one."

"See if she has an extra flue first," Ronda said. "I think there's an old stove in our barn."

"I did see one a while back," Joe said, disappearing down the stairs.

"Are you sure that would be okay?" Ronda asked. "I'd still feel better if we moved down to the basement."

"You won't do that," Ella said firmly. "You are the ones payin' the rent. And I'm going to the basement."

"I guess that settles that," Ronda said, giving in, "but we will try to be good renters."

"There's no question in my mind."

"Joe wants so bad to get our own place — a farm where he can do the milking," Ronda said wistfully. "With farm prices like they are, it may take awhile yet."

"Yes, I think it surely will. Prices seem high these days," Ella said.

Joe came up the basement stairs. His voice sounded cheerful when he came through the door and said, "Yep. There's a flue down there, just as I thought there would be."

"Why didn't I see it?" Ella asked.

"They left it covered up till it was needed," Joe said.

"Nothing like a man in the house," Ronda said, fairly bursting with delight, and Ella nodded. She had been given a *gut* gift in this young couple.

THIRTY-TWO

The clock on the wall showed that it was now past noon. *Ronda and Joe should have been back with their wagonload of furniture. Where are they? Yet, the afternoon still lay ahead, and there is plenty of time, no matter the holdup.*

Now that they discovered the chimney flue in the basement, Ella could move downstairs. That did change everything. There was no longer any reason to use the upstairs during the week when Preacher Stutzman's girls were there. Now she just needed curtains for the basement windows. As for sleeping, the bed they recently moved upstairs could stay there. If she placed foam mattresses on the basement floor and moved the crib down, she would be all set for the weekdays.

The more she thought about it, the more Ella liked the setup. It would prove more efficient while the girls were here, and weekends upstairs would provide relief from basement life.

Three o'clock came, and still there was no Joe or Ronda. A glance down the road produced no sight of anyone. Ella thought to hitch the horse to the buggy and go look for them. *How silly that would look. Even if there had been an accident or some such calamity, what could I do? Waiting really is the only option.*

Ella busied herself with packing for the girls. Preacher Stutzman would come sometime this evening for his daughters. He hadn't said exactly what time. *Is he a scheduled person, who will show up each week at the same time or only comes when it suits him? If his fiery sermons are any indication, the latter seems likely. I'll simply have to be ready either way.*

Ella took all three girls upstairs with her and began to pack their bags. Mary didn't say anything. *Should I explain this and perhaps establish order to this routine that will reoccur every Friday for some time to come?*

"Your daett will come soon to pick you up," she said gently.

Mary looked long at the suitcase but said nothing.

"You'll go home for the weekend and then come back here on Monday."

"This is home now," Mary said. "Why doesn't Daett come here?"

"No, dear," Ella said, shocking herself with her tone. "Look, Mary, I just take care of you — like your Aunt Susanna does — and then your daett takes you home again for the weekend."

"Yah," Mary said, staring off into space.

Carefully Ella placed all their clothing in the suitcase, adding the washed diapers. The dirty ones could stay. This was the way she wanted it. All clean clothes should go back with Preacher Stutzman on Friday nights, even though the girls would return on Monday.

The sound of steel wheels rattling up the driveway caused Ella to run to the window. *Who's bringing a wagon in?* She gasped at the sight below. *So this is why Joe and Ronda had been delayed!* A hay wagon stood in the yard near the front door. A cook stove was propped in the middle, and some beds were set on the end along with the furniture Joe and Ronda had gone to retrieve. Out by the hitching post, Joe tied the horse. Ronda was already at the front door. She gestured with her hands to her dad, who had come with them, and pointed toward the basement door.

"Ronda and Joe are here," Ella said loudly,

and Mary jumped up to run to the window.

"Come," Ella said, taking the baby and encouraging the girls to follow. At the top of the stairs she paused and took Sarah's hand in hers. Mary held onto the handrail but still kept up with them. Ella quickly left the baby on the blanket, shooing the girls over to the living room window. She really needed to get outside to help.

"Oh, I was so worried," Ella said, opening the front door and stepping out onto the porch.

"I just knew you would be," Ronda said, wrinkling her brow, "but what was there to do? Dad offered to bring the stove today, and he even had the wagon hitched up already. Then the stove wasn't in the barn but over at my brother's. He was done with it, though. They just used it last winter."

"You're sure?"

"Certain," Ronda said. "He bought himself a new one for his shop. This is more of a cook stove. I think he was a little embarrassed with a kitchen stove in his shop."

"I guess Daett would feel the same."

"So you see it all took time, but now it's done, and am I thankful. How Daett and Joe plan to carry the thing into the basement, I don't know. But they are confident." Ronda then noticed the girls in the window.

"They're still here? When does he pick them up?"

"I don't know," Ella said. "This is our first week. Soon, I think."

"It would be like him to be late."

Ella went over to where Joe and Ronda's father, Jesse, was surveying the stove. The older man kept eyeing the size of the stove in comparison to the basement door.

"Ach, good afternoon," he said with a smile. "Just tryin' to see how to get this thing down there."

He was a big, muscular man who was obviously used to hard farm work. Still, this would be quite some task.

"It took four people to load it," Ronda said. "Don't you think you'd better wait for help?"

"Wait?" Jesse said, rolling the words out in a roar of laughter. "Not with me and Joe here. Why would we need more men?"

"I think it'll help if we take these fire bricks out," Joe said, bringing his head back out from behind the stove. "All I need is a screwdriver, and the job's as good as done."

"You have one?" Ronda asked Ella.

"Nee," Ella said.

"There's one in my toolbox, which is still in the buggy. Ronda knows where it is."

Ronda ran quickly toward the buggy,

retrieved the screwdriver, and handed it to Joe. After some tinkering with it out of sight, Joe finally hollered in triumphant, "Finally got it!" He handed the gray fire bricks to Jesse who placed them carefully on the wagon. When the last one was out, they heaved together. Their faces quickly reddened, but they managed with some struggling to navigate the steps. Ella ran ahead and held the basement door open as they staggered in.

"Put it down. Rest a little," she said.

Jesse roared and heaved harder than before, and Joe followed along with him, making it over to the chimney.

"There! We did it!" Jesse said, leaning against the stove and gasping for air. "A little rough on an old man, but we made it."

Ella grabbed a rag and began to scrub the stove top. The dust rose thickly. She coughed and then laughed. Dust could also explain the tears in her eyes.

Joe disappeared up the basement steps and returned with different lengths of stove pipe. He laid them out on the basement floor. Picking out one piece, he began to connect the end of the stove to the chimney.

"You can do that later," Jesse said. "Let's get this furniture unloaded so I can get back for chores."

"No problem," Joe said, getting up off his knees. "I think I have everything I need."

"This is so nice of both of you," Ella said, following them upstairs. "This stove is exactly what I need."

"You're the one who has helped Joe and Ronda," Jesse said. "This is the least we could do, and you just keep the stove until you don't need it anymore."

"But I can't keep it that long," Ella protested. "I don't know how long that will be."

"Might the young bishop have something to say about that?" Jesse said with a mischievous glint in his eye.

"Oh?" Ella said, feeling the blood rush to her face. "Him?"

"We were glad to hear the news," Jesse said, smiling broadly. "The young bishop has needed a wife now for some time. Is it not the will of *Da Hah* that a man find his life's companion? He couldn't have done any better."

What am I to say? Her face turned bright red, and a cry of agony rose from her heart. *Surely this is a nightmare from which I will soon awake. Can Jesse read my face? What does it say about my feelings for the bishop?*

Ella dared to look at him only to find he was turned toward the wagon, readying himself to move the furniture.

Joe lifted a table from the top of the wagon and lowered it to the two women and Jesse on the ground. Then Joe jumped down to help carry it into the house. At the front door, Jesse went first, holding the table sideways, while Joe maneuvered the legs through.

"Don't scratch the door," Jesse said.

"I'm more concerned about the table," Ella said, trying to help.

"You just hold the door open all the way, and we'll get through."

Ella held the door and her breath as they slowly went inside.

"That was awesome," Ronda said, once they were inside. "You two sure know how to move furniture."

"She's just tryin' to butter you up," Jesse said, laughing. "Just be warned, now, son."

Joe grinned and glanced at Ronda.

It almost looked like the man grew a few inches taller. Something about the way Joe and Ronda looked at each other brought a brief pang to Ella's heart. But it quickly passed — more quickly than it would have only a month ago, she realized.

Jesse paused at the front door and then came back to give Ronda a hug. "I have to go now. Both of you take care," he said, giving Joe a stern look. "Take care of that wife of yours — real *gut* care."

"I will," Joe said. His voice was rich with emotion as he added, "She's well worth it."

Jesse rattled out of the driveway, hollering at the horses to hurry. Ronda made Ella sit on the couch while she raced around getting supper ready. "You and the girls will eat with us," she said, "especially since Preacher Stutzman hasn't come yet."

"We can eat our supper just as well in the basement. I can prepare something. After all, it's your first night in your new house."

"No, we won't hear of it," Ronda said. "Now stay on the couch."

"I guess it would be nice," Ella said, leaning back on the couch and accepting the unexpected rest.

"It'll be a casserole Mamm sent along," Ronda said, "but it's a really *gut* casserole. And she sent along fresh bread and jam."

Ella got up from the couch and said, "You can, at least, let me set the table."

Ronda waved her arm in the direction of the cupboards. "Help yourself, and then we can eat."

"Come, girls," Ella said once the table was set. Mary and Sarah climbed up onto the bench, and Ella held baby Barbara. Joe led out in prayer with a voice that was deep and

320

steady. What a joy it was to have a male voice in the house who could lead in an audible address to the Almighty. Somehow it made the house truly a home.

After prayer, they ate their meal and listened to the girls chatter lightly. Ronda and Ella washed dishes while Joe sat in the living room. Neither Mary nor Sarah asked to help. When they were finished, Preacher Stutzman still hadn't come.

"I guess I'll take them downstairs," Ella said.

"What a man," Ronda whispered, and they exchanged looks.

How such a man could have three darling girls, really is a wonder. She took Sarah's hand, held the baby in the other arm, and encouraged Mary to hold the handrail again. Together all three moved down the basement steps.

"Be careful," she said in Mary's direction.

"I can do it," Mary said, protesting. She jumped off the last step and landed with perfect timing. Her face was a picture of delight.

THIRTY-THREE

Preacher Stutzman drove his buggy hurriedly toward Chapman Road. He was late, but he could rationalize it by the fact that the chores had gone long. One cow was down with mastitis, and another had a lesion on her foot. The walk down to the phone booth was necessary, as well as the call placed to the veterinarian. Since he couldn't come out till the morning, Preacher Stutzman wrapped the cow's leg with salve. The mastitis would have to wait until the morning. He simply dumped her milk into the gutter.

He slapped the reins, hurrying the horse on. *Perhaps I should have left earlier. Might Ella feel taken advantage of? What if she already has the girls in bed, gave up on me, and figured I hadn't meant what I said? Lois never questioned me. She trusted me completely, whether I was late or on time. Ella might be different, though. Why do her feel-*

ings on the subject even bother me? Why should I care what she thinks? Ivan shifted on the buggy seat and slapped the reins again.

He had his reasons for why he was late, and that was just that, whether Ella understood them or not. With a pull of the line, he turned on to Chapman Road. The dim light from Ella's living room window was just ahead. Framed around the glow of the lantern was the outline of the house. A shadowy fog crept over the soft rays from the window. The horse seemed to turn into the driveway on its own, which was disturbing. *How does the animal remember the driveway from the few visits I've made?*

With the horse tied at the hitching post, Ivan knocked on the front door and was met with silence. He repeated the motion, louder this time. *Surely Ella wouldn't ignore me on purpose.* Quick steps sounded from behind the closed door. *So she is ignoring me.* He got ready for Ella to open the door and noticed that his palms were sweaty. The confident words of excuse were all gone, long before the knob turned.

"Good evening," he said before the door was halfway open.

"Yah," a young woman said.

"The girls," he said, "I have come for

them." *If only my voice wasn't so weak,* he thought as he kept his eyes directed at the doorknob.

"They are in the basement," the woman said in a sharp and strange voice.

Is Ella irate with me, and why are the girls in the basement by themselves?

"In the basement?" he asked, lifting his eyes to the face of the one who had been speaking and saw that she was not Ella. *Who, then? Does she have visitors who answer her door?*

"Joe and I moved in this week," the woman said, "and Ella gave us the first floor. She took the basement."

"Moved in?" Ivan exclaimed. He was confused and didn't move from his spot in front of the open door.

"Perhaps she didn't tell you," the woman said.

Now she sounds amused! Ivan struggled to find his voice. "No, she didn't tell me, but I guess it doesn't matter."

"She's down there," the woman said, opening the door wider and pointing down the basement steps.

"Yah," he said, but she had already shut the door on him. Her steps faded away inside like hollow echoes, which finally were no more.

With a deep breath, Ivan took the steps one at a time. A dim light came from the basement window and shined onto the concrete walk. He approached the door and carefully knocked on it. Inside he heard no footsteps, but the door opened at once.

"Good evening," he said through his tense throat.

"Come in," Ella said. "The girls are ready."

He nodded, stepped inside, and caught sight of Mary, who squealed with delight and ran toward him. Sarah wasn't far behind. For the moment, he forgot all else, dropped his hat on the floor, caught them in his arms, and held them both tightly. Mary wiggled and protested first, and so he let her down. Sarah laid her head on his shoulder and clung to him.

"I heard you knock upstairs," Ella said, "but I didn't get out before Ronda answered. I guess you didn't know they had moved in."

"No, I didn't know," he said, "but that's okay. It looks like you have plenty of room down here." He looked around and took in the layout of the basement. *It looks nice. Ella can obviously make even a basement look good. Lois could have also,* but he pushed that thought away. *This ability might be a trait all Amish women have, for all I know.*

His nervousness threatened to return. Behind him, his hat lay on the floor, and he bent over to pick it up.

"Well," Ella said, "here's the girls' bag. I packed it earlier. I didn't know when you would come."

"I didn't either," he said, offering nothing more. *Why should I explain to her?*

"Ella showed me how to eat," Sarah said in his ear, distracting him.

"She's a nice mamm," Mary said, tugging on his arm. "Can she go home with us?"

Ivan looked down at the floor. *What in the world am I supposed to say?* Ella's laugh went all the way through him.

"I'm glad they liked being here," she said. Thankfully she didn't try to embarrass him, but his throat was dry. This might be the bishop's wife-to-be, but she did take care of his girls. He smiled, nodded his head, and took a deep breath. "Did you have any problems this week?"

"With the girls?" Ella asked. "No, they are really sweet. I had no problems at all."

"You need anything from the house? Maybe I can pay you each week?"

Ella shook her head. "I'm okay, and the end of the month is fine. The girls are like little angels."

"You plan to continue, then?" he asked, feeling the words stick in his throat and hating himself for it. *Somehow I'll have to bring my emotions under control.*

"Oh," she said, "of course. If you want to . . . up until you have the wedding."

He felt his face flush red.

"Not that it's any of my business," she continued, "but the bishop said you had plans, and I have no problem with their care until that time. In fact, I would like it very much."

Ivan stroked his beard with trembling fingers. *How in the world does the bishop know?*

As if she understood his unspoken question, Ella said, "I suppose he heard it from Susanna — and they do need a mamm."

"We have one now," Mary said, pointing all of her fingers in Ella's direction. The comment went ignored by both Ella and Ivan.

"Ach, you know how people talk," he said. "Susanna doesn't always know everything."

"No, but I'm sure she's right in that the girls do need a mamm," she said. "A good one, but you know that, of course."

"I do," he said. *Perhaps she means nothing by this. Lois would have said the same words with that same look in her eyes. Women might be all the same around children they care about.*

"I don't mean to interfere," she said. "I really don't. It is just that, of course, you want the best for the girls."

He brushed his hand over Mary's head. "Would it be okay if I sat for a moment?"

"Of course. I should have known you'd be tired."

He touched Mary on the shoulder. "Why don't you girls go play for a little bit. It won't be too long, and then we can go."

"We like to play here," Mary said, smiling and moving away.

He took the nearest chair, lowering his body gently down.

"I don't mean to take your time," he said, "but perhaps I'd best explain myself."

"You don't have to," she said. "You really don't. My concern for the girls was perhaps out of order. I'm sorry."

"No, your concern is very much in order," he said. "It really is. See —" He choked a bit and cleared his throat. "I loved Lois. I never thought *Da Hah* would take her from me. Not even once did I consider it. I guess I took Lois for granted. I didn't really know how much I loved her until we were on the way to the clinic. I knew then that I would never arrive in time and that she would die, but still I drove like a madman — because that's all I could do."

What does she think of my weakness? It doesn't matter. The words must be spoken. They must. "I think, perhaps, I have sinned before *Da Hah* with my love for Lois. *Da Hah* is a jealous God, great in might and power. He will take no place but the first. In this we cannot be too careful. So for now another wife seems not be *Da Hah's villa* for me. I tell you this so you will know what to expect with the girls' care . . . that it may be a longer time than we think."

He glanced at her, but she had her eyelids lowered, staring at the tabletop.

"Before you had consented to take care of them, I didn't know what to do. You don't know how much you have answered the cry of my heart. I dared not even hope for someone to give them care. Now you do not only that, but you love them. *Da Hah* is truly a great and a merciful God — that is if we humble ourselves and walk in His will."

Did I say too much, and yet the relief is so real. This woman unarms me and opens my heart. Perhaps I had best go now before I say something I shouldn't.

"Yah, I understand," she said, watching him get to his feet.

Her comment caught him off guard. *Lois would have said exactly that.*

Ella continued, "I loved too. As much as you loved Lois, I loved Aden, and *Da Hah* has also taken him."

"Yah," he said, turning back to his girls. *I must go now.*

"I will take care of your girls until you wish otherwise," she said in a calm and certain voice, as if the matter were completely settled and would never be raised again.

"Come," he said, bending over to pick up the baby and then the bag. With Mary and Sarah beside him, he walked to the front door. But he couldn't leave like this. *I have to say something, and yet can I stand to meet her eyes?*

"Here," she said, lifting Sarah into her arms. "I'll come with you out to the buggy. It's dark outside already, and Sarah's tired."

"I am," Sarah said, nestling her head on Ella's shoulder.

Carefully he found his way up the steps. Mary walked beside him all the way out to the buggy. He laid the baby on the seat, lifted Mary up to her seat, and turned to take Sarah from Ella's arms.

"She's almost asleep," Ella whispered in the darkness.

"Thank you . . . for everything," he said. Surely the buggy lights didn't show the feelings on his face.

"You're welcome," she said, holding his horse while he climbed in and then letting go when he was ready.

It was all unnecessary, but so were a lot of things about Ella. She had more graces than a morning sunrise or *Da Hah*'s most beautiful mountaintops.

"Good night," he said, slapping the reins.

"Good night," she said.

Mary's form was dimly lit by the buggy's lights as he swept by and down the incline to the end of the driveway. The buggy bounced at the bump and then settled down. Beside him, Mary sat close, holding the baby. Sarah sat on the other side of her sister. The two pulled the buggy blanket snuggly around them to stay warm in the cool night air.

How he wanted her to be with them. He wanted her sitting next to him and holding Sarah in her lap — and not left to walk back into the house alone. But how could it be otherwise? She belonged to someone else, and *Da Hah* was against him.

THIRTY-FOUR

The aloneness of the night wrapped itself around Ella as she walked slowly back to the basement. They were gone. The sound of Preacher Stutzman's horse was faint in the distance. At least the girls loved their father. Their reaction to his arrival earlier spoke for itself. That was a sign that the man did have some soft spots in his life, even if he thundered in his Sunday sermons.

Perhaps the man needs to talk to someone more often than he does. I've been glad to listen. It's odd, but I find that the way he says his words, with the obvious brokenness in his voice, soothes my own pain. Well, he doesn't need to be figured out. There are enough problems in life already.

Ella stopped and turned her face upward to the heavens. The full moon hung heavy; low down like a weight in the sky and seemingly upheld by the wispy clouds beneath.

Where is Aden tonight? In heaven, yes, but

where is that? Does the Promised Land lay beyond the moon and stars? Is the only entrance death, and is it guarded by the angels? Death — so cold and dark — with the earth beneath her bare feet warm in comparison.

Yet the angels, sent by Da Hah, *had come to take Aden's spirit home. Had* Da Hah *known that comfort was needed for those left behind when three deaths so quickly followed each other?* Ella dug her toes into the dirt, feeling more of the damp warmth beneath. *These things are too high for me and best left to the preachers to figure out. Someday, when it is time, heaven will come for me too. Perhaps it won't happen till I am well into my old age, when I am broken in body and weary with years. Yet the angels will be there — if I obey God and am not ashamed of His name or His people.* Ella looked back toward the house and made her way down the steps to her basement.

This is my home now. It is such a gut one, given by the mercy of God. There is much to be thankful for. She walked over to the couch and on impulse knelt and whispered the words that came to her.

"Thank You, dear Lord, for all You have given me. I don't understand You or what You do. Just help me as You already have.

Be with Preacher Stutzman's little girls. Thank You that they have a father who loves them. It would seem too much to have their mother taken and no father around who cared.

"Thank You for Ronda and Joe, who have come to live with me. They already mean so much. Thank You for the quilt I've already sold, and I ask for the strength to work on it. Thanks for my mamm and daett, Dora and Clara, Eli and Monroe. You know the trouble Eli is in. You know he's stubborn and thinks he knows what's best. Would You forgive him and have mercy on him? He needs mercy like we all do. I, perhaps the most of them all. Amen."

Ella got up and prepared to go upstairs to bed. With the girls gone, she would spend the weekend sleeping in her own upstairs bedroom. Knowing she would miss the girls, at least she would have her own bed to take comfort in.

Is there time yet to write tonight, to place my thoughts on paper? Surely there is. Carefully Ella turned out the gas lantern and took the kerosene lamp with her. The basement steps creaked under her feet as she crept upward and onto the first floor. Down the hall, she could see that the living room light was still on, but there was no sign of either Joe or Ronda.

Ella continued up the stairs. The bedroom door opened under her hand without a sound. It's newness was evident in the very feel of the wood and the ease with which the knob turned. The journal was still in its place in the cedar chest, covered by the protective dresses.

Ella set the kerosene lamp on the dresser. With her journal in hand, she walked over to the bed, sat down, flipped through the pages until a blank one came up, and then began at once to write the thoughts that came to her.

Preacher Stutzman just left. It was a good week . . . taking care of his girls. I didn't quite know what to expect, but he does love his girls. Ronda and Joe are here now and fully moved in. That has been such a blessing. Now, if we could just find an answer to the problem of Eli. Yes, he is a problem in his own right. A big one, but how I do love him.

I was just a little girl, too young to remember much, when Eli was born. Dora and I played together outside in the yard or in the barn in those days. He was just the little bundle Mamm would lay down on a blanket beside the wash line while she worked. That much I do remember.

When I first learned to love him, I don't know. Perhaps it happened the day he could run faster than me, chasing after our collie, Bessie, who had stolen my doll. Dora couldn't keep up either with the naughty creature. The dog meant no harm, I'm sure. We left our dolls lying around the yard all the time while we played.

That day the collie took off with mine, dragging the poor rag doll by its head. Horrified, I screamed at the sight of such abuse happening to my beloved treasure. Dora didn't help things by yelling. I thought the doll would soon be all torn up with nothing much left to it. Bessie wouldn't listen to any of our pleas to stop.

It was Eli who caught her running out of the barn. How he could run! I can still see him. He wasn't that big, but he looked like the best sight I'd seen all day. He told Bessie to stop in his little voice. He told her what a bad dog she was, and for some reason, it worked.

Eli scolded Bessie some more — his hands tight around her neck — while I went to pick up my doll from the ground. Other than some tiny teeth marks, I couldn't see what harm had been done. Somehow I knew Bessie would never do

336

such a thing again, and during the next few years, while we played with dolls, she never did.

On the day she died from old age and arthritis, Eli carried her body in the little wagon all the way down to the creek. I didn't go along because Mamm had work for us to do. Dora didn't want to go, but I would have. Eli said he buried her under the oak tree — the big one. I wasn't sure, but I think he meant the one within sight of the water.

I remember how glad I was when he was old enough to accompany us girls to the youth gatherings and singings. That was the year before Aden came into my life. When I first noticed Aden and saw him smile, I thought my heart would jump right out of my skin. I couldn't imagine how I would ever say no to anything he asked of me. Yet, I would have tried if he hadn't been as nice as Eli.

Eli is stubborn, and yet his heart is so soft underneath. I wonder if it's always so. I guess it isn't because Aden wasn't stubborn, just strong, and he was even nicer than Eli. How then could my brother have gone so wrong — to think he can date an Englisha girl? I still can't believe it.

I wonder if the bishop knows how much

he has won over our hearts because of his spiritual concern for Eli. I guess everyone wanted me to marry the bishop the first time he came around. Well, his genuine interest in Eli has played a big part in my decision.

How will we live with ourselves if Eli actually marries an Englisha girl? It will be like a part of our own body has been ripped from us. The preachers say Da Hah gives grace for all trials, and I guess He gave me grace to bear Aden's death. I don't know how else I'd still continue on with life.

It certainly can't be for love. I don't think there's enough grace in heaven or earth for me to love a man again. Oh, I suppose the calm, settled kind who some speak of could come later.

Bishop will make that kind of husband. I can respect him. He'll marry me — even if my heart doesn't throb at the sight of his face. He will likely tell me that is how it should be and that his love is enough for any girl. I suppose he's right because he is right on most things.

I will be known as the bishop's wife and have no cause for regret, I guess. But my heart will never forget Aden. I will always remember — even when I am old and crippled with age — what it was like to have loved a man with all my heart. I think the bishop knows that. He'll say his wife's obedience to him is sufficient and will not care about the rest.

In some way, I think he should care, but I'm not sure why.

Ella thought for a moment but found no more to write. She carefully closed the journal and slid the tablet back under the dresses.

Slowly she walked over to the window. The night sky was now inky black and the moon still hung in the sky. The view was much better up here and made her feel like one riding above the earth. *Why can't I sleep up here every night? Nee, it isn't possible with the girls. It's better that I stay in the basement. Any small sacrifice for their comfort is well worth the effort.*

She changed, blew out the kerosene lamp, and climbed under the covers. Sleep came easily enough, and the dream just as easy. Before her eyes the dream unfolded. She saw the familiar barnyard, the house, the couples seated in front, and her own face across from the bishop's. With a gasp, she woke. The moon was bright in the window, and the hour was somewhere close to morning. *Why did I dream that same dream again, and why are my hands sweating and gripping the edge of the sheets so fearfully?*

THIRTY-FIVE

Ella stood by the bed. The light that streamed through the window framed her figure. *How did I oversleep by so long? It must be past seven already.* Quickly she dressed, stopping for a moment when she heard the sounds Ronda made in the kitchen downstairs. *Ronda is up, but does that mean I have to be? This is Saturday, and the girls are at home with Preacher Stutzman. Why can't I sleep as long as I wish? There is no one around but Joe and Ronda, and they won't hold it against me.*

Still, it can't be right. Daett would never approve of his girls sleeping in. There is no acceptable excuse — not even the hours I lost after that dream.

Why did the dream return? It seems senseless, so without merit, and a thing of the darkness that came uninvited. It troubled her greatly. *Perhaps, as foolish as my fears are, it might be best to share the matter with some-*

one. The young bishop is a gut man.

Ella opened the bedroom door, which caused the noise from downstairs to sound louder. She could tell that Joe and Ronda had finished their breakfast. *Maybe this is the very answer I am looking for. Ronda is a true friend — and married. That carries a lot of weight, even if she is younger.*

Opening the stair door, Ella peeked into the living room. There was no sign of Joe, but Ronda was washing dishes at the sink. Ella walked across the hardwood floor in her house slippers.

"Good morning," she whispered, but Ronda still jumped.

"I thought I heard somethin'," Ronda said with a laugh. "I'm not used to being alone in a big house yet."

"I thought I'd see how you're doing. Is Joe gone?" Ella asked. Glancing toward the plates on the table, she walked over and gathered them up for Ronda.

"Yah," Ronda said, "he has to work on Saturday — at least through the summer, especially since we lost a few days for the wedding. And we do need the income."

"Mind if I sit down?" Ella said. "I overslept badly as you can see."

"Please sit. I hope I didn't wake you. I had to start the bread dough early. This is my first time as a married woman."

"It'll turn out fine," Ella said as she sat down.

"I sure hope so," Ronda replied.

Silence settled on the room. *Should I say anything about the dream? It might be better to wait until after I eat breakfast.* "I'd better get breakfast before I faint," Ella said, getting up.

"I have oatmeal left. I made too much for the two of us. You're welcome to have some."

"Thanks," Ella said. "That's nice of you."

Ronda moved toward the stove. "See? I kept the oatmeal warm just in case. What for, I wasn't sure. But I couldn't bring myself to throw it away. I even imagined myself eating oatmeal for lunch."

Ella put a dab of oatmeal in her bowl and poured in the milk. She added a small spoonful of sugar and slowly stirred the mixture. Ronda watched her with a curious look on her face.

"What?" Ella asked, noticing Ronda's expression.

"I've been wanting to ask you if it's true you're seein' the bishop — the young Bishop Miller."

"Yah," Ella said, "I suppose it's true."

"What's love like the second time around?

I can't imagine losin' Joe and loving someone new."

"It's not the same, of course. Not even
love, really. A little more down to earth,"
Ella said, shrugging, "but I guess that will
come. They all say so, at least."

"It'll be the bishop's first courting time,"
Ronda said. "Does that bother you?"

"I hadn't thought of that, but I don't think
it bothers me."

"Yah," Ronda said, obviously alert and
waiting for Ella to continue.

Ella took a deep breath and cleared her
throat. *Why not take the plunge? Ronda can
be trusted.*

"Ronda, I want to tell you something. It's
this dream I keep having about the bishop
and me getting married — our wedding and
all. I had it again last night. I even saw in
the dream where our wedding takes place."

"You know where you and the bishop are
getting married?"

"Yah. It's at the same place where you had
your wedding."

"Our wedding?" Ronda said, looking surprised.

"It wasn't your wedding in the dream,"
Ella said. "The wedding in my dream just
happens at the same place."

"I know other people have gotten married

344

there. Several already," Ronda said.

"I guess that's true. I hadn't really thought of that."

"Yah." Ronda said. "What's wrong, then, about such a dream?"

"It's frightens me . . . for some reason. Seein' myself at my own wedding . . . with the bishop. I stayed awake last night for a long time after I dreamed it again. I think that's why I overslept this morning."

"Maybe it's a warnin'."

"A warnin'? But about what?'

"About the bishop."

"You think he's to be feared?"

"Not likely," Ronda said, shrugging. "They say there hasn't been a better bishop among our people in years."

"Then why am I afraid?" Ella said, leaning forward. "He's comin' over tonight. Mamm and Daett think he's perfect for me, and everyone else does too. Even Preacher Stutzman's sermon last Sunday sounded like he thought so too."

"Preacher Stutzman?"

"Yah. You weren't there, but he talked about Rebecca in the Bible and how *Da Hah* had chosen her husband for her."

"He ought to be more careful about his preachin'," Ronda said as a sour look crossed her face. "I've heard a lot about him and his preachin'. He's quite somethin', they say. I guess Joe and I will get to experience it now that we live in the district."

"He says things he shouldn't. You should have heard him at Aden's funeral. He was thunderin' about the judgment of God."

"That's strange," Ronda said, dipping a glass of water from the bucket and setting it down on the table.

"It's more than strange. It's disrespectful."

"Not that. I mean *you*." Ronda said, tapping Ella on the hand.

"Me?"

"Yah, you. You just took Preacher Stutzman to task . . . and rightfully so, I would say. Yet, you take care of his girls. That might not be a good sign, and your dream might be a warnin' — perhaps from *Da Hah* Himself. He does work in such ways. I had a dream about a boy once myself, just before Joe came along. It kept me from sayin' yes . . . even when Daett liked the boy."

"You had a dream?"

"Yah," Ronda said, "only I just dreamed it once. It was about the Yost boy, Benjamin, who's from our district. He was a looker, that's for sure. Joe is too but just not quite like that. Anyway, I caught his eye at the youth gathering. It was by accident, it seemed to me, but he really got to me. I knew he would ask me pretty soon. I also knew I would say yes, even when I saw that another girl was after him. You could tell by the way she hung around him. Everyone expected he'd ask to take her home. It was a pleasant thought to pull something off like that — against that other girl."

"I don't remember any of that," Ella said.

"She was from the south districts. Anyway, I went home that night and made my plans. I thought about it all that week — how it would be when he asked me, how that special feelin' would be there, and how much I'd enjoy the time with him when I got into his buggy. I even thought of our life together, about the time when we'd be married, of our children, and everything. It all seemed as plain as day. Then Dad found out about how I felt. He found out from my brother, I think. He must have noticed because I sure didn't tell him.

"Then on the Sunday night before Benjamin asked me, I dreamed the dream. I saw him drive his buggy down by the road south of us. I clearly saw him driving right off the road and crash into the trees. He got his horse all tangled up in the bushes, and the buggy was in an awful wreck. It frightened me, but it was when I saw him pull me out that I really got scared. I didn't move even when he called my name."

"That's awful," Ella said.

"I know," Ronda said, shivering. "So when Benjamin did ask me, I said no, all because of that dream. When Dad found out I said no, he raised a fuss. He told me I never could find a better boy than Benjamin. I didn't tell him about my dream. I haven't told anyone before. I suspected they'd think me stupid or something, like I shouldn't be makin' life's decisions based on a dream. But it was *real,* Ella. Really real!"

"Do you think maybe my dream means something, then?"

"I don't know," Ronda said. "What do you think?"

"It just makes no sense to me at all."

"I think *Da Hah* is tryin' to send you a message just like He sent one to me. You just don't see what's in front of your nose."

"Yah," Ella said.

"And there's something else," Ronda said with a serious tone in her voice. "I noticed it last night . . . with you and his girls, but I wasn't going to say anything."

What is the woman talking about?

When Ella said nothing, Ronda continued. "You're so blind, Ella. It's Preacher Stutzman. Why can't you see it? I can."

"I have no idea what you mean," Ella said, fearing what Ronda might say next.

"The man *likes* you," Ronda said, waving her arms. "No, it's more than that. The man is completely taken up with you. He almost adores the dust on your feet."

"Preacher Stutzman?" Ella almost laughed out loud. "How can you say that? How could anyone have any feelings for him at all? Least of all me?"

Ronda leaned forward, kept her voice low, and said, "You don't have feelings for the bishop either."

"That's different," Ella said. "He's half decent at least."

"Have it your way," Ronda said, getting up. "What do I know? I'm a simple-minded Amish girl, just married, and ignorant in her ways."

"Well, I didn't mean it that way. Sure, I love his girls. Who wouldn't? They do need a good mamm, and I mean to take care of them until Stutzman finds one."

"You know, Ella," Ronda said, placing her hands on the table, "for as sensible a girl as you are, you don't have a whole lot of sense on this one. You would make Preacher Stutzman an amazing wife. His girls . . . Well, you would make the best mother they could have. And the man is all soft inside his rough edges. You should have seen him last night when I answered the door."

"That's so funny," Ella said, laughing. "You base this all on my dream? Just like that?"

"No, I base it on a lot of things — like seein' the way he acted with you last night."

Ella, wanting to end the discussion, glanced at the clock. "I think you're wrong, and that's all there is to it. The day is moving on, and I think we should too. Can I help you with anything?"

"No, I need to learn to care for a house by myself, I guess," Ronda said, squaring her shoulders, "but I will cry for help if things get out of hand."

"Do that," Ella said with a strained laugh. *Truly* Da Hah *has sent me a great friend even if she has some strange ideas.*

THIRTY-SIX

Ella paused a moment to watch the load of diapers roll out on the clothesline. Already the white wash had begun to move gently in the breeze. *When the wind picks up, it will flap and dry quickly in the warm sun.*

Ella smiled. *Ronda certainly has wild ideas about me and Preacher Stutzman. The girl does have a lively imagination. Yes, the preacher has turned out to be nice to his girls, but otherwise he is impossible. Plus I don't have the slightest feeling for him, not even the kind of warm family feeling I get when everyone's at home sitting around in the living room with the gas lantern hissing above. I watch his girls, but that is all there is to it. So Ronda thinks the dream is meant to warn me? Well, she is just plain wrong.*

"Bread's arisin'," Ronda called from the kitchen window, thoroughly cheerful. "I think it's workin' fine, like usual."

"Gut," Ella said, hollering back. "Don't

351

punch it down — not yet." The girl was a dear, a gift to Ella, and there was no question about that. She was a misguided gift, perhaps, but a pleasant one.

"Oh, how do I tell when to punch it down? Mamm always told me."

"When it looks ready to pop, and just remember that bigger is better."

"You'd better come and see," Ronda said, sounding worried.

Ella laughed but walked over to the kitchen window and looked in. Two mounds of dough lay on the counter, puffed high into the air.

"I'd say that's about right," she said, squinting through the screen. "You want the dough to rise enough."

"Can it go too high?"

"Not really. I wouldn't worry about that. An hour is usually enough."

Ronda glanced at the clock. "Oh, it's been well over that."

"Then stomp it down and into the pans," Ella said, laughing.

"Oh my! I do hope Joe doesn't find out I had to ask. He'll think he married a *dummkopf*."

"I won't tell," Ella said, "and Joe wouldn't care anyway."

"I don't think he would either," Ronda

said with her hands deep in bread dough, "but what if he does?"

"He likes you well enough," Ella said, leaving the window and walking back to her wash. Ronda would soon gain confidence. The girl was quite capable. She would also make a great mother for the children who were sure to come along, would be an asset to both Joe and the community, as all Amish women were supposed to be.

Would I be an asset to the bishop? He is coming tonight, and there are many things to discuss. Life's situations need to be dealt with head-on, and if the bishop wants me as his wife, he might as well get used to the way I am. That's the way I've been raised. Mamm and Daett always spoke about their problems as the need came up. Bishop or no bishop, I won't lose that trait. Surely the bishop won't feel otherwise.

Ella finished her wash, cleaned up the basement, and prepared to begin her quilt.

"Come and eat lunch with me," Ronda hollered down the stairs.

"Really? Well, I'm not going to turn that down."

She ran up the steps, and helped set the table as Ronda brought the sandwiches out. They bowed their heads in silence before beginning to eat.

"This house already seems like my home," Ronda said.

Ella nodded. "And I was thinking of this as your kitchen when I was in the basement. Isn't that something?"

"I still think you should be up here. I feel bad about that."

"You shouldn't. I'm fine."

In a few minutes they had finished, and Ronda said, "There's no way you're going to help clean up."

"Then it's back to my quilt," Ella said, walking down the stairs.

She laid out the quilt, stretched the frame, and drew in the lines of the blocks. The house in the center would have to wait until she rolled the quilt in.

When she heard Joe's buggy wheels rattling faintly in the driveway, she knew he was home for the afternoon. *When will the bishop arrive?* she wondered. *We didn't discuss a time. Usually people wait until dusk or after supper because, if for no other reason, they are simply shy. But, of course, the bishop isn't shy. Of all his traits I know of, that's one he lacks. From the first time he came over after Aden's death, his boldness and confidence were what attracted me — if attraction is what that feeling could be called.* Ella blushed even though no one was around. *If*

I plan to marry the man, feelings of some sort help. Surely this isn't being disloyal to Aden's memory since these are entirely different feelings. Her thoughts of Aden had set her heart to pounding. *The bishop definitely doesn't do that to me. With him, my emotions are hardly involved at all, but perhaps that is how it is supposed to be the second time around.*

Surely there is time for supper yet. Ella retrieved a jar of canned tomato soup from the shelves near the root cellar. She would have her own garden next year, but thankfully Lizzie had sent a variety of canned items along from the well-stocked shelves at Seager Hill.

Ella started the fire in the oven and stirred the contents in the small kettle as it heated. When the soup boiled, she transferred the contents to a bowl, cut a slice of bread, and retrieved jam and butter from the root cellar. It would be a *gut* supper, plenty and enough for one person.

A soft knock came on the door before she had time to reach the table. She jumped, and the soup almost slopped out of the bowl. *Surely the bishop isn't here already. No one has driven in. Perhaps it's a late customer who was drawn in by the quilt sign and is stopping in.*

Cautiously Ella opened the basement

door. The straw hat came into her line of vision first, and her smile wavered.

"Good evening," she said, opening the door wider.

His blue eyes were intense and seemed to search her face. "Good evening."

The man sure is confident enough.

"Am I early?" he asked. "I didn't really set a time, but *Da Hah* says we are to walk in the light, same as He is in the light. It seemed right to come while the sun was still up. Yet there is honor and no reproach at all between the love of a man and woman. We must always remember that."

"Yah," Ella said, hoping the red in her neck didn't spread up her face. She motioned around the room with her hand. "This is all I have. I guess we'll have to sit on the couch."

"You have not eaten, I see. I hope my presence won't disturb your supper." He removed his straw hat and held it firmly with both hands.

"I can eat now, if you don't mind," she said. *Perhaps I am getting used to him.* "Or I can wait till later, but I haven't eaten since noon." *Where does such courage come from? With this much grace given,* Da Hah *must be for me and this relationship.*

"Why don't I eat a little with you?" he

said, laying his hat on the floor. "I had supper, but your soup looks good. I have to see how you cook, now, don't I?" He laughed softly.

"How do you know I didn't take special care?" Ella asked, getting an extra bowl.

"I doubt it," he said with a smile. "Your family has quite a few good cooks, from what I hear, and I don't think your mom failed to teach you. Am I not right?"

Ella felt her neck grow red again. *Why am I always embarrassed when he talks like this? Aden said much nicer things, and I don't remember any redness, just the pounding of my heart.*

"Depends on who you ask, I guess," she finally said, not showing him her face. *He likely read way too much into my reaction already and doesn't need further encouragement. Besides, I need my courage.*

"I think I'll live with food like this . . . might even get fat on it," he said.

This remark confirmed her fears. He was definitely looking at her as his future wife. She looked at the soup bowl. *How am I going to eat my soup now with my stomach churning and the memory of my dream racing through my mind like ghosts returning to haunt me?*

"I saw your sign for the quilt shop," he

said, holding out his bowl as she ladled soup into it.

"Yah," she said, dipping what was left into her own bowl.

He cleared his throat. "I thought perhaps you didn't think this through all the way. The sign is a little on the edge . . . I was thinking this could cause trouble for our people and the *Ordnung*."

"Trouble? My sign could cause trouble?"

A smile filled his face. "I see you're innocent, which is understandable. I'm sure you just didn't think of the sign in quite the way I would. Perhaps it's because this is your first time with a business. I'm sure you're more than willing to correct the problem."

She met his eyes. *What is the man talking about?*

"I thought so," he said with an even wider smile. "Anyone could make the mistake. Although I must say I am a little surprised, perhaps even a little disappointed."

"I don't understand," Ella said, finding her voice.

"Our people," he said in a voice that resonated against the basement walls, "they believe in humility, a bowed walk before *Da Hah* and His Word. This befits us and our way of life. This is how we have been taught by our forefathers to live. Many of them gave their lives for the faith."

"Yah?" Ella said. *The man sure can make a lot of words. They flow off his tongue like he has them stored up in abundance.*

"Your sign shouldn't mention your name. Really, it shouldn't. It reads, *Ella's Quilt Shop.* This is not fitting at all. But I'm sure you'll agree and are willing to change the sign as soon as possible."

"My name," she said, vaguely comprehending. "I hadn't thought about how that would look. Not in such terms. I thought the name might bring in more customers and sort of make it personal."

"That is understandable," he said, allowing his smile to fade a little, "yet it does seem as if you have placed a lot of thought into this. I had hoped it wasn't so. I had thought perhaps you had made the sign — how can I say it — sort of by accident. But this doesn't sound as if you have. You must have thought about it. I must say I am a bit disappointed. You do come from a good family, though, and I'm sure your father has taught you about humility."

"He has," Ella said, forgetting her soup. "I'm sure this is not Daett's fault. Perhaps my inexperience is to blame, but certainly not his. I will paint my name off the sign even tonight . . . if you so wish."

"That's not necessary," he said, seeming to relax. "Like I said, we are all human and prone to error — all of us, even those who are called to lead the people. A wife of such a man should have the same expectations but also the same weakness, I suppose. You are willing to take correction, for which I am grateful. This is a good sign of humility. Those who do not receive correction, well, it is hard to keep hope for such. They are prone to greater and greater error . . . and are almost impossible to turn back toward the good."

"Yah," Ella said, dropping her head when his eyes searched her face. *What is wrong with the man? I did not expect this condemnation, this weight of guilt, over such a small matter. Daett would often bring correction — to all the children — yet this was not like Daett's correction.*

"I'm sure it won't happen again," he said.

Ella looked up at him. "I would have changed the sign quite willingly. That's all you would have had to say."

"Perhaps. But it's good to search the heart, even as *Da Hah* does with all His people. Sometimes we spend too much time with the fruit of the tree and not with the root. The root is where all things spring from and is the source of the matter. Our people gave us a great root — over five hundred years ago — from which we have sprung up. They gave up their lives for the faith, and with their blood and their testimony, they sealed their witness. It is this root we must strive to be like. We must, like them, seek to be a humble people who walk the earth as obedient servants of the most high God. All of us should be pilgrims and strangers in this land."

Ella nodded. The soup bowl was cold between her hands, but the bishop didn't seem to notice. His own bowl was already empty. *When did the man eat? I can't remember seeing his spoon going to his mouth.*

"The Scriptures," he said with an intent look on his face, "they speak of a virtuous woman — one whose price is far above rubies. Such a woman brings honor to her husband. She brings grace into his home and rears godly children. It is for this woman I have prayed and longed for, Ella. You know that. Surely you do. This is the desire of my heart, and I believe *Da Hah* has finally allowed me to be satisfied with you — after all these years. He has brought me a wonderful woman. Perhaps you can understand my disappointment in your actions. It's not that serious. Yah, perhaps not really. But one must deal with what is at hand. I am glad to be able to speak with you on this matter, and I am glad you are willing to correct it."

"I am sorry I have disappointed you," she said as the words caught in her throat. "I'm not perfect."

"Yah, none of us are," he said.

He obviously meant to comfort, but the words clamped around her heart like frozen blocks of ice. Forbidden thoughts sprung to her mind. They were thoughts she knew she shouldn't harbor, but it was already too late.

She saw Aden, as clearly as if he stood in front of her, with a gentle smile on his face. "You're lovely Ella," he whispered. "Almost perfect. And the little leftover part . . . is the best of all." He had said the words down by the stream and beside the little bridge where the water ran the fastest. He said them on the Sunday afternoon he drew her to him and tightly embraced her. His lips were gentle in their kiss.

"Have I said something, perhaps? Something out of order?" the bishop asked. His voice reached her through the fog. "You don't look well."

Her face was pale as she looked away. *What would he think if he knew what I had just remembered?* "I was just troubled."

He pulled his chair closer, took her hand, and wrapped his fingers tightly around hers. "Your sorrow is befitting," he said gently. "I must say I am deeply touched. *Da Hah* has indeed given me a virtuous woman. Yes, you are human, but then we all are. We are all given to mistakes. I make them, and so will you. Yet, with this repentance you show, well, no man could ask for more. I would like to marry you soon, Ella. As soon as possible. I need a wife."

Is the man pressuring me already — just after the correction he gave me? "But I must have time," she whispered.

"You are twenty-one," he said as he searched her face. "I'm not young anymore. You are what I have waited for all these years. Why should we wait, Ella? There is no need. Enough time has already gone by. As much time as is necessary since Aden's death. Even by the measure of our people it has. Is more than the sorrow, perhaps, holding you back?"

Ella was still unable to look at him. She shook her head in silence.

"Then you have moved on . . . as it should be. Perhaps even more healing will still come . . . with the love that you and I will share. Is this not *Da Hah*'s way, Ella, for you and me?"

"I have to take care of Preacher Stutzman's girls," she said, getting the words out.

"Stutzman's girls? Anyone can take care of them. I'm sure his sister Susanna can — at least for some time. Both she and Stutzman will understand when they hear of our plans. Everyone will understand. Other than Susanna, there are many of his relatives — perhaps younger ones — who can take over the care of his girls. I also believe Stutzman himself has a wedding coming up and perhaps soon. There is no reason for further delay, Ella. None at all."

She knew she shouldn't speak it, but the words came out. "Preacher Stutzman isn't gettin' married. Not anytime soon."

"You know this?" he asked, speaking the short words abruptly.

Ella nodded. "He told me." Again, she knew she was speaking out of turn, and yet she could not do otherwise.

"Ivan told you himself?"

"Yah."

"Why would he be speaking to you on this matter of his marriage? I don't understand. This is not an appropriate thing to speak of with an unmarried woman — especially one who isn't his relative."

"It was not so intended," Ella said, remembering how she insisted he find a good mother for the children. *Clearly those words would also be misunderstood by the bishop if I were to say them.*

"You defend him, Ella? Ivan is not a very tempered man. He's much subject to emotions," the bishop said. Then, after a silence, he continued, "Surely you don't feel your heart drawn to him. I would expect better of you. You belong with me. You belong as *Da Hah* has willed it."

"My heart is not drawn to him," she said, "but I'm sorry I have disappointed you again."

"You only disappoint me in your defense of him . . . and in what seems a very inappropriate conversation with the man about his marriage. This is not the way of our women."

"Perhaps . . ." She spoke slowly but with a strange sense of deliberation. "Perhaps, I am not meant for this . . . to be your wife. It is true that Aden still keeps a place close to my heart. I've not made a secret of this with you or with anyone else. A single life is not outside of my wishes."

"I cannot consent to such a thing." He said the words quickly. "Never have I seen a woman I loved so much. You are what *Da Hah* has willed for me. Of this I am certain. We must not let such little trouble come between us. Especially on this first night. You have been so troubled. You have not eaten your supper yet."

So he did notice. "It can wait," Ella said, brushing the air over the bowl of soup. Fueled — and surprised — by her own boldness, Ella began again, "I must be clear about this matter relating to the care of Preacher Stutzman's girls. Their care will continue and will be done by me. That is until the man marries or he changes his mind about the need for my help. I care too much about the girls to back down on the subject."

"But this is unreasonable, Ella," the bishop said, "and I don't like it. I don't like it at all. You and he surely speak together often. Such an appearance is very inappropriate, to say the least. What will people say?"

When Ella didn't have an answer, the bishop said, "I'll tell you what I will do. Next week I will speak with Ivan about this matter. He will understand and can then find someone else to take care of his girls."

Ella took a deep breath. The words would have to be spoken. "If you do that, then you might as well forget about marrying me."

"Oh," he said, looking as if she had thrown a bucket of sink water over his head.

"It's your choice," she said. "I love those little dears. They are precious, motherless girls. It's not right to throw them around in circles from one person to another. Preacher Stutzman will marry eventually. Then I will be free. You have waited this long. Perhaps you can wait longer. It will also give me more time to heal from the loss of Aden. It might be for the best anyway."

"I do not agree," he said, "and I think it's very inappropriate, but your care for his girls is touching. It shows your tender heart, and in this I can see virtue. For that reason alone, perhaps I should consider it — if you assure me there are no feelings between you and Ivan."

"I have already said there are none on my part," she said, finally looking at him as she spoke.

"And his feelings toward you?" he asked. His eyes blazed.

"I have not spoken to him on the matter," she said. "It would not be seemly."

"Has he given you cause to think he cares for you? Has he asked for your hand in marriage?"

Ella laughed. "No, he certainly has not."

The bishop settled back in his chair. "One never knows, even with our own people, what they will do. Some do inappropriate things — even men like Ivan — because in the matters of the heart, only *Da Hah* can know them. Like a serpent on a rock, says the Holy Book, so is the way of a man with a maid."

"You will not speak with him, then?" Ella asked.

"I make no promises," he said, folding his hands.

"It would be best not to speak to him," she said firmly, making sure her meaning was unmistakable.

Silence fell between them, and then he sat straight up in his chair. "Your supper. I have kept you from it with my talk. What sort of man am I?"

"It's okay," she said weakly.

"It's not — most assuredly not. Supper is no longer to be kept from you."

With that, he sprang to his feet, grabbed her soup bowl, and took it over to the stove. With expert care he fanned the fire that had died down to embers, stoked the ashes, and proceeded to reheat her soup. "I wasn't a bachelor all these years for nothing," he said with a grin. After a couple of silent minutes, he said, "There, now. Nice and warm, are we. And the bread, I will warm it over the oven."

"You are good," she said as she took the

first spoonful.

"Not at all," he said, brushing off the compliment with a wave of his hand. "Soup isn't so hard to warm up."

"Do you want some more?" she asked. "There's plenty."

"I had enough, so I'll just watch you eat."

"That doesn't help," she said. The red was creeping up her face again.

"Well, then," he said, laughing, "let me tell you a story."

"Yah," she said. *Anything! Just stop watching me.*

"Last week one of my cows got out of the pasture. It's the usual rowdy one," he said, smiling warmly. "She always looks for the way through the fence and seems to find it when I'm not looking or when the barbed wire has gotten even the slightest bit loose. She finds it — always does. And she's my best milker. She drops heifer calves every year, as dependable as can be, so I don't ever consider taking her to the sale barn.

"Anyway, she got out on the road again by pushing the wire back with her neck. I didn't notice anything amiss until a car in the road blew its horn. I had to leave my team in the middle of the field to tend to the problem. The nice man and lady in the car were tourists who seemed amused to find an Amish cow — by their description — out in the middle of the road.

"They helped me get the cow back in. They said they used to be farmers before they retired in Florida, and I could believe it. After we got the cow back safe and sound inside the fence, they stayed and chatted. I watched the horses out of the corner of my eye the whole time, but they didn't move, as good as gold they were. They probably were thankful for the long rest."

Ella finished the last bite of her soup and waited for more of the story. When nothing more seemed to be coming, she said, "Why are you telling me this? Am I missing the point?"

"Just that I suspect you're a little bit like that cow," he said with a twinkle in his eye. "You're not quite willing to be content until you see what's on the other side."

Rather than press the point, Ella simply smiled and decided she might as well change the subject to her concerns about Eli. She didn't want him to leave without knowing what had been happening with her brother.

"Eli's in trouble again," she said, noticing the bishop didn't look too surprised. "Dora thinks he's seen the *Englisha* girl again. I don't know what gets into him. We all thought your talk had done him so much good, but Eli's always been that way — stubborn."

The bishop spoke slowly. "I'm disappointed . . . but not too surprised. This is a serious matter. It's of grave concern for one of our boys to see an *Englisha* girl. Sure, the *Englisha* are good people. They have their own way with *Da Hah,* as we have ours. But the two must be kept separate. They cannot mix, Ella. I'm sure you know that."

"I do," she said, "but we always have our wild boys."

"I see you defend him," he said, smiling. "I guess it's because he's your brother. Perhaps that blinds you to the seriousness of this matter. Yah, we have our wild ones, those who push the fence during their young years. But to love an *Englisha* is very wrong, Ella. We tempt *Da Hah* Himself with such a sin. I will speak with your father about this matter. I think perhaps it would be best if Eli left home until he repents fully of his error."

She stood to her feet. "No, you must not do that. You must not speak to my father. He would have to obey you . . . and Eli must stay at home. Daett needs him. He needs him a lot. I wouldn't want to see Daett suffer more than he already has. And this could drive away Eli for good. I believe Eli will choose the faith in the end. I just know he will."

He studied her for a long moment. "As I said, you're a lot like my cow. You always push the fence. You always find the loose wire. Yet in spite of that, you are the best woman I have ever seen. I find my heart pulls me in one direction, Ella, and my good sense pulls me in another. You really ought to learn the ways of an Amish woman's meek and quiet spirit. Has your *Daett* not taught you this?"

"You don't have to marry me," Ella whispered. "I still think the single life may be for me, but you must not speak with Daett about Eli."

"Yah," he said with a slight smile on his face, "I see you also speak your mind. Perhaps we should leave these matters alone for now. I will think some more about the subjects, both Eli and Ivan's girls. But I do have peace in my heart on one matter. *Da Hah* has given you to me for a wife — of this I am sure. I will humble my heart to accept His good will. Much work will be needed, I see. Yet His will is always the best."

"I have not yet agreed," Ella said, finding her voice.

"But you will," he said, speaking with a firm voice and standing to go. "Enough for tonight. Two hearts must grow together slowly. I see we have more time than I thought, and that too, I must get used to. I had hoped to marry you very soon, but I see I must wait. You are worth it, Ella."

"I am not so sure," Ella said, holding on to the sides of the chair and remembering her dream.

"I am," he said with his hand on the door. "Good night, now. *Da Hah's villa* be done. Until next Saturday, then, if you will?"

"I will see you then," she said. *What else is there to say?*

His steps were soundless as he climbed the stairs, but his buggy wheels rattled loudly as he drove out the driveway. Ella stood by the basement window to listen until the sound had died away into the distance.

THIRTY-SEVEN

Thankfully Preacher Stutzman didn't preach on Sunday. To have to listen to the thunder in his voice, hear the condemnation he brought, and face her disappointment in another man seemed too much to bear. After church Ella helped with the tables, ate quickly, and then headed home, staying in the basement for the rest of the afternoon.

Bright and early Monday morning, Preacher Stutzman pulled in the driveway with his girls, tied his horse at the hitching post, and, leaving baby Barbara in the buggy for the moment, approached the basement door, twirling his hat round and round in his hands.

Mary ran as she neared Ella and sprang into her arms with shrieks of delight. Sarah came much slower but smiled happily at Ella as she reached her.

"I see they still like me," Ella said with a smile.

"Of course they do," Stutzman said in a voice barely above a whisper.

"I suppose they would like anyone who takes care of them," Ella said. "It's not just about me."

"Yah," he said, "perhaps they would." His hat went around and around in his fingers.

"We didn't see you on Sunday," Mary said, "but Daett said you were in church."

"I do go to your district, and I was there," Ella said, "but it was crowded." She wasn't about to give the reason why the girls hadn't seen her — her deliberate attempt to avoid the attention and affection they had just shown her. In public this display would attract much more attention than she needed.

"But we like you," Mary said, "and we wanted to see you, but now we're back for all week. That's what Daett said."

"I'm glad too," Ella said, giving both girls a hug. "Now we have to get your sister from the buggy."

"Be good girls," Stutzman said with his hat on his head now. He walked to the buggy, brought the baby back with him, and handed her to Ella. He then knelt down, ruffling Mary's hair in front of her little white *kapp.* He gave Mary and Sarah a hug.

"I must be going now. There's hay to make and silage before too long."

"Of course, they will be *gut*," Ella said, "because they just are *gut*."

Stutzman smiled weakly, nodded, and then walked back to his buggy. Ella took the girls' hands and led them to the house, making sure they stopped to wave at their daett from the top of the basement stairs. Their father didn't seem to notice, his attention already elsewhere, as his horse hit the main road. *How like a man. They love their families, and then they leave. Perhaps he does have plenty on his mind, like he said. Still, he could have waved to his girls.*

"Well, what have we here?" Ronda asked from the open living room window. Her head was almost a whole floor above them. "The three little angels are back with us."

Mary laughed. Her voice bounced in the morning air. Sarah joined in.

"You're just girls, aren't you?" Ella said, pulling both of them toward her for a quick hug, while holding the baby in her other arm.

"Yah, that's all we are," Mary said, nodding like she understood.

"You're comin' up here for lunch later, aren't you?" Ronda asked.

"I can't be putting you out all the time,"

Ella said. "You'll spoil us all."

"It won't be every day. You know that. Joe's gone for the first time since the weekend. I guess I'm lonely in this big house. It just feels so good to have someone downstairs."

"Then we'll come. How about it, girls? Shall we go up for lunch with Ronda?"

They both nodded, and the matter was settled.

"Aren't they dears?" Ronda cooed. "How they can come from such a hard man, I have no idea. He sure has his eyes out for you."

"Shhh," Ella said, motioning toward the girls.

"Ach, you stick up for him," Ronda said. "The girls don't understand, but you must have taken my words to heart by the expression on your face."

"Would you quit it?" Ella said, mouthing the words to Ronda and making her laugh.

"I guess I am about as changeable as the wind. Mamm always said so anyway. I must say that bishop of yours is a much nicer prospect."

Ella glared at her, which only produced laughter from the window.

"Well, I've got work to do," Ronda said, shutting the window.

Work — seemingly things always came

down to that. Life was full of work. "Come," she said, taking Sarah's hand. "We also have to get to work, don't we? Did you girls have breakfast?"

"Yah," Mary said, "Daett made some oatmeal and fried eggs."

"Oh." Ella said, holding open the door. *It's tough to imagine Preacher Stutzman fixing eggs and oatmeal in any edible condition.*

Ella had no sooner settled the girls in the basement than she heard buggy wheels in the driveway. Above her, the basement door to the house opened, and she heard Ronda say, "It's him. He's back. What did you do to him?"

"Shhh." Ella whispered, looking over at Mary and Sarah, who were already busy at play on the floor.

"I best stay with them," Ronda said, "while you go out. I'm sure he's not back for nothin'."

"Maybe he forgot something," Ella said. "I have no idea what else it could be."

"Who does with that man," Ronda said, now standing at the bottom of the stairs. "Go outside quick . . . before he comes in."

Ella turned to Mary and Sarah and said, "Girls, I'll be right back. Ronda will stay with you until I return." Both girls looked briefly to Ronda and went back to their play.

As Ella walked outside, Preacher Stutzman was tying his horse. When he saw her,
he waited. That could only mean one thing.
He wanted to speak in private, away from
the house.

"Ronda is with the girls," Ella said, uncertain as to how she should act.

He nodded. His hat was not in his hands,
as it usually was when he talked to her. It
was seated firmly on his head.

"I had to speak with you," he said with a
determined voice.

*Oh, he's using his Sunday voice, but some-
thing is different about it.* The Sunday passion was there, but it also held a sort of
gentleness she hadn't expected.

"Yah?" she said, looking up to his face.

"I am not a man of great words. Yet I cannot let this go on like it is. I must speak to
you of what is right."

At once Ella knew what was to come,
though he hadn't yet said the words. Like
the sun rising over the hill with light and
brilliance, it was clear. How she knew, she
couldn't say. But perhaps it was always this
way when a man spoke his heart.

"My daughters need a mother, and it
seems they have found one in you. I cannot
but speak for them . . . and ask for your
hand in marriage."

Ella weighed her words. "You know I'm seeing the bishop. For that reason, I'm not free to give you an answer."

"Then you do not say no?"

"I do not say no . . ." she said, "nor do I say yes. May I ask what you think the bishop will say when he hears of this?" Ella met his eyes. Soon his hat would come off, and he would begin circling it in his fingers. He reached for his hat as she waited.

He took the rim in his fingers, lowered it, and held the hat tight by his side. "The bishop can say what he wishes. I will tell him to his face the rightness of my question. My daughters need the mother *Da Hah* has sent them."

"And you?" she asked. "What am I to you?"

The red started at his neck and spread till it filled his face, but his eyes blazed. "You are more than any man deserves. Least of all me."

"Then you do not ask for yourself but for only your daughters?"

How the man struggled with the answer. His hands clenched, his jaw tightened, and he stared only at the ground. "Yah. I ask also for myself. And may *Da Hah* forgive me."

"Does He need to forgive such things?

That you love a woman?"

The hat came up in his fingers, turning slowly in his hands. "For me, yah, He needs to forgive. I loved Lois more than *Da Hah* allows. That is why He took her."

"Perhaps He had other reasons. He took Aden too. Did I love too much?"

"I know not your heart, and I cannot speak for another."

"You certainly seem to do so on Sundays," Ella said with a sharp tone to her voice.

"In this I have a great weakness," he whispered.

"Yah, you do," Ella said, now searching his face.

"Like at Aden's funeral," he said. "I was hard that day because I was thinking only of myself and that *Da Hah* had also taken Lois. I should not say such things especially in such times. My words were not from *Da Hah*."

"Yah, you should not have spoken so," Ella said, surprised at her boldness. This, after all, was Preacher Stutzman. The thundering voice of many a sermon.

"I am weak . . . and am made from the clay of the ground. You must not hold me as perfect."

"I do not," she said. "Of that, you can be certain."

"Can you forgive me? I do need your forgiveness."

Ella took a deep breath. "Yah," she said slowly, "I can forgive you."

A slight smile played on his face. "What, then, is your answer to my question?"

"I cannot give it now."

"I am a very sinful man to even ask."

"Perhaps you should not judge your own heart so harshly," Ella said.

"Then you can give me good news — more than I dared hope for."

"I promise nothing," she said quickly.

"But you will think about it?"

"Yah, but you should understand that I have no feelings for you."

His gaze fell to the ground again, and his face looked troubled. Finally the smile came back, and he met her eyes. "Then I can wait. Perhaps your heart will turn in time."

"I make no promises, and I will still see the bishop," Ella said, hearing her own voice from a great distance.

"Then I will speak with him too," he said, his eyes flashing.

Ella shook her head. "Nee. The bishop must not know that we have spoken. That will only keep the girls from me. I will speak to him when I have decided."

Silence hung between the two of them.

Then the preacher said, "I have spoken my mind. It is enough, then. You can give me your answer when you are ready. I will say no more."

He turned and walked to his buggy, loosened the tie rope, climbed in, and slapped the reins. His buggy wheels spun on the gravel as he turned. Then, for just the briefest of moments, at the end of the driveway, he turned and glanced back.

THIRTY-EIGHT

"Well, what did he want?" Ronda asked. "Ella, your face has gone white. Did he really? Oh, Ella, I can't believe it!"

"Don't go looking at me like that. This has all become very crazy all of a sudden," Ella said, lowering herself into her chair. Mary and Sarah were playing with their dolls while the baby was in her crib, kicking her legs and cooing.

"But Preacher Stutzman. Really!" Ronda said, waving her hands around. "Ach, the way he preaches. Did he actually ask to come courting?"

"Something like that."

"Ach, he asked to marry you, didn't he? Tell me all about it."

"I can't," Ella said. "It's too much."

"Well, at least you have a choice now — the bishop or the preacher. That's the bright side."

"Oh," Ella gasped, "the sign! I forgot

about the sign. I have to change it right away. Bishop wants me to, and I should have done it first thing since I couldn't yesterday."

"What are you talking about?" Ronda said. "Forget about your sign right now, whatever that means. I want to hear what you told Preacher Stutzman."

"Bishop wants the sign changed right away. He gave me a lecture on it Saturday night. I'd best run out and at least bring the sign in. I'll be right back."

"Would you explain?" Ronda said as Ella disappeared out the door.

Ella ran swiftly past the barn, past the fresh buggy marks in the driveway, out to the road, and retrieved her sign.

When she came back inside, Ronda had picked up the quilt Ella had started for her customer and began to stitch on it. "I hope you don't mind," Ronda said. "I like to quilt. And it was just laying here. Please let me help with it."

"That would be helpful, I guess. I told her I'd have it ready as soon as I could." Ella took up the other end of the quilt and began her handwork on it.

"So what will you do?" Ronda asked.

"I don't know," Ella said. "I planned on staying single after Aden died. Now I have two men after me, and what can I say but no."

"But you shouldn't," Ronda said. "Marriage is a *gut* thing. So what did you tell him?"

"I told him I'd have to think about his question and that I really have no feelings for him."

"But you'd consider it, and I know why," Ronda said, nodding toward the girls.

"Yah," Ella said.

"Perhaps Preacher Stutzman *would* be better than the bossy bishop," Ronda said, glancing at the sign now propped against the living room wall. "It sounds like he's already ordering you around, and Stuzman's more worthy of you. He wouldn't be reminding you of your faults all your life. And then there's the matter of the girls to think of."

"Bishop was within his rights to speak to me about the sign," Ella said. "And I suppose I should work on submitting myself better. Aden might have been too *gut* for me in that way."

"Don't be sayin' such things." Ronda motioned toward the sign. "You're going to repaint it, aren't you?"

"Yah," Ella said, standing. Ready to put action to her words, she retrieved her paint box and brushes from a closet, sat down at the table, and prepared to repaint the sign. She opened the box and selected the brush she wanted, unscrewed the small paint jar lid, and dipped the bristles in. With a gentle sweep, she placed fresh paint over the letters of her name. Glancing over at Ronda's work on the quilt, she said, "You do good work — and fast. Look at how much you've done already."

"I like to quilt," Ronda said. "Mamm taught us well. You have to like it, though. My older sister never did. She'll quilt when she has to but not much more than that, though. Me? I can work at it all day."

Ella set the sign on the table, touching it with her fingers. It was nearly blank now. She washed her hands at the wash basin and said, "If you really want to help that much, I'll pay you for your work."

"I guess I'd take something but not much. How soon does this one have to be done?"

"There's no deadline. I told the lady I'd complete it as soon as possible."

"Are there any more orders after this? I haven't seen anyone stop by."

"No," Ella said. "I suspect there will be, though. All the other quilt shops do well. Mine's just not that well-known yet. Clara's bringing some drawings over for me to try to sell."

"Drawings? Of people?" Ronda asked, holding her needle suddenly still.

Ella laughed. "Of course not."

"I suppose the bishop won't say anything, then."

"I hope not. Mamm let me use Clara's drawing for this quilt. That's where it comes from."

"This house?" Ronda asked, motioning with her chin. Her hands were busy stitching again.

"Yah. She's good, isn't she?"

"It sure looks like this house."

"Yah," Ella said, smiling, "it really does. I planned it that way."

Ronda's eyes lighted up. "You can sell those drawings easily, I would think. When people see the house and the quilt together, they should sell quickly. I never would have thought of it."

"That's why the lady purchased this one. It seemed an easy sale to make."

"See, you're *gut*," Ronda said. "Really *gut*."

"Not sure about that," Ella said, wrinkling up her face.

Mary set down her doll, came up to Ella, and pulled on her dress. "Can we go outside?" she asked. "Sarah and I?"

"I don't know," Ella said, getting up to glance out the window. "It's not raining or too hot. You have to stay close to the house and don't go out toward the road."

"We won't," Mary said with a solemn shake of her head.

Ella held the basement door open for them as they ran outside. Childhood was such a joyful time; so innocent of the troubles of the world. Surely it was the mercy of *Da Hah* on the little children.

They climbed to the top of the steps and then stopped. A shiny white stone Mary found beside the driveway captured their interest. Mary held the stone in her hand and gave it to Sarah when she showed interest.

How darling they really are. I could do this . . . be their mother. Where did that thought come from? Yet for the first time since Aden's death, something in her life began to make some sense. *Don't I want to be the girls' mother? But is it worth the sacrifice of also being Preacher Stutzman's wife?*

Back inside, Ella placed baby Barbara on a blanket on the floor, took her place at the quilt, and got to work in earnest. Her stitches easily matched Ronda's in both speed and quality.

"You're good too," Ronda said. "I don't think anyone could tell our work apart."

"Yah," Ella said, nodding, "we work together well."

Silence settled on the house, and their hands stayed busy. The clock on the wall ticked away, marking off the minutes. Every fifteen minutes or so, Ella got up to walk to the window and check on the girls.

Ronda got up at eleven to go upstairs. "I'm hungry. I'll go prepare lunch and holler when it's ready."

"Yah," Ella said, "quilting makes for as good an appetite as farmwork."

"Don't expect Joe to believe that," Ronda said from the foot of the stairs.

"They know it, though," Ella said. "You couldn't get them to quilt either way, I think."

"Now that's a fact," Ronda said, laughing and climbing up the stairs.

Concentrating on the fabric, Ella prepared to stitch around a little animal. For effect she needed darker thread and checked her own quilt on the wall for the right color. In every way this should be an exact copy. The woman had liked what she'd seen.

When Ronda called, Ella picked up the baby and went outside to collect the two girls. Little Barbara blinked at the bright sunlight, and Ella shielded her eyes with her hand. She found the girls having a pleasant discussion in the barn. She paused to listen in.

"He's too brown," Mary said. "Much too brown. I like Daett's horse better."

Sarah nodded.

"He looks mean," Mary said. "He looks like he could bite you, and I'm stayin' right here. You should too, Sarah. You'd better be careful. You don't like him, do you?"

Sarah shook her head vigorously.

"I don't either," Mary said and then grinned sheepishly when Ella cleared her throat.

"So you don't like my horse?" Ella asked with a smile.

"We were just playin'," Mary said.

"He's a nice horse, but you had best stay away from him. In fact, you should stay away from all horses until you're bigger. Horses can step on little people."

"That's what Daett says," Mary said.

"Oh, he does?" Ella asked.

"Yah, he takes us out to the barn with him sometimes when Aunt Susanna can't watch us. We have to be careful then."

"That's good," Ella said, picking Sarah up in her free arm. "It's time for lunch now. Are you hungry?"

They both nodded.

Ella walked toward the house. *Will I really become the mother of these children?* It seemed as if the choice was hers. To do so she would have to become Stutzman's wife. That was the price to pay.

Ronda had the sandwiches ready. They washed their hands at her washbowl and wiped them on the towel. At the table, they bowed their heads in silent prayer for the proper length of time, which was governed by some inner sense developed from youth.

"It's good," Mary said after the first bite.

"Yah, they are," Ella said. "Ronda's a good cook."

"I'll be gettin' Joe fat yet," Ronda said, giggling. "That's what he said last night."

Sarah dropped her sandwich, and Ella bent over to pick it up.

Ronda seems happy with Joe as her husband. What would it be like to have Stutzman as my husband? With Aden I knew what to expect. Here, the future stretches out dark and unknown. Only these three children can shed light on the journey. I love them, but could I ever love their daett? Certainly not like I loved Aden, but does that matter?

With Sarah's sandwich back where it belonged, Ella bit into her own. *What would Ronda think if she knew my thoughts? Ronda didn't ever date one man while having thoughts of another. She's calmly looking out the window, so she must not have noticed my distress.*

"I'll help clean up," Ella said when they were done eating.

"You have more to do than I do," Ronda said, motioning with her hand. "Just get on back to your work."

"We'll help," Mary said with bright eyes.

"See?" Ronda said, smiling. "Everything's taken care of."

"I guess it is," Ella said, getting up and taking baby Barbara in her arms. "Thanks so much for lunch, but we can't do this every day."

"Only when necessary," Ronda said, sweeping the crumbs from the table. "I like it. I really do. That's what's so nice about this — I can invite you up whenever."

"Nice on my part," Ella said. This was why she liked Ronda. Not because she invited her to lunch, but because she was a real friend.

Downstairs Ella returned to her work on the quilt. When the girls came down after helping Ronda, Ella settled the girls down for naps.

"I'm not sleepy," Mary said but fell asleep quickly. Sarah still had her eyes open and her thumb in her mouth.

That was one thing that would have to change as soon as possible. Ella's mamm never let her brother and sisters suck their thumbs very long. It deformed the teeth, her mamm had often said.

Silence settled on the basement, and the stitches stretched out before her. *How glad I am for Ronda's help. Many hours will go into this quilt, but in the end, the effort will be worth it. The finished product will warm the buyer's heart — and mine too.*

"*Da Hah*'s way of blessing," her daett said. "When one works with the hands, the blessing goes to both the giver and the receiver."

Feeling the need for a break from the needlework, Ella thought about her journal. *Would this not be an excellent time to write in it?* By tonight, the first day the girls were back, she would be too tired to write.

The news from this morning almost demanded it, and so with a silent step, she slipped upstairs, hoping each step didn't squeak too much and that Ronda wouldn't wonder why she went upstairs in the middle of the afternoon. Grabbing her journal, she also picked up the repainted sign and went outside and hung it on the hooks.

Back down in the basement, she opened the tablet and began.

Dear Journal,

How strange life can get. Preacher Stutzman proposed to me this morning, just like that. I don't know what the man was thinking. Surely he could see that I have no feelings whatsoever for him, and yet I love his daughters. The most surprising thing is that I didn't say no. Could this be Da Hah's way, or is my life all messed up?

I'm sure I know what the bishop will say — if I ever tell him.

I have no idea what my answer will be. The man even apologized for the hard preaching at Aden's funeral, as if he knew this bothered me . . . even when I had never told him so. He's a strange man, but then all of life is very strange right now.

I suppose I could just tell them both no and remain single, like I planned all along. The thought of being someone's wife after losing Aden is hard to imagine. How will it feel to have another man's arms around me? I don't even like to think about it.

I think, though, that I will have to say yes to one of them. The hard part is to just make the best choice possible. What God has in mind, only He knows. I sure don't. There are still moments of bitterness when I wonder why, but as strange as it may seem, the girls have softened those feelings faster than anything else has.

Could this be a sign of what I am supposed to do? I don't know. I wish Aden would send some sign, like it seemed he did when I had to make the decision about the house. But all is silent in the heavens. Maybe he thinks I can make my own decisions now. That would so be like him — not to interfere in my choices. He would want the best for me now that he's no longer here. Yet what is that?

Can't he see that better than I can? Can't he send an angel back to tell me or do some little thing to show me the way to go? Yet, I'm just Ella, one girl among millions on this earth. Many are in worse shape than I am, and I'd best be thankful for what I have.

I need some answers, and that right soon. Perhaps my answer will be evident by seeing if the bishop makes a move. I don't really know why what he does is so important to me, but somehow it is. I should know by Saturday — whether he does what I expect him to do. He'll be back that night, and we'll have to see.

Ella shut the pages gently, slid the tablet under the couch, and returned to her quilt, humming a hymn softly to entertain herself.

Minutes later gravel crunched in the driveway. Stretching her fingers, Ella got up, glanced out the basement window, and saw a car parked by the barn. A lady, in her thirties or so, had stepped out of the car, and a young girl — a daughter perhaps — followed her. The two looked around, said something to each other, and then walked toward the house. *Are they here to see the quilt shop?*

The children were still asleep, and Ella hoped they wouldn't be awakened. Business came first, anyway. The girls could go to bed early tonight, if necessary.

"Good afternoon," she said, greeting the woman at the door.

"Good afternoon," the woman said with a nod. "Is this the quilt shop?"

"Yah," Ella said, motioning them inside. "I have girls sleeping, but don't worry about them. It goes with having a business in your basement."

"Oh, we can come back later," the woman said, stopping just inside the door.

"Nee," Ella said, "please come on in. I don't have much to show anyway because we just opened. But you can see the quilt we're working on right now."

The woman crossed the room with her

daughter close by her side. She ran her fingers across the stitches on the new quilt and then raised her head to look at the quilt displayed on the wall.

"That's our sample," Ella said, "and right now we're just making this one kind. The centerpiece is a copy of the house."

"I noticed," the woman said, smiling. "Is this one sold?"

"Yah," Ella said.

"Have you another ready to sell?"

"Nee," Ella said, "not yet."

"I'd take one if you did. Perhaps we can stop by next time we are through here. Maybe then you'll have more like this one?"

"Yah," Ella said. It was clear that she could make quilts ahead of time, and then sell them.

"Your girls are still sleeping," the woman whispered with a soft smile. "Thanks for the tour."

Ella held the door open for her. *I will enjoy making and selling quilts.* Da Hah *has been gracious by giving this idea to me.*

Toward evening and just before Joe came home, Ronda called to Ella from the top of the basement stairs, "What did that lady want? Did you sell a quilt?"

"She would have bought one," Ella said,

398

"if we had one ready."

"We need to work steadily and have more quilts ready to sell on the spot," Ronda said, smiling from ear to ear.

"I think so too. I'm thrilled at the opportunity, but it does look like we have a lot of work to do."

"Yah, it does," Ronda said as buggy wheels turned into the driveway. She quickly closed the basement door, and soon Ella heard the front door open. Next she heard excited voices and then the heavy steps of a man on the hardwood floor above.

Ella fixed soup for supper, fed the girls, and had them in bed by eight. She stepped outside when the stars came out. It was a clear night with not a cloud in sight from horizon to horizon.

The bright sweep of the stars seemed silent tonight. Gazing up at the sky, she sought out the familiar figures she knew — the seven sisters, the little dipper, and the sword that hung from the hunter's belt.

"Dear God, please help me," she prayed, but there seemed to be no answers tonight. Ella pulled her gaze away, stepped back inside the house, and prepared for bed. She needed her sleep for the week ahead.

THIRTY-NINE

Ella started the washing machine early the next morning and carried the finished laundry outside to hang on the line. She set up a ladder so Mary could climb up, help pin the clothes to the line, and then turn the wheel, which sent the wash out toward the windmill. Sarah squealed with delight and handed the clothespins up to her sister until she tired of the exercise. Mary stuck it out until the last piece of wash was rolled out.

"Good morning," Ronda called from the kitchen window.

"Yah, that it is," Ella said, waving. The morning air improved her spirits a little.

Back in the basement, Ella completed the next load of wash and made another trip to the line with the girls. She held Mary's and Sarah's hands on the walk back while Mary dragged the hamper with her other hand.

"Let me take that," Ella said when they

came to the driveway. "I don't want it to drag on the stones."

"When I'm big, I will carry it like you do," Mary said, beaming.

"Yah, you will," Ella said, thinking how great it would be to be Mary's mamm and watch her grow up. Ella pushed the thought away.

She worked on the quilt till lunch and then fixed soup for the girls.

Soon afterward an older lady drove her car up the driveway. Ella opened the basement door for the woman while holding baby Barbara in her arms. "Hello. Please come in," she said warmly.

"Oh, she's such a cute baby," the woman cooed. "Such a darling."

"Yah, she is," Ella agreed.

"You have quilts?" the woman asked and stepped inside.

"Only the one we're making," Ella said, pointing to the quilt she and Ronda were working on. "There's the display of the finished product. We just make that one kind right now."

"Oh, just the one," the woman said. Ella couldn't tell if there was disappointment in her voice.

"We're just starting up," Ella said. "We might branch out later, but not for now. We just have the one, and the one we're working on is already sold."

"Ah, then, you must take orders and ship them? I hope you do because we live in Ohio and can't come through here that often."

"I do. In fact we plan to ship this one when we're finished."

"Do you have anyone to help you? With three children —"

"Yah, the lady who lives upstairs helps me. We could have another quilt done in four months, we think."

"Then I'll take it," the woman said. "It's a beautiful design. I'll just leave my address and such."

"Yah, that will be fine. We will ship the quilt C.O.D. Is that okay?"

"Oh sure," the woman said, writing her name and address on the piece of paper Ella gave her.

Ella drew in her breath. *What if I can't get it done in time — even with Ronda's help?*

"It's good doing business with you," the woman said as Ella held the door open for her.

Only moments later Ronda opened the basement door and called down the stairs, "Was that another sale?"

"It was," Ella said, laughing nervously. "I

think I'd better take the sign down now. I can't go on selling like this, and we can't work this fast."

"Then I'd best get busy," Ronda said. "My, but this is fun. And don't take the sign down. They can always just look. You want your shop to be well-known so people will stop by. Just think, they'll soon be standin' in line at the door."

"I doubt that," Ella said, relaxing a little.

"Your mom just drove in with Clara," Ronda said. "I suppose you didn't hear them with the *Englisha* car driving out."

"Ach," Ella gasped, "Mamm's here, and the house is all a mess."

"It's not," Ronda said. "Stop worrying. It just looks worked in. Isn't that good? Your mamm will understand."

Ella still rushed behind the curtains where the girls were playing, picked up things, and then grabbed the dolls the girls had left on the couch.

"Who comes?" Mary asked. "Is it someone to look at the quilts again?"

"No. Mamm's coming."

"Mamm?" Mary asked, wrinkling her brow. "But we have a mamm. How can she come?"

"It's *my* mamm," Ella said.

"You'd better marry him," Ronda said

403

from the top of the stairs. "Don't say I didn't tell you." Then she closed the door.

Ella stopped her straightening for a moment, wrapped her arm around Mary, and looked at her eye-to-eye. "Mary, I just take care of you. Your real mamm is up in heaven. Your daett will find a good mamm for you some day."

Mary's eyes clouded over. "But I already have one. There's one in heaven, and then there's you."

Ella bit her lip. She glanced up to see her mom walking past the basement window and carrying a paper bag. Clara walked behind her.

She hurried to the door and pulled it open. "Ach, it's so good to see you." Quickly she gave her mom and then Clara a hug.

As she pulled back from her hug, Mamm searched Ella's face. Ella didn't say anything but just wrapped her arms around her mom again, clinging to her for a long moment.

"Is there bad news?" Mamm asked in the wake of the second hug. "Has there been trouble? Is Ronda makin' trouble?"

Ella shook her head. "Ronda couldn't be sweeter. *Da Hah* has blessed me with havin' her here. I can't say how much I appreciate her."

"Then what is it? Somethin's troublin' you."

Ella shook her head. Now wasn't the moment.

"It's this livin' alone in this big house," Mamm said. "I never did like the idea. You ought to have a man around like normal people do. I should have insisted on it before I ever let you leave."

"It's not that, Mamm. Really," Ella said, trying to smile.

"At least you can smile yet," Mamm said, sitting down on the couch and looking around the room. "Have you been workin' too hard? Are you out of money? I see the quilt's being worked on. Can't you sell it? I know *something's* wrong. A mother knows."

"I've sold two, Mamm," Ella said. "It's about other things. Perhaps later we can talk."

"I want Ella to see my drawings," Clara said. "Show them to Ella — quick."

"I will," Mamm said, lifting the first of the framed drawings from the paper bag she carried. She held them up for Ella to see. "Clara begged and begged, and so I finally allowed it. I suppose people might want to buy things like this. I must say the work is good enough."

"It is. It is," Clara said, pointing to the

landscape drawing of plowed fields and touching the barn and cattle in the distance.

"I would say they are *gut,*" Ella said, reaching for the frame. "I'll hang it on the wall and we'll see what we can get for it. You can have all the money, Clara. It'll make you a little extra to spend, yah?"

"It best not be too much money," Mamm said.

"She sure can draw," Ella said, still holding the framed picture. "We'll just have to see."

"I'm so happy," Clara said, picking up baby Barbara.

Mary tugged at Clara's arm and asked, "Can you tell me and Sarah a story?"

Clara didn't think too long. "Yah," she said, taking Mary's hand. With Sarah following, she walked over to the baby's blanket by the quilt and nestled down with the three girls around her.

"So tell me your troubles," Mamm said. "Would they perhaps be about the bishop?"

"What about Clara?" Ella whispered, glancing in her sister's direction.

Mamm shook her head. "Clara can hear, but I suspect she's too busy to listen. Is there trouble with him?"

"Preacher Stutzman asked for my hand in marriage," she blurted out.

"Preacher Stutzman? How dare he! Doesn't he know about the bishop?"

"He knows."

"Surely you have said no, Ella."

Ella's silence was answer enough.

"Has your heart gone toward him? The daett of the three girls you are taking care of?" Mamm asked, leaning forward on the couch.

"Yes, my heart has gone toward the girls but not their daett," Ella said. "They already call me their mamm."

"But you cannot let children decide for you. Marriage to a man is for life, Ella. You know that."

"Yes, I do. I know that. But I also know my heart is not drawn to the bishop. I fear him, Mamm. I've had dreams about our wedding — dreams in which I wake up in great terror. I don't know why. In my dreams, I fear him. Yet he's nice enough, yah, but that's not enough."

"He loves you, Ella. I can see it in his eyes. Surely you have not told him you won't marry him."

Ella shook her head.

"Then why these fears?"

"I don't know. They come without being sought. They come in the nighttime when I least expect them."

"Has he spoken harshly to you or given you reason to fear him?"

"Ach, nee. He has corrected me, yah, but even Ronda could understand that. I do things without thinkin' at times."

"Then perhaps it's nothing of concern. You can tell Preacher Stutzman you are already promised. You are, aren't you?"

Ella shook her head again.

"This is not good," Mamm said, pondering for a long moment. "Is your heart holdin' back, then?"

"It is, and then part of it is because I can't forget Aden the way people seem to think I should. I can't put aside what I felt for him. How can I let another man put his arms around me, Mamm? Only Aden has ever held me close."

"Then that's what this is. You fear him as a man you do not know well enough to love yet. That will leave, Ella, when the marriage promises are made. *Da Hah* will see to it."

"But it wasn't so with Aden. I looked forward to marrying him. I loved him before we were to be married. I wanted his love more than almost anything in the world. Why was he taken from me?"

"Is this bitterness, then — a withholding of your mind against the will of the Almighty One?"

"I don't think so," Ella said, meeting her mom's eyes. "My heart is clear with *Da Hah*. I have blamed Him at first, yah, but I know His will is for the best."

"Then perhaps you just need time. Surely the bishop should understand that."

"Mamm," Ella said, wondering how to explain, "you have to understand. Preacher Stutzman's girls are the only reason my heart has opened to a man. Since Aden's passing, they are the only reason why I have hope. Yet, I have told Preacher Stutzman that I don't have feelings for him. That's what's so strange about this. In spite of not having feelings for him, I really am considering his proposal."

"You are sure of this? He preaches so harshly sometimes. He may be a hard man to be married to."

"Yah, he preaches hard, but he has another side to him. He even said he was sorry about the sermon he preached at Aden's funeral."

Mamm raised her eyebrows. "I remember that. I remember hoping it hadn't bothered you too much. Had you told Stutzman about this? Is that why he apologized?"

Ella shook her head.

"So the man isn't playin' with your heart. He doesn't seem the kind to do so."

"I do know I don't fear him as I do the bishop," Ella said, "but neither do I love him, Mamm. Can marriage still be *gut* if you don't love the man?"

"Marriage is holy, Ella, no matter what our feelings are. Are you sure you have no feelings for the bishop? He loves you, you know."

Ella shrugged. "He's attractive, but I don't trust him. His face smiles, but his eyes don't reach all the way to his heart. He seems far from me."

"Are you sure Aden hasn't left you with too many dreams? He's gone, Ella. Why it happened, we don't know. But *Da Hah* knows best. You must not hang onto Aden. No man will ever be like him. You know that our women marry again. They take husbands after their loved ones have passed. They can't expect another love to be the same as the one that was taken. You know that, Ella, don't you?"

"Yah, but I wish you could at least tell me what to do. It's hard to figure out myself."

Mamm got up and glanced toward Clara, who was deep in whispers with baby Barbara and still busy with the three girls. Mary chattered away beside her. Gently Mamm wrapped Ella in both arms, kissed her on the forehead, and held her close.

"Your heart has been broken, Ella. We try to understand, but only *Da Hah* really can. He's the one who has borne our sins on the cross and can fully know our pain. You must trust Him. It's not Aden who can give you direction, it's Him from heaven. He cares about you . . . about your broken heart . . . about your tears. He really understands, Ella."

Ella allowed the comfort of her mother's embrace to flow through her, and then she wiggled loose with a sheepish grin.

"Ach, Mamm, I'm not a little girl anymore," she said.

"I know," Lizzie said, running her hand over Ella's forehead. "I wish you'd have stayed small . . . that all of you had, so I could take care of your hurts. But now you are in *Da Hah*'s hands. I must trust Him too. You asked me if a woman can marry a man for whom she has no feelings. Sometimes a woman turns slowly to love. You may not love him until you belong to him. I know it was not so with Aden, but each man is different, Ella."

"Is the love for his children enough?"

"It may be enough to begin on."

"That is my only hope," Ella said. "Did you love Daett before you married him?"

Mamm's face lighted up. "Yah, he was a

good man. I knew so from the start. He is not hard to love."

Ella nodded and dropped her gaze. "Am I strange, Mamm? I feel so . . . torn up. I don't do things the same as the other women do."

"You are loved," Lizzie said, stroking her forehead again. "In that way you are the same as the others."

Ella didn't dare lift her head. "I love you, Mamm. You know that?"

"Yah, I know. And all of you are precious to me."

"Did the bishop come over to speak with Daett or Eli?"

Lizzie shook her head. "Not that I know of. I'm sorry Eli is makin' trouble again. Daett has spoken with him, but he is very stubborn."

"He will come on Saturday, if he comes . . ."

Mamm looked questioningly at her.

"It's just something I need to know," Ella said.

Mamm relented and said, "Ella, while we're here, is there something Clara and I can do to help you? We have to be getting back soon, but we can give you an hour."

"No, I'm fine," Ella said. "You have already given me plenty with your advice."

A smile played on Mamm's face. "There is always work to do. Don't tell me there isn't."

"Well, there's the quilt. Ronda and I could use some help with it, I suppose."

"Then let's get to it. Clara can keep the girls busy. If you call Ronda, perhaps she can help too."

"I'll check," Ella said, taking the basement steps two at a time. She found Ronda upstairs in the kitchen with her cookbook open in front of her.

"Your mamm left?" Ronda asked, looking up. "I didn't hear her leave."

"Nee. She's going to help with the quilt for an hour or so. We just wondered if you could help, but I see you're busy."

"This?" Ronda said, laughing. "It's for supper. It can wait for now, and I'd love to help." She turned the cookbook upside down on the counter and followed Ella downstairs.

"Are we taking you away from something?" Mamm asked.

"Nothing that can't wait," Ronda said, pulling up a chair and finding her familiar spot with her needle already strung with thread.

"So, have you and Joe settled in?" Lizzie asked.

"I think so, but there really wasn't that much to do. Mamm and Daett helped us move and got everything in order. Now if I can just keep things so."

"You'll learn what works, as the rest of us did," Mamm said

"It's all worth it, though, with Joe as wonderful as he is," Ronda said. With a sly smile, she added, "And perhaps soon the *bobli* might be on its way."

Ella felt red creep up her neck at this plain talk.

"That's *Da Hah*'s way," Lizzie said, nodding. "We love a man, we have children, and we grow old. Then we leave those behind who follow us onward."

Ella listened to their voices as a vision of Preacher Stutzman rose before her. His arms were outstretched as he thundered in his Sunday sermon. *Would he make a good husband?*

FORTY

The week sped by quickly as Ronda and Ella worked on the quilt during every spare moment. The Stutzman girls were predictably easy to care for. And it was again with reluctance that when Friday arrived, Ella washed the girls' clothes and packed their suitcases for the weekend at home.

"Is Daett coming soon?" Mary asked.

"Yah, soon," Ella said, giving a weak smile. "You'll be going home with him for the weekend, just like usual."

"Why are you not coming?"

"Because I live here. This is my home."

Mary smiled and stared off into space. Ella paced the floor with baby Barbara in her arms. If Preacher Stutzman didn't show up soon, she would place the baby on the blanket and work on her quilt some more. The house outline still needed stitches. They had rolled up the edges of the quilt on either side. Only a foot and a half was left exposed

415

in the center.

"Daett's here now," Mary said, making the announcement from the basement window.

Ella jumped. There had been no rattle of buggy wheels in the driveway. Quickly she grabbed the girls' suitcase, took Sarah by the hand, and went up the steps. She wanted to meet with him outside in case a conversation ensued. It would be best for that to happen — if it happened — away from the house and any listening ears. Not that Ronda would listen on purpose, but it might be best not to tempt her.

Mary ran ahead of her, and her father scooped her up in his arms. "So how has my girl been this week?"

"Gut," Mary said, hugging him tightly.

Ella walked toward them. Her smile looked as crooked as a barnyard mud trail.

The preacher's eyes were as intense as they were tender when they met hers. He nodded and then reached for Sarah, who ran the last few steps into his arms.

"How are you?" he asked, giving her a hug.

"Gut," Sarah said in an imitation of her sister's tone.

"And the baby?"

"Good as can be. Not a problem all

week," Ella said. The words tumbled out in a rush.

"They have a good keeper," he said, reaching for the baby.

For the slightest moment, his fingers brushed hers, and she met his eyes.

"I will have them back on Monday," he said, laying baby Barbara on the seat of the buggy.

Ella didn't want to turn and leave, so she held his horse for him. It felt more appropriate doing that than just standing there or walking back to the house while he climbed into the buggy.

The man nodded and offered a brief smile as he slapped the reins and she let go. *Is this to be our ritual? Am I to hold the horse so he can leave with his daughters?* She had done it twice now.

She watched the buggy disappear around the corner. The sight of him was blocked out quickly by the woods, and the sound of his horse's hooves faded into the distance. Turning toward the house, she walked slowly, thinking about so many things.

"That was such a dear sight," Ronda said, standing by the front door, "you holdin' on to his horse. I could just see you in the buggy with him. You look so like you belong there."

"You weren't supposed to be watching," Ella said, making as if she would walk on past.

"I really wasn't," Ronda said. "I just came to the door at the last minute. I thought I heard somethin'. You didn't do anything wrong."

"I felt nervous," Ella said. "I think that's why I hold his horse for him. It's something to do while waiting."

"Ach, that's a good sign," Ronda said, laughing. "A real *gut* sign."

"It's doesn't feel like Aden . . . that I do know."

"They say it's never the same the second time around. I know no one would ever be the same as Joe."

"I hope you never have to find out."

Ella watched Ronda nod slowly, sure she saw tears in her friend's eyes.

FORTY-ONE

Ella heard the bishop arriving long before he even reached the driveway. The evening was still, the air heavy, and his horse's hooves beat hard on the road. A sharp rattle of stones sounded when he turned in at the road. Ella spread the last of the white frosting on the cake she had just baked and scraped the knife clean on the bowl's edge.

She was unexpectedly calm. *Perhaps this is another of Ronda's* gut *signs. But what if he has been to see my parents and demanded that Eli no longer be allowed to stay at home? This is what he had wanted to do, and if he had followed through in spite of my objections, it will make the evening much more difficult.*

Yet, perhaps, it would be simpler. *Dealing with the bishop is like walking on the edge of a wooden fence rail. The thin board presses hard on the soles of my feet, and the pull of gravity is strong on either side.*

A visit to my parents against my expressed

wishes would show the bishop's depth of character. Though I don't want him to have made that visit, I have to admit such a visit would show that he is willing to risk our relationship to do what he feels is right. I would have to find some respect in my heart for that aspect of it.

She got two plates and a knife out of the cupboard, set them on the table, and went to the door. The bishop's shiny black shoes were already halfway down the basement steps. He was wearing his best Sunday suit coat. He had dressed up for her.

Ella opened the door for him.

"Good evening," he said. "Am I too early?"

She shook her head. "I just finished my cake. I would say you timed it pretty well."

"Ach, *vell,* such things happen. I'm glad to hear it."

She motioned with her hand toward the couch.

He took his seat and said, "So the girls leave on Friday, and you've been by yourself all day. Is it a relief to get away from them after the stress, you know, of three little girls who aren't your own?"

"I suppose even mothers have such times with their own children," she said, sitting beside him on the couch.

420

"Then I imagine you must be ready to get away from them even more than real mothers. I must say, you don't look tired. And I like that about you. You do all that work during the week — taking care of two little girls and a baby and running the quilt shop — yet you look as fresh as a bright new day. You are a very *gut* and wonderful woman, Ella."

Ella wondered why red didn't creep up her neck. *It certainly would have if Stutzman said such things, but then, of course, he wouldn't.* With a start, Ella shifted on the couch away from the bishop. For the first time, she was comparing him with Preacher Stutzman and leaving Aden out of the comparison. *Have I really moved so far away from my memories? Apparently so.*

"Did I say something?" the bishop asked. "This is true, you know, that you are an exceptional woman among women, as the Good Book says. Like I have said before, I never expected the day to come when I would say such a thing. You must not let the praise alarm you. Surely Aden told you the same?"

"He did," she said, moving even further away from him, "though not in those exact words. It was different somehow."

"Yah, I understand," he said, nodding.

421

"Yet you must not let this difference stand in the way of our relationship. *Da Hah* can bring about love again — in a different way perhaps — but something just as precious. He would not have taken Aden if He did not know that life could still be just as good for you, Ella, as it was before. You must believe that — believe that a woman should take a husband. That it is *Da Hah*'s *villa.*"

"Did you speak with my parents about Eli staying at home?" she said, letting the words out quickly.

He studied her for a moment. His face darkened, and then a smile reappeared. "So you did expect me to rush over to your parents and, thus, give you reason to hold something against me. You should know me better than that, Ella. I wouldn't do something so out of order. Not after you said what you did."

"But you still feel as if Eli should not stay at home?"

"That is another matter entirely, Ella. You told me not to go, and I have not gone. Is that not good enough? I listened and heard what you said. I simply felt that at this time it would be best if the matter was left alone."

"And would you listen to me about this matter . . . if we were married?"

His hand jerked on the couch and joined

422

the other. As he rubbed them together, he said, "Yah." He paused and then continued, "Perhaps I should explain. My work for the church often calls for hard choices. Sometimes things might even go against one's own family. It's not easy, and the calling is sacred. I am sure you understand that. But for now, I can do what you say — if it makes things easier for you. Then perhaps later . . . it will not be as hard."

"Then this is just for a time. Until later — when someone like Eli would be dealt with in another manner than he now is?"

"Perhaps," he said as he laced his fingers tightly together, "but you must not hold that against me. I do not want to offend you now. Have you changed your mind about Eli? I would respect you for that change . . . greatly in fact. This is a weakness in you, Ella. I know Eli is your family, but one must put that aside to do the work of God. Our forefathers left their property and their loved ones — even their own lives — all for the faith. We cannot do less than they did, Ella. We really can't."

"If you believe that, then it would have been best if you had gone to my parents and spoken with them."

"So you *have* changed your mind, then," he said, letting a smile warm his face. He wet his lips. "I cannot say how glad I am of this. I had some doubts about you, Ella, but I see again you are able to receive correction. As you know, this virtue is greatly valued among our people. It's also a virtue of great value in a wife."

"But I didn't mean that I have changed my mind," Ella said, clearing her throat. "In fact, I have not changed my mind about Eli, even if it comes to him leaving the home place, which it well might. I just think it might have been best if you had gone anyway . . . even though I told you not to. This way I could have decided better about what I think of you. Now it has been decided for me."

"I don't understand," the bishop said, leaning forward. "What has been decided for you? I do not see. You expressed your concern, and I tried not to offend you. Yah, perhaps later you will understand these matters, but you do not now."

"Our relationship. I cannot continue. I fear it."

"You fear, but there is nothing to fear, Ella. I have told you the truth, have I not? Many would not have. Perhaps they would have held back part of the truth from you. I hope our people would not do such things, but one never knows in this day of sin and darkness. I love you, Ella, as I have never loved any other girl. Yah, never have I loved so much. There is nothing to fear from me. *Da Hah* will be with us. He has promised."

"I've had a dream about us," Ella said, meeting his eyes. "In this dream I see a wedding. The buggies are parked outside, the people are gathered in the house, and then when I come inside, it is you and me. We are seated in front, ready to be married. Then a great fear comes upon me, and I don't know why."

"Ah, so it is a dream that holds you back," the bishop said, looking relieved. "I had thought it was some other thing. Perhaps Stutzman or his girls have gotten to you. I had hoped you wouldn't fall for the charms of his children. You must not make that mistake. This dream, though, I would think it is a good sign — a *gut* indication that *Da Hah* has willed it so and has shown you ahead of time. You must take comfort in this — not fear."

Ella stood. *This is so hard.* "I find in my heart that I can't continue seeing you. I'm sorry if I have disappointed you," she said.

"Ella," he said, rising to his feet. His hands reached out, grasping both of hers in his. "Ella, don't make this mistake. There is no one else I want to marry. I need a wife . . .

and not just any wife. Look at what life could hold for you . . . for us. I will treat you right, Ella. You don't have to be afraid."

"I have my mind made up," she said firmly.

"You are serious?" he said, dropping her hands. "And there's nothing I can say?"

"There is nothing."

"Stutzman has spoken to you. He has asked your hand in marriage."

"Yes, he has."

"And you have given him your answer?"

"No."

"Then you looked for a fault in me and searched this out on purpose to see whether I would fall and stumble in your eyes."

"Perhaps I did. I don't really know."

"This is not the proper manner in which one finds a husband, Ella. Stutzman should be held accountable for this."

"Even our people do not hold it against a man who follows his heart in love, do they?"

The bishop relented. "They do not. Do you love him, then?"

"Is this not a matter between him and me?"

"It is, yes, but your face betrays you, Ella. I know you do not love him. And I know I love you. Are you sure you will not reconsider?"

"I'm sure," Ella said, holding his gaze.

"Then *Da Hah*'s *villa* be done. It is not in me to stand in the way of what is to be. Just be sure of this, Ella. Look carefully about yourself and not just at your fears. Perhaps you will yet see the right way before it's too late. Once you have made the promises, it will be too late to change your mind. Remember that, Ella."

"I will," she said as the bishop walked to the door, opened it himself, and stepped out into the night. His buggy wheels rattled on the gravel a few minutes later. She stared blankly at the untouched cake on the table. *Did I just make an awful mistake? Did I drive a wonderful man of my people away? Now surely Eli will receive no more help from the church. He is as good as lost.*

Ella sat down. Slowly she took the fork, cut a piece of cake, and brought it to her mouth. It softly melted on her tongue as her thoughts settled on the truth.

I'll live alone in this house if it comes to that. If Preacher Stutzman and I can't make a go of it, I'll be just fine. It can be explained to the girls that things couldn't be worked out. They might understand, and they might not. But whatever happens now, I've brought it on myself.

She set the fork down on the tabletop,

making the metal rattle lightly on the wood, and then lowered her head onto her arms.

FORTY-TWO

Ella sat in church and listened to the main sermon. As decided in the earlier ministers' conference upstairs, it was Preacher Stutzman's turn to preach. He now stood between the living room and kitchen with his hands clasped on his chest. From where Ella sat, surrounded by the other single girls, she could see only the side of his face. It was better that way; a small gift from *Da Hah*. Had she sat facing him, perhaps their eyes would have met. He then could have seen her answer in her eyes and wouldn't have been able to continue preaching.

He was now in the middle of a story about Queen Esther. "And after the terrible day arrived when the wicked Haman got it into his head that all the Jews of the kingdom must be destroyed . . ."

Wherever he intends to go with the message, it isn't unusual as Amish sermons go. What's unusual is his tone. Already he has passed several points in the story that pro-vided excellent opportunities for his usual diatribes. Yet he missed them. Has anyone else noticed? Did I really see the bishop glancing strangely at Stutzman? Twice already?

The bishop looked comfortable and well settled on the bench. His back was bent, his shoulders drooped, and his long beard was bent at a forty-five degree angle to his chest. Stutzman was now at the place in the story where Mordecai had to make a choice. Would he bow at the gate to the evil Haman or not? Preacher Stutzman paused and took a deep breath. His eyes were focused on the hardwood floor.

"So *Da Hah* has called each of us to make a choice. Will we serve Him or will we serve the world? Will we bow to the god of this world, or will we bow to the will of *Da Hah* in heaven? Will we submit to the will of His church on this earth? Many are the temptations we face. They come and go, and each of us makes daily decisions as to how to respond. Let us all be like Mordecai, who feared not the wrath of evil, but obeyed the Lord." Stutzman took a deep breath, and his voice rose higher. "Each of us can count on being caught for our sins. Men and women think they can hide . . . that they are smart enough to escape punishment. Yet we see from this example that things do not turn out so. *Da Hah* sees to it that sin has its reward — a reward of death and not of life."

The bishop nodded his head vigorously. The sermon came to an end, and the preacher asked the bishop and two other men to give testimony. The men's voices droned on, and then the final song was announced and sung.

Ella got up to help with serving by taking bowls of peanut butter to the women's table. That was about all she could handle today. Thankfully no one directed her over to the men's table.

Moments later the bishop announced the closing prayer for those eating, and the tables cleared out. Quickly the girls moved down the sides, washing the utensils and rinsing out the coffee cups. The tables began filling again. Ella waited, saw that there would be room, and slid onto the bench.

"So how are the Stutzman girls doing for you?" Aden's mamm asked from across the table. "I heard you are taking care of them."

"Gut," Ella said, clutching the peanut butter sandwich in her hand. "They are little angels." What would Aden's mother say if she knew? Would it bother her to know that two men now wanted to take the place in

her heart so long held by Aden?

"I can imagine they are," Aden's mamm said. "They can use a *gut* mamm again."

"Oh, I just take care of them during the week," she gasped, glancing at the sandwich as the peanut butter ran over the edge and dripped onto the tablecloth. *What a* dumm-kopf *I am.*

Ella wiped the peanut butter off the tablecloth. It could happen to anyone, but today it had to happen to her. She glanced up, but Aden's mamm had turned to someone beside her and was now deep in conversation. Soon the bishop would announce prayer again, and she could get out of here. It wouldn't be a moment too soon. Perhaps next Sunday her nerves would be more under control. Surely things had to get better.

"Now that we have eaten, let us pray," the bishop said with a clear voice that carried all the way through the house.

Ella bowed her head and waited through the prayer. When it ended, she rose quickly and moved toward the front utility room to collect her bonnet and shawl. A few women nodded at her as she squeezed through the kitchen. She found her things and opened the utility room door. With her shawl wrapped tightly around her, she approached her buggy. *Now how am I going to get my horse from the barn? Will any of the younger boys offer, or should I just go myself?* The men sat on benches out under the big trees, but no one seemed to be looking in her direction. *I'll go and get the horse myself. It is better that way.*

Just then the barn door opened, and the young bishop came out, leading her horse. *What is he up to? What might people think? Didn't my words last night take hold?* She grabbed the buggy shafts and lifted them high.

"Good afternoon," he said, swinging her horse in place.

"Good afternoon," she said as cheerfully as she could.

"I can still be nice to you," he said, pushing the tugs on, "with the hope you'll reconsider."

"I won't reconsider," she said, meeting his eyes as she climbed into the buggy.

He nodded and held the bridle until she was settled in, and then she slapped the horse lightly on the neck. Holding the reins tightly, Ella steered past the bishop. *He has some nerve, but that's just the way he is.*

When the alarm clock shrieked its fury in the early morning darkness, Ella pushed the covers back and crawled out of bed. Although there had been no dream about the bishop last night, she slept fitfully. No doubt it was because today was the day she would tell Preacher Stutzman her answer.

That I will marry him? No. That is too much. Just that I will see him? Perhaps whenever he wishes? Something like that. After the bishop, Saturday nights don't seem appropriate. Perhaps we could have an understanding between ourselves and maybe agree at first to something like little chats when we see each other while out and about. Maybe my heart will have time to make a decision if it's not rushed.

Ella dressed and went down the stairs, stepping outside to reach the basement. Already the late summer air had a brisk feel to it. She paused to look toward the sunrise. The sky had no color and held no clouds. Only the first rays of the sun's white light burst over the horizon in bold streaks.

Where has the summer gone? One day follows another so quickly. Do the years do the same? Will marriage come that quickly? Will one bobli *be born, only to be followed by another and another — mine and Stutzman's children — until we are old and gray? Is that how it will be?*

Will Aden be there on the day my eyes close

and I cross over the river? Will Aden look the same? How will I speak with him after things have turned out so differently than we had planned? Surely he understands that the best must be made of things and that life does, indeed, go on.

As for loving again, do I even dare after having loved so deeply? Ella brushed back the hair from her face. *The faith expressly speaks that such a thing is allowed after a death separates a man and a woman. Perhaps I can learn to love again — with time and patience. Preacher Stutzman — no, I might as well call him Ivan now. Ivan might understand and be patient with me. I will simply have to see.*

With one last look at the sky, Ella walked down the steps, careful not to trip in the faint light. The girls would have had breakfast before they arrived. *Ivan is a* gut *father — there is no question about that. Surely he will be* gut *to me also.* She rubbed the goose bumps on her skin.

She struck a match, and after moving the kindling into place, the fire caught easily enough. Ella then lit the kerosene lamp. Its flickering light danced on the quilt and accented each thread, creating a quick flash here and there.

She drew in her breath. Da Hah *loves me.*

Signs of this are everywhere! I can see it in Ronda and Joe — my friends — living in the rooms above me, the quilt shop with new orders already, the matter with the bishop resolved, and the house itself. So easily everything could have failed, and I would have been forced to move back to Seager Hill. Yet failure was not my lot.

Now there are three little girls who cast the light of joy in my life, and add to that their father. Can I love him? Perhaps a quiet settled love would have to suffice, and I can only hope for more. Is Ivan willing to wait with patience . . . even if the love never comes?

Ella heated the water for her oatmeal and stirred in the flakes when it boiled. She cut a slice of bread, spread it with butter and jam, and then dipped out a generous portion of oatmeal and poured it into the bowl. The milk splashed and almost spilled when she poured it on top of the oatmeal. She jerked the pitcher upright and stirred the oatmeal before adding more milk to the bowl. When it was just right, she prayed silently and then ate quickly. She heard the sound of the buggy wheels rattling in the driveway as she washed the dishes.

Ella took a deep breath, wiped her wet hands on her apron, and went up the basement steps. It was important to reach Ivan

436

before he got close to the house.

"Good morning," she said. He had his back turned to her as he lifted baby Barbara off the buggy seat.

"Good morning," he said, turning and smiling weakly.

Noticing his hat askew, Ella almost laughed. Never in her wildest dreams had the image of her lover been like the man who now stood in front of her. *Da Hah* surely had a *gut* sense of humor.

"We have come back," Mary said with a sleepy voice. "Daett gave us breakfast already."

"I thought he would," Ella said, reaching down and giving her a hug. "And, Sarah, how are you?"

Sarah said nothing even after Ella's hug.

Ivan handed Ella the baby, nodded, and stood ready to climb back into the buggy. "The day is full for me, as usual. I hope you have a good week," he said as he turned to leave.

Ella cleared her throat. "About your question —"

"Yah," he said, looking back and pausing. His foot was already on the buggy step.

"I do not know the final answer yet or when I will know, but you are welcome to visit . . . if you still wish."

"But the bishop," he said, taking his foot off the buggy step.

Ella took a deep breath. "He's not coming back."

He turned to look fully at her. The sunshine caught the side of his face, lit up his beard, and made his eyes blaze with light, "Ach, Ella, this is too much for me."

"Perhaps for me too, but not in the way you mean."

"I understand," he said softly. "I am not worthy even of this."

She was surprised to see tears in his eyes. "You may come to visit," she said. After a pause, she continued. "Let me say it another way. I would like it if you would come to visit. Perhaps we can get to know each other slowly . . . a little at a time if it suits you."

He reached out and touched her hand. "Perhaps it would be best that way. More can come later perhaps — as *Da Hah* moves. I do not wish to act too quickly."

"Yah, that would be best."

"Then we understand each other," he said, touching her hand again.

She nodded and watched him step up into the buggy, slap the reins, and touch the brim of his hat by way of saying goodbye. Then he was gone. Still she stood and watched until his buggy disappeared in the early morning light.

"Are we going in the house?" Mary asked, tugging on her dress.

"Yah," Ella said, "we are. Come, let's go."

By midmorning Ronda came down the basement steps and knocked gently on the wood railing. "I'm ready to quilt. Is it okay if I come down?"

"You are always welcome," Ella said.

The two women quilted quickly, adjusting the frame twice before the lunch hour approached. Finally, after a particular long silence, Ronda cleared her throat as if to speak.

Ella waited, keeping the smile off her face.

"Did you and the bishop get things worked out?" Ronda asked, trying to sound casual.

"Yah, satisfactorily I think," Ella said, maintaining a straight face.

"Oh, Ella, don't keep me in suspense any longer! You've been torturing me all morning. And what were you and Preacher Stutzman talking about this morning?"

"He just dropped off the girls."

"Ella, I'm going to scream!"

Ella burst out laughing.

"Well, at least it must not be bad news," Ronda said. "Did you get things patched up, then?"

"I have made up my mind," Ella whispered. "I told the bishop not to come back, and I told Ivan this morning he could start seeing me. I have decided to follow my heart in loving the girls. Time will tell if my heart will also lead me to Ivan."

"Ivan, is it? What did he say?"

"He was nice enough. He didn't push things."

"And he'd better not," Ronda said, glaring out the window, "or he will have to answer to me. He should appreciate what he's getting. And what did the poor bishop have to say? I do sort of feel sorry for him. He just lost the best girl he could ever have gotten."

"The bishop thinks I'm making a mistake, of course."

Ronda simply sighed.

"And now," Ella said, "we had best focus our attention on this quilt. We have a business to attend to."

Late that evening and after the girls were in bed, breathing deep even breaths, Ella sat down to write by the light of the kerosene lamp.

Dear Journal,

Another day has passed with my girls. I now call them "my girls," but only to myself. They are so dear and make their way deeper into my heart every day. Who would ever have thought it would happen so.

I told Ivan today that he could see me. We are starting slow. I don't trust myself completely yet, and I don't know if I can ever really love him. I suppose, in a way, it doesn't seem right to give the man hope, but Mamm thinks there is no wrong in it, and so I guess I will try.

Ivan seems very understanding. He touched my hand this morning in a way that only a man could. And even though my heart didn't jump with joy, as it would have if Aden had touched me, at least it didn't grow cold around the edges as it did when the bishop did so.

As for the bishop, I do hope he finds happiness with someone. It's strange that I should be the one who turned him down — the first woman he says he's really loved. But if you ask me, all of life is strange in that way. The bishop might as well find out the same thing.

I'm not sure he's fully aware that his chances with me are really over. I expect he'll wait to see what happens with Ivan and me.

Good night, Journal. I plan to sleep well tonight. I can hardly keep my eyes open. The house is still and peaceful this evening. It is full of people, as houses are meant to be, and well kept — not by me, I should hasten to say — but by Da Hah's gracious care.

DISCUSSION QUESTIONS

1. *Ella's Wish* opens with Clara and Ella relaxing in Ella's new home. What do you think is at the root of Ella's desire to be left alone? Should she have stood by that resolve?

2. Do you think Ella handled Daniel properly when he arrived to declare his love?

3. As Bishop Miller and Preacher Stutzman's profiles are given, where do your sympathies lie?

4. Ella spends a day at her parents' home helping in the hay field. Do you think this strengthened and encouraged her for the conversation the family had that evening?

5. Did Ella take too much responsibility for Eli's waywardness?

6. Was Ella wise to rent out the upper level of her home to Joe and Ronda?

7. Do you think Preacher Stutzman was looking for reasons to pursue a relationship with Ella when he went to her home to ask if she could watch his girls?

8. Why do you think Ella had recurring dreams about marrying Bishop Miller?

9. Would a relationship between Preacher Stutzman and Nancy Weaver have worked out?

10. Why did Ella continue the relationship with Bishop Miller for as long as she did?

11. Why didn't Ella accept Preacher Stutzman's marriage proposal?

12. Do you think Ella will marry in book three? If so, to whom?

ABOUT THE AUTHOR

As a boy, **Jerry Eicher** spent eight years in Honduras, where his grandfather helped found an Amish community outreach. As an adult, Jerry taught for two terms in parochial Amish and Mennonite schools in Ohio and Illinois. He has been involved in church renewal for 14 years and has preached in churches and conducted weekend meetings of in-depth Bible teaching. Jerry lives with his wife, Tina, and their four children in Virginia.